Welsh Requiem

(Welsh Village Murder Mysteries)

K T Mill

dark neon

ISBN: 978-1-913132-17-0
Published by: **dark neon**

http://www.darkneon.com/

The Welsh Village Murder Mysteries

Welsh Requiem is the first book in the series of Welsh Village Murder Mysteries. It is followed by…

Who Killed Inspector Stoat?

Table Of Contents

CHAPTER 1

It all began with the thing on the rocks. It was lying at the bottom of the cliff on the northern side of the bay. Ruby thought it might be a seal but she was unable see it clearly because the morning was gloomy and the air was thick with sea mist. From where she was standing, on the beach, all she could see was a dark shape which might or might not be a seal.

It was not her habit to go scrabbling about over the rocks. Usually she walked along the sand, listening to the surge of the sea and watching the lines of seagulls shuffling back and forth at the tide's edge. But her curiosity was piqued. She had heard people say that seals sometimes came ashore but she had never seen one. She thought it would make an interesting picture.

Ruby had already taken a few photographs that morning using the camera in her phone. The light had an attractive silvery quality and the cliffs, seen vaguely through the mist, would make a good subject for a painting. Watercolour painting was a hobby of Ruby's. She would have been the first to admit that she was not really a very good artist but it gave her pleasure.

It must have been about half past six when Ruby noticed the thing on the rocks. She had not slept well the night before and, since she could not bear lying awake in bed, at the first light of dawn she got up, got dressed and went down to the shore to try to blow the cobwebs out of her head. Once she had walked the length of the bay, she had intended to walk back up the hill to her cottage and have breakfast. For the past few weeks, since the mornings had become light enough, this had become her routine: wake, walk, breakfast.

She had only been living in Rose Cottage for a couple of months. She had inherited the cottage from a great aunt, Mrs Guinevere Probert, whom she had never met. The fact that they had never met probably explained why Ruby was the sole beneficiary. Ruby had been told that her great aunt had not much cared for those members of her family whom she *had* met – a prejudice which Ruby found entirely understandable.

Ruby tried to take a photo of the seal by zooming in using the highest magnification of her phone's camera. But when she looked at the phone's small screen the picture did not show much more than she could see with the naked eye – just weed-covered rocks with a big, black thing lying on top of them. That was when she realised that she would have to go scrambling over the rocks to get closer.

The rocks were wet and slippery and her progress was slow. She was worried that, by the time she got close enough, the seal would have taken panic, waddled its way over the rocks down to the sea and swum away. It was hard for Ruby to keep her balance. She slipped on slimy bladder wrack, plunged her foot into a pool of cold water and, in trying to break her fall, put out a hand and cut it on some barnacles. She was pretty fed up by that time but that only made her more determined to get close enough to take a picture of the basking seal.

When she got there she found that it was not a seal at all. It was a man. And he was not basking. He was dead – very definitely dead.

CHAPTER 2

By the time Ruby had finished talking to the police, the morning was well advanced. By the time she arrived back home it was almost eleven o'clock. As she pushed open the little, creaking wooden gate and walked up the cobblestoned path she could not help but smile. Rose Cottage was the sort of place she had always dreamed of. It was an old, stone-walled house with bottle-glass windows, roses scrambling up a trellis and a gnarly wisteria bush trailing over the front door.

Rather than going straight into the cottage, she walked along the narrow gravel path that led into the back garden. Rose Cottage perched on the highest point of Fern Hill and Ruby's back garden overlooked the great expanse of Clogwyn Bach Bay extending from a rocky promontory at its southern end to another rocky promontory at its northern end. It was beneath the cliffs at the northern end that she had found the body.

On that clear, mild May morning, the view from her garden seemed to Ruby the most beautiful sight in the world. In the short time she had been there she had become very fond of Clogwyn Bach. The scenery was magnificent, the locals were – with one or two exceptions – friendly, and the village itself had a timeless quality. It was slow and sleepy in its isolation, giving the impression that the modern world has passed it by and it really did not care.

The name Clogwyn Bach means 'Little Cliff' in Welsh. It is the smaller of the two Clogwyns which are situated on the south west coast of Wales. The larger town of Clogwyn Mawr ('Big Cliff') lies some ten miles to its north. To the disapproval of the few remaining Welsh speakers, many of the locals now call the towns by the Anglicised names, 'Little Cloggy' and 'Big Cloggy'. Clogwyn Bach or 'Little Cloggy' was, in Ruby's view, by far the nicer of the two Clogwyns. The locals called it a town but it was really no more than a village with dreams of greatness. What it lacked in amenities it made up for in its simple, unspoiled beauty. It sat at the bottom of the half-bowl of land formed by the semi-circular, tree-covered hills surrounding the bay. It was so idyllic that Ruby felt almost guilty for being unable to find the peace and contentment for which she longed.

Ruby had barely had a good night's sleep for the past month. She had been suffering from anxiety attacks and she did not know why. She assumed it might be something to do with the sudden change from the frenetic pace of her former life in London to the altogether more leisurely pace of her life in Clogwyn Bach.

Ruby was an actress. Her younger friends told her that she should refer to herself as an 'actor' because the word 'actress' was sexist and old-fashioned. But she had grown up idolising Marlene Dietrich, Greta Garbo and all those other great Hollywood stars. She could not think of them as actors no matter how hard she tried, and if the word 'actress' was good enough for Marlene Dietrich then it was jolly well good enough for Ruby Lake.

While she had never been a very famous actress, she had made a reasonably successful career in both the theatre and on television. She often played 'character' parts such as vicars' housekeepers, slightly dodgy lady villains or the strange woman in the corner house who spies on neighbours from behind the net curtains. She had never understood why people considered her to be particularly well-suited to those roles. She had always believed that she would be rather good at Lady Macbeth or Cleopatra but directors and producers did not share her conviction. On the other hand, if a television drama required a vicar's housekeeper or a small-time lady crook, Ruby's name would very probably be close to the top of the list.

Even if you have not seen Ruby on TV, you may have heard of her thanks to the notorious 'Lipstick Poisoner' murder case (as the press called it). In fact, much to her chagrin, Ruby seemed to be more famous for that than for her acting. It happened while she was playing the part of the Fairy Godmother in the Christmas panto at Milchester-Mire; half way through the second half, one of the Ugly Sisters suddenly clutched her throat and collapsed on stage – stone, cold dead. The identity of the murderer might never have been uncovered but for Ruby's observation of the lipstick on the whisky glass. However, that is quite another story and we shall have no more to say about it here.

Ruby was not always in work, of course. She did not care to admit to it but she had, in fact, spent quite a bit of time 'resting', which is what actors do when there is nothing to be acted in. During her resting periods, she had filled in the time doing everything from selling advertising for a local newspaper to stacking shelves in a supermarket. She had also made a few TV commercials. She was one of the dancing kittens in the cat food advertisement which you have no doubt seen – "So tasty, they'll eat it to the last miaow." And she had also recorded quite a few radio commercials. You know the sort of thing – "Snibbet's Intimate Deodorant, available from selected dealers, while stocks last, one purchase per household, subject to status, over 18s only, be sure to read the safety precautions, terms and conditions apply…" and so on and so forth. She considered radio commercials to be demeaning. They were certainly not what she had had in mind when she had been at drama school. She had gone through long years of training and had learnt to squeeze every last ounce of emotion out of everything from Brecht's 'Caucasian Chalk Circle' to Osborne's 'Look Back In Anger' – and what did she end up doing? Recording commercials for underarm deodorants and funeral saving plans!

CHAPTER 3

Unable either to relax or to concentrate on getting any work done, Ruby went next door to see her neighbour, Bessie Morgan, who lived in a cottage with the unpronounceable name 'Awyr Môr' which apparently means 'Sea Air', so why it could not have been called 'Sea Air' Ruby did not know. Ruby's knowledge of the Welsh language was limited to a few place names and two or three of the more colourful swear words. She had been born in the little village of Slackton Ings in what she still called the West Riding Of Yorkshire (ignoring the fact that the Yorkshire 'ridings' had been disbanded decades earlier by government officials with no poetry in the souls). While her family had some Welsh connections, none of them spoke Welsh and Ruby always felt slightly intimidated by anyone who could not only pronounce the words but also understood what they meant.

Bessie took Ruby into her kitchen, made some tea and brought out a plate of Welsh cakes, which was Bessie's way of dealing with any sort of crisis. Bessie's kitchen was warm, comfortable, old-fashioned and typically Welsh; just like Bessie herself. It had whitewashed walls, a slate-tiled floor, an oil-powered Aga range-cooker and a big oak table right in the middle of the room. On one wall there was a framed embroidery of the quotation, "One is nearer God's Heart in a garden than anywhere else on earth." Close by was a beautifully hand-written text, also framed, "Gweddi'r Arglwydd – Ein tad, yr hwn wyt yn y nefoedd" which Bessie had told Ruby was the Lord's Prayer in Welsh, "Our father who art in Heaven." In principle, Bessie was a Methodist though she claimed that she had "lapsed" long ago. On the mantelpiece over the fireplace there was a black-and-white photograph of Bessie as a young woman, holding hands with a smiling young man. They were at the seaside somewhere and the sun was shining in their faces. They looked radiantly happy.

Ruby sat at the table and immediately jumped up again so suddenly that she very nearly knocked over her chair. "Something brushed against my ankles!" she said, "I think there's a rat there!"

"That's not a rat," said Bessie, "That's Harry."

"Harry. Who's Harry?"

"My hedgehog."

"Your hedgehog?"

"He's having his breakfast."

"A hedgehog is having breakfast in your kitchen?" Ruby glanced under the table and, sure enough, there was a hedgehog tucking into a hearty meal of some unpleasant-looking brown mush in a saucer.

"What's he eating?"

"Dog food."

"I thought hedgehogs ate cheese and drank milk?"

"Then you thought wrong. Milk, you see, gives them diarrhoea. Now then, just you sit yourself down again and don't you go paying any attention to Harry. Well! You've been in the wars by the looks of it."

"What?"

"Your hand. That's a nasty graze you've got there. Been fighting, have you?"

Ruby told Bessie that she had slipped on some seaweed and scratched her hand on a barnacle-covered rock. It was really nothing, she said, but Bessie insisted on attending to it.

"Yow!" Ruby yelled as Bessie dabbed a spot of iodine onto the cut. "Is that stuff safe? I didn't think people still used it."

Bessie patted away the excess iodine using a paper towel and then she put a small plaster over the cut. "There now," she said, "drink up your tea and you'll feel all the better for it." She put the bottle of iodine back into an old toffee tin in which she kept a range of medicines and ointments, many of which Ruby had not seen since her childhood. "It's a big shock you've had, you see," said Bessie, "It'll have upset you, no doubt. Take things easy is what you should do now, to give yourself chance to get over it."

"For goodness' sake, Bessie, it's only a little cut. I'm not in shock!"

"I wouldn't be so sure. After what you've been through this morning. A terrible shock that must be."

Ruby considered that. "No. Not really. Why do you think that?"

"Enough to upset anyone, I should say. Finding a dead body. Well! It doesn't bear thinking about."

"Actually, it was quite exciting."

Bessie was in the process of crumbling a piece of bread into a saucer. "There's a thing to say!" She tutted her disapproval, "But there, you see, you don't know what you are saying. On account of the shock." She poured some milk over the bread and then poured some tea onto it.

"Oh, I know what I'm saying all right," Ruby insisted, "Nothing happens here usually, so finding a corpse! In mysterious circumstances! That certainly livens things up!"

Bessie frowned. Ruby was not herself that morning. In the two months since Ruby had moved into Rose Cottage, Bessie had not heard her talk about anything more exciting than the weather forecast. In fact, Ruby had given every indication of being an entirely calm and sensible sort of person. She swept her path, she kept her front doorstep clean and she never got drunk and sang bawdy songs while dancing stark naked around her garden in the early hours of the morning (unlike old Mrs Probert, the previous occupant of Rose Cottage). So, on the whole, Bessie had thought she had done well to gain such a nice, uncomplicated, pleasantly dull neighbour.

"The police were marvellous," Ruby enthused, "And so many of them! It was just like one of those shows on the telly."

Bessie took the saucer of tea-soaked bread and put it alongside the saucer of dog food under the table. The hedgehog twitched his nose at it then stumped over and started eating from the new saucer.

"I thought you said hedgehogs shouldn't have milk," said Ruby.

"That's not milk," Bessie protested, "It's *bara-te*, bread in tea. Very good for hedgehogs. And he's got to have milk in his tea, hasn't he?"

When Ruby had first met her, she had thought Bessie was slightly eccentric. In the past couple of months, she had modified that opinion. She now thought that Bessie's eccentricity was of such a high calibre that it would give hatters and March hares pause for thought.

While on most topics Bessie gave every impression of being rational, when it came to animals her rationality deserted her. It was not just that she *liked* animals. She also *befriended* them. Worse still, she was quite undiscerning in precisely which animals she befriended. Ruby had no objection to cuddly, well-behaved animals. Cats, guinea pigs and hamsters were, in Ruby's view, entirely reasonable creatures to have scurrying around in your kitchen. Bessie, however, was just as likely to have rats, toads and snakes hopping and slithering about. When visiting Bessie, it was always a good idea to check that some venomous creature had not already taken occupancy of a chair before you sat down upon it.

"There was a what-d'you call it?" Ruby went on, "A Scene Of Crime Officer, I think they're called. And a photographer. There were police in uniforms. And some others wearing white overalls and gloves – those were the forensics people. I was in an episode of Line Of Duty once. Did I tell you?"

Bessie did not seem interested. She was stooping to watch Harry the hedgehog eating his bread and tea.

"I was the neighbour," Ruby continued, "I'd seen the perpetrator and I had several lines to say when the forensic team arrived."

"Oh, there's lovely," said Bessie abstractedly, "Only I don't watch much telly, do you see. Well, except for the gardening programmes, of course, and the Inspector Stoat Mysteries, so I don't really know what you are talking about."

"Ah. Well, anyway, that's how I know. About the forensic team. What are the Inspector Stoat Mysteries?" Bessie was not listening so Ruby nibbled a piece of a Welsh cake and went on: "Of course, they tried to tape it all off at first, the scene of the crime, but that's not so easy when there are rocks and seaweed all over the place. And on top of all that, the tide was coming in!" Ruby laughed, "Oh dear, it would have been funny if only…well, you know."

From the look on her face, Bessie did not give the impression that she saw the funny side at all. "You're gibbering," she said.

"Gibbering?"

"It's the shock. Takes people in different ways shock does. Some go quiet. Some feel faint. Some gibber. You are one of the gibberers."

"I've told you, Bessie. I'm not in shock!"

"Maybe you don't think you are. But people never do, do they?"

"Don't they?"

Bessie shook her head. "Never. That's a well known fact."

"Is it?"

"Oh yes."

Ruby took another Welsh cake from the plate. She had not had any breakfast and the excitement of the morning had given her an appetite. "You don't have to worry about me," she said, "I'm tougher than I look. It'll take more than a corpse on the rocks to unsettle me."

Still, there was no getting away from the fact that finding a dead body had upset her plans for the day. She had dialled 999 on her mobile phone and less than twenty minutes later a constable had arrived. She had told him all she knew, which was no more than he could see with his own eyes – namely that there was a man's body lying on the rocks. The constable had made a call on his phone and within half an hour the rocks and beach were swarming with police of various descriptions.

"They interrogated me, of course," Ruby said.

"They took a statement, do you mean?"

"Is there a difference?"

"Did they take you into a darkened room and shine a light in your eyes?"

"No."

"Then they took a statement."

"How do you know all this?"

"If you watched Inspector Stoat you'd know it too."

Ruby ignored that comment. "A young woman police officer did most of the talking. She wanted to know why I was on the beach so early in the morning. I told her I couldn't sleep. She sympathised. Apparently she'd been having similar problems. So I sympathised with her. I suppose it must be stressful, mustn't it, being a police officer these days. Murders from one day to the next."

"Not many murders around her, I shouldn't think," said Bessie, "A quiet and safe sort of place Clogwyn Bach is."

"I'm not so sure about that," said Ruby, "An old gent flung to his death from the clifftops. That's not what I'd call quiet and safe!"

"Flung to his…?" Bessie raised a sceptical eyebrow, "Letting your imagination get the better of you is what you're doing. The clifftop path is unsafe. Been dangerous for years. It's too close to the edge, for one thing. Bits of it are always crumbling away. The council should have done something about it ages ago."

"You really think it was an accident? That he just fell from the top of the cliff?"

"I remember, oh, ten years ago it must be, an old lady, a holidaymaker, was standing right on the edge when it suddenly gave way. Then last year a dog fell over…"

"Oh no!" Ruby gasped, "How awful!"

"Do you mean the old lady or the dog?"

"Well, the dog of course!"

Bessie smiled. "You needn't worry. The coastguard sent a helicopter to get him. Winched him back to safety. A little brown and white spaniel he was. None the worse for his adventure."

"Oh, thank God for that!"

"The old lady, however…" Bessie cast her eyes to the floor but Ruby showed no interest in the old lady's fate.

Bessie changed the subject: "You must have been out at the crack of dawn this morning, then?"

Bessie knew all about Ruby's sleep problems. When Ruby had first mentioned them, Bessie had suggested camomile tea. That had not worked. Then she had suggested single malt whisky. That had not worked either but it tasted better than camomile tea so Ruby had continued self-administering a dram or two at night.

"I'm still not getting as much sleep as I'd like," Ruby said, which was an understatement, "But it's not a big problem," which was a downright lie.

"See the doctor is what you should do. Get some pills."

"No. Sleeping pills are not the answer. Something to occupy my mind is what I need."

"Get yourself a hobby, then. There's all kinds of things going on in the village: jam-making classes, yoga, art. You should give it a go."

Bessie's idea of an exciting night on the town was not the same as Ruby's. Besides which, Ruby rarely ate jam and had not the slightest interest in learning how to make it. Yoga was out of the question. Even if she were capable of tying herself into knots (which she sincerely doubted), it would be undignified for a respectable middle-aged woman to be seen in public wearing a leotard and legwarmers (which she presumed were *de rigeur* for yoga). As for art, however… well, that was a possibility. She had always enjoyed sketching and painting. She was not very good at anatomy or perspective but she was not too bad at landscapes.

It was Ruby's hope that one day she would be able to paint something good enough to offer to Bessie. Bessie liked paintings. She had a few framed watercolours on the walls of her hallway and living room. And, of course, there were the framed embroidery and calligraphy on the walls of the kitchen. She did not have any photographs, however, apart from one that was given pride of place on the mantelpiece in which Bessie was a slim young woman, shyly holding the hand of a good-looking young man.

Ruby wondered who the young man was but Bessie rarely talked about her private life and Ruby did not think it polite to ask. She drank her tea and looked out of the window. In the far distance, sunlight glittered on the sea in the bay down below.

"I wonder…" Bessie said, "who it was? The man you found. I suppose it might be somebody I know mightn't it?"

That possibility had not occurred to Ruby. She suddenly felt ashamed and insensitive for giving the impression that finding the body had been a bit of a lark.

"You didn't see his face, I suppose?" Bessie asked.

"No, I didn't. He was lying face down. He had grey hair, he was wearing a long black coat, fairly ordinary brown shoes. That's all I saw."

"It could have been almost anyone, then," said Bessie, "Any old man at all." She crumbled a piece of a Welsh cake in her fingers, stooped to look beneath the table and was about to add the crumbs to the saucer of tea and bread; but the hedgehog was nowhere to be seen. Bessie stood up and started gathering up the dirty plates and cups. "A lot of old men there are in Clogwyn Bach. We'll have to wait and see which one of them has gone missing."

CHAPTER 4

It was almost one o'clock when Ruby left Bessie's cottage. She had been planning to bake a cake but she felt too tired. At the best of times her cake-baking was a hit-and-miss affair. When she had lived in London she had never cooked anything more complicated than a Marks and Spencer's ready meal. Now that she was living out in the sticks, with no ready access to a local supermarket, she was either going to have to live on baked beans and frozen pizzas or she would have to learn to cook for herself. She had decided on the latter course of action. Progress was slow though she had been pleased by the last cake she had baked which had been edible even if the top was a bit blackened and all the fruit had sunk to the bottom.

She glanced at the recipe for 'Pineapple Upside-down Cake' in her cookery book. It looked impenetrably complicated. Cursing her insomnia, she yawned and put the book back on the shelf.

As it was a fine afternoon and quite warm for early May she considered working in the garden. In its present state the garden was no more than a scruffy, weed-infested square of grass at the back of the cottage but Ruby had resolved to transform it into a thing of beauty. Unfortunately, she was not good at keeping resolutions and, apart from half-heartedly snipping at a straggly rosemary bush with a pair of secateurs, she had not yet commenced upon the substantial landscaping that she had in mind. This afternoon, she told herself, she would make up for lost time. She would pull up the dandelions, prune the roses and double-dig the vegetable patch. But first she would have a cup of tea.

Having made the tea, she sat on a stool by the kitchen window and stared out at the breath-taking scenery. On an impulse, she took her mobile phone from the pocket of her jacket, which was slung over the back of a chair, and dialled her agent.

"Max," she said, "Where've you been? I've been expecting you to call."

There was a brief pause at the other end of the line. She had a horrible feeling that Max was trying to place her voice. She had only been gone two months. Surely he cannot have forgotten her so soon. But then came the gushing, enthusiastic tone that Max always used when he had no work for her – "Ruby, darling, how lovely to hear from you. How's life out in the back of beyond?"

"Eventful," she said.

"Really? That's good. What sort of events?"

"This morning, for example, I found a dead body."

Max laughed uncertainly. He was waiting for the punchline. When it did not arrive, he said, "A body, did you say?"

Ruby told him all about the events of the morning, from finding the body to all that fuss with the police. Max actually sounded interested for once.

"Have you been interviewed?" he said.

"By the police, you mean? I gave a statement of sorts. There wasn't really much to say, though."

"By the media," Max said, "TV, newspapers, that sort of thing."

"Interviewed? No, of course not."

"Oh, you should. It could be very useful."

"Useful. How?"

"Publicity, darling. The first person on the scene of the crime and all that. The newspapers would love it."

Ruby was about to say "So you think it's a murder, do you?" But that would only encourage Max in his quest for free publicity.

"Scene of *what* crime?" she said, "Really, Max, I think you're letting your imagination run away with you. A man fell from the clifftop path. Might have had a heart attack for all I know. All very sad but not exactly the sort of thing that would make the front page of The Times."

"But you said a lot of police turned up. They wouldn't do that if the chap had croaked from a heart attack, would they?"

"Wouldn't they? I don't know. It's probably standard procedure, I should think. They had no reason to suppose there was anything untoward…"

"As far as *you* know," said Max, "The police might have all kinds of information of which you are blissfully unaware."

"Oh, for heaven's sake, Max! Believe me, this is not the kind of place where murders happen. It's, well, quiet and safe here. He was an old man. I found him at the foot of a cliff. He lost his footing. Obviously. You should see the cliff paths. There are no barriers, they are right next to the edge and the mud is as slippery as hell thanks to all the rain we get."

"Yes," Max conceded with some reluctance, "You may be right. Still, it wouldn't do any harm to phone up the local TV station and see if they'd be interested…"

"Max! Don't be ghoulish. I have no intention of using a poor man's death to try to whip up some cheap publicity. Anyway, that's not why I called you. The reason I called is…"

"The commercial for the whipped cream substitute? Have you finished it?"

Ruby tried to think what on earth Max was talking about. Then, with a start, she remembered. A couple of weeks ago, Max had sent her the scripts for two radio commercials. One was for an insurance company and another was for a "delicious whipped cream substitute that will have you begging for more".

Ruby muttered something unintelligible that included the words "soon" and "at any moment".

"What? This is a terrible line. I can barely hear you. Shall I phone you back?"

It would not take her long to record those dreary commercials but in her present mood Ruby did not think she would be able to invest them with the right amount of false sincerity.

"Well, actually, it was the other job you mentioned…"

"Which other job?"

"The narration. You mentioned the possibility of…"

"Oh, so you've had second thoughts?"

"I'm still not keen, to be honest, but then again, I have some time on my hands so I suppose I could try one. Just to see how I get on with it. I mean, if it's not too much of a hassle…"

"I have just the thing. It'll be absolutely perfect for you, darling. I'll email it to you. I'm sure you'll love it. Believe me, sweetie, it's easy money. For someone of your talents."

After Max rang off, Ruby made another cup of tea and sat in the kitchen, staring out of the window. A bee was buzzing around a big yellow flower that poked up bravely among a clump of brambles in her garden. She wondered if the flower was something that should be fertilized and tended or a weed that she should pull up at her earliest opportunity. She would have to get a book about gardening to find out.

Bees were buzzing around the flower while singing "Hi-Ho! Hi-Ho! It's off to work we go," when all of a sudden an electronic beeping noise disturbed them, the bees flew off singing "Wake me up before you go-go," and that's when Ruby realised she had been asleep, her head resting in the crook of her right elbow, slumped across the kitchen table. It was the laptop computer on the desk in her upstairs office that had been making the beeping noise to indicate that some email had arrived.

Ruby stood, yawned, stretched, rubbed her eyes, yawned again and then stumped wearily up the staircase to her little office overlooking the back garden. Looking at her computer screen, she saw that there was an email from Max with a document attached called *passbuck.pdf*. She saved the file onto her computer's hard disk and then opened it to see what it contained. It was the text of a novel called "Passions of a Regency Buck". It was not a book she had heard of. As far as she could recall, it had not been discussed on the Radio 4 Book Programme. She did not hold that against it. The Radio 4 Book Program tended to favour novels about people suffering angst in Hampstead. Frankly, a passionate Regency buck sounded like more fun. She would start work on the narration tomorrow, she decided. Glancing at her watch, she saw it was already almost five o'clock. She went to the kitchen and made herself some beans on toast. After eating that, she went into her living room and turned on the TV to watch the local news.

There was a strike somewhere, some villagers somewhere else were complaining about potholes, a woman in Cardiff had won an international guinea-pig-grooming competition and there was still no news on when the lava-bread shortage would be over. Then there was a report on a terrible accident at the idyllic seaside resort of Clogwyn Bach. A woman reporter was shown standing on a beach while she solemnly informed viewers that a man's body had been discovered "by a member of the public" and "a spokesperson for the police has said that the death is not being treated as suspicious." And that was it. Then they moved swiftly on to a story about an all-women rugby team doing a charity match in support of the Welsh Crested Newt Trust.

Oh well, that's the end of it, then – Ruby thought. She had found a dead body. It had made a brief news item on the telly. End of story. She could now forget about it all and get on with the rest of her life.

She could not have been more wrong.

CHAPTER 5

Ruby could not think what to do with the rest of the evening. She picked up the newspaper and flicked to the television listings. There was a documentary on about wars in the Middle East, a programme about midlife obesity and a situation comedy set in a sewage reprocessing plant. Curiously, none of these appealed to her. What about reading a book, then? There were a couple of paperback thrillers and a new crime novel lying on the floor next to her favourite armchair. But after the events of the day, she really was not in the mood for murders. The simple truth was that she needed to get out, to *do* something, to be with other people.

Bessie was right. Ruby should find an interest. She should throw herself headlong into the life of the village. Assuming, that is, that there was any "life" there into which to throw herself. Bessie had mentioned an art class. The local newspaper would probably have the details.

She picked up the crumpled copy of last week's Clogwyn Clarion which she had bundled among some glossy magazines in her magazine rack. The lead story concerned a wine bar that was due to open at the end of the month. Since, in Ruby's opinion, the village was singularly lacking in night life, the addition of a wine bar would be a significant improvement.

She turned to the "What's On" section on the inside back page of the newspaper. There were numerous events listed for the bigger town of Clogwyn Mawr, ten miles to the north, but the range of activities on offer in Clogwyn Bach was much more limited: a coffee morning at the vicarage on Tuesday morning; a choir practice in the Methodist Chapel on Wednesday evening; in the village hall there was jam-making on Tuesday afternoon, yoga on Wednesday morning and art on Thursday evening.

Today was Thursday! According to Ruby's watch it was already nearly ten-past seven. The listing in the newspaper said that the class began at half-past seven. Ruby came to a snap decision. She would go. She brushed her hair, put on a pair of walking shoes and a light overcoat and set off on a brisk walk down to the village. The road that led down to the village was steep, narrow and lined with trees. It was a pleasant evening and she felt in a surprisingly good mood. It was good to get out of the cottage, good to be meeting people, good to be starting something new. She had always been an enthusiastic amateur sketcher. With a bit of expert tuition, who knows, maybe she would be finally able to take her artistic skills to a more professional level?

Who was she kidding? Expert tuition? In the village hall of Clogwyn Bach! She could imagine the sort of person who would be teaching art there. It would be some frumpy old biddy who had taught herself to draw from a book and now spent her days painting endless awful pictures of her overweight tabby cat and vases of wilted chrysanthemums.

By the time she arrived in the village, Ruby had almost convinced herself that it would be much the best decision to turn around and go back home again instead of wasting her time painting cats and chrysanthemums in a cold village hall. But she had nothing to go home to – just an empty house with nobody to talk to (not even a cat) so on the whole she might as well give the art class a try, even if she did not actually learn anything about art.

The village hall was a bland one-storey, white-painted, boxy sort of building with a few steps leading up to the front door. Ruby glanced at her watch: twenty-to-eight. The walk had taken longer than she had anticipated. Still, she had no doubt that she would not have missed much – just a lot of dull, old people drawing flowers or fruit in a wooden bowl. She was wrong. When she pushed open the door she was surprised to see, reclining on a chair set upon a raised platform at the centre of the room, a completely naked man.

CHAPTER 6

Ruby had always had a tendency to blush. To that tendency she now gave full vent. Had a mirror been placed before her, she suspected that she would have seen reflected in it a face resembling an over-boiled beetroot. It was not that she was prudish; she was not. She had seen naked men before. On several occasions. When on holiday in Florence a few years previously she had spent some considerable time gazing at every curve, bulge and wrinkle of Michelangelo's David without the slightest embarrassment. But Michelangelo's David was made of marble whereas the man sitting on the platform at the centre of the Village Hall was self-evidently made of flesh – and a great deal of it. What's more, David was a perfectly-proportioned, athletic demigod whereas the man on the platform looked as though he had not taken any exercise for the last seventy years or so.

Ruby was so startled to see the naked man that it took her several seconds to realise that the room contained about a dozen other (fully clothed) people too, all of whom were staring at Ruby.

"Hello. Have you come to join our class?" A tall, slim, elegant young man with honey-coloured blond hair stepped forward.

"Well, I, er…"

The man on the platform cackled, "Women are drawn to me like moths to a flame. Isn't that right, Ruby?"

Ruby was surprised to hear her name. She glanced at the man again and realised with a shock that she knew him. It was old Tom Crockley, the sheep farmer from Craigwen Farm. He sold lamb chops and sausages in the farmer's markets in the village square. Usually he wore dark green overalls and mud-spattered Wellington boots. Without them he looked completely different. And not in a good way.

"Well, I er…"

The elegant young man pointed to a vacant desk. "If you seat yourself there I'll just get you some paper and pencils. We are trying to find the essential form of our subject tonight. We are not aiming for realism, just the planes, the volumes, the light, the shadow…"

"Ah." Ruby could not think what to say, which was most unlike her. She was rarely at a loss for words. This was one of those rare occasions.

Desks had been arranged in a circle around the platform on which Tom Crockley was perched. At each desk sat a student drawing upon a large sheet of paper using an assortment of pencils. Some students had their paper clipped to an angled drawing board propped up on the desktop; others had their paper laid out flat. The vacant desk to which Ruby was directed was positioned to the rear of the model. The view thus presented of old Tom Crockley was neither the most artistically challenging nor the most flattering.

"I didn't know you was into all this art stuff," a rasping female voice said to Ruby's right. It was Maggie Pountice. She was famous in the village due to her being (so she claimed) a psychic.

"I heard about that terrible business this morning," said a voice from the desk on Ruby's left. That was Muriel Greenalge who ran the local "Food'n'News" shop.

"Sir Clifford," Maggie Pountice said, "That's what I heard, anyway."

"Who's Sir Clifford?" Ruby asked.

"You don't know who Sir Clifford is!" Maggie exclaimed.

"You don't know who Sir Clifford is!" Muriel echoed, just in case Ruby had not heard Maggie saying exactly the same thing.

Ruby felt almost embarrassed to admit it but she assured them that she did not know who Sir Clifford was.

"She doesn't know who Sir Clifford is," Maggie told Muriel. They were having difficulty in comprehending such invincible ignorance.

"Sir Clifford," said Muriel importantly, "is Sir Clifford Coot."

"Or 'was' at any rate," Maggie added, "Until this morning."

"Ah." Ruby tried to give the impression that all was now made abundantly clear. In fact, she had not the slightest idea who Sir Clifford Coot might have been.

"You it was who found his body, wasn't it?" said Maggie, "That's what I heard anyway."

"Well, as a matter of fact..."

"Now, now, ladies..." The young, elegant gentleman whom Ruby assumed to be the teacher had strolled across the room towards them. He was nothing like the flouncy old biddy she had expected. "Tea break will be in half an hour," he said, "There'll be plenty of time for gossip then. For now, though, I want you to concentrate on finding the essential details of our model."

Tom Crockley began laughing – "Essential details! I've heard them called all sorts of things but 'essential details' is a new one, all right."

"Bloody Hell!" grumbled Maggie Pountice, "When he laughs everything starts wobbling! How am I supposed to draw him when everything between his chin and his knees is bouncing around like a bloody jelly?"

Ruby could not concentrate on drawing. For the next half hour all she could think about was what Muriel and Maggie had said. The body which she had found on the rocks was someone called Sir Clifford Coot. It was clear from the reverential tones in their voices that Sir Clifford Coot was quite a big deal. Then it suddenly came to her: she *had* heard the name before. He was a composer. She had heard his music played on the radio. Lush, swelling orchestral music with lots of violins and the odd blare of the brass to wake you up when you felt you might be drifting off.

"Good Lord!" she thought, "The corpse I found was famous!" She would have to tell Max. He would probably want her to do TV interviews in which she would claim that she and Sir Clifford had been intimate friends in spite of the fact that she had never met the man.

"Right, ladies, time for a break!" the teacher eventually called out. "You can put on your robe now, Tom," he added for the benefit of their model.

Ruby looked at the clock on the wall by the door. It was quarter past eight already. The teacher came over to take a look at what she had drawn. It was not much. It looked like a big spongy blob with a smaller spongy blob stuck on top of it. The big blob was Tom's body, the small blob was his head.

"Interesting," said the teacher, "I'm Chris Chamberlain, by the way. And you are…?"

"Ruby. Ruby Lake."

The light of recognition came into Chris's eyes. If he did not recognise Ruby by sight, he had clearly heard her name. "You are the, um… I mean, it was you who…"

It did not take Ruby more than a second to work out what he was referring to, so she filled in the gaps for him. "I found the body, yes. On the rocks. This morning."

"How ghastly!" said Chris, with feeling.

"Well, it certainly wasn't what I was expecting."

"Look, we have a short break now. Tea is on offer in the kitchen," he pointed to an open door at the far end of the hall to which all the other students were already gravitating, "Please avail yourself of the biscuits. We don't charge."

"Oh!" Ruby suddenly realised that she had not paid for the class, "How much does it cost to…?"

"First lesson is free," Chris smiled. He had a dazzling smile. "If you come back next week," Chris added, "it's five pounds per class."

"Such good value!" Ruby gushed.

There was a babble of conversation coming from the small kitchen. The babble stopped the moment Ruby arrived. All eyes turned to look at her. She had the distinct impression that she had been the principal topic of discussion.

"Here, have a mug of tea," the gravelly voice of Maggie Pountice said as she handed a mug to Ruby, "You'll be needing it after the shock you had."

"Seeing me in my natural condition, you mean?" Tom Crockley said with a leering wink. Ruby was glad to see that he was now wearing a white towelling robe which concealed most of his 'natural condition'.

"There were lots of police there, so I heard." That was Muriel Greenalge again.

"I don't know what we'll do about the concert now," said a gloomy-looking middle-aged man.

"The concert?"

The man held out his hand, "Elfyd Davies."

"He's our local doctor," Muriel explained, "Maybe you've been to see him?"

Elfyd smiled, "Now then, Muriel, you know I can't talk about my patients' matters in public."

"No," Ruby interrupted, "I haven't been to see him."

"You should," said Elfyd, "You're looking a bit peaky as a matter of fact. Are you sleeping all right?"

Ruby raised an eyebrow impressively, as only a trained actor can: "I thought you couldn't talk about your patients' matters in public."

Elfyd grinned. "You're not my patient though, are you! Yet."

Ruby lowered the eyebrow, but only slightly. She did not care to talk about her health so she changed the subject. "What was the concert you mentioned?"

"Oh, well, the Clogwyn Bach Male Voice Choir, isn't it," Elfyd Davies explained.

"Male Chauvinist Choir," a dark-haired young woman interjected.

"We've been rehearsing Sir Clifford's latest piece," Elfyd went on, "It was supposed to be for the Summer Fayre."

"We have a Summer Fayre every year," Muriel explained, "It's quite a big thing."

"It's a bit like Glyndebourne," Elfyd added, "Only on a smaller scale. But whether Lady Coot will want us to perform it now, well, your guess is as good as mine."

"Lady Coot?"

"Sir Clifford's wife. Or widow, I should say. Lady Patricia Coot."

"Getting to know everyone, I trust, Ruby?" Chris, the art teacher, interjected. He had a very cultured voice, Ruby noticed. Certainly not a local. He also had a very lovely smile which he was using to good effect. "I hope you are enjoying the class."

"Oh, yes, thank you," Ruby simpered, "Most enjoyable."

"Right then, come along ladies and gentlemen! Time to put away the teacups and pick up your pencils. We have art to create!"

CHAPTER 7

"He was lovely," Muriel said, "No one had a bad word to say about him."

The art class had finished at nine o'clock at which time everyone walked down the street towards the Cat and Ferret pub. Nobody had said, "Shall we go to the pub?" or "Anyone fancy a pint?" – they were drawn towards the pub as inexorably as iron filings are drawn towards a magnet.

The pub was of the old-fashioned country variety: wooden tables and chairs, with a big dark wooden settle against a wall next to the open log fire. The fire took the edge off the night's coolness. The men congregated down one end of the pub to do some serious beer drinking. Ruby, Muriel Greenalge and the dark-haired girl who had expressed her disapproval of the choir's male chauvinism went to the other end to share a bottle of chilled sauvignon blanc. Maggie Pountice sat with them drinking a pint of best bitter.

"How do you know it was Sir Clifford?" Ruby asked, "Did the police say?"

"This is a tight-knit community," Maggie Pountice rumbled, "We don't need no police to tell us what is and isn't going on."

"Oh, it was Sir Clifford for sure," Muriel said, "Rona told me."

"Rona?"

"That's me," said the dark-haired girl.

"Ah, and where did you hear it from?"

"From Bronwen."

"Bronwen Price?" said Maggie.

Rona nodded.

"Bron does some cleaning for Lady Coot," Muriel explained.

"I know Bronwen!" Ruby said, "She does some cleaning for me too."

Muriel gave Ruby an odd look – "It's all very well for those who can afford hired help, I suppose."

Ruby opened her mouth and was about to say "She's cheap," but thought better of it and contented herself with smiling anaemically.

"Well, anyway," Muriel went on, "the police were up at Coot Hall when Bron was doing the dusting and polishing. Bron overheard a few snippets that were said and pieced it all together."

"And Bron told me," said Rona.

"And Rona told me," added Muriel.

"And I knew anyway," said Maggie, "It was in the cards."

"The what?" Ruby asked.

"Maggie reads the tarot cards," Muriel explained, "She has the second sight."

Ruby sipped her wine. Down at the other end of the bar, the men had started singing rude songs. In Welsh. Ruby did not understand the words but she could tell that they were rude because the chorus came with a number of easily recognisable gesticulations.

"Poor Lady Coot," Ruby said, "She must be grief-stricken."

"Pah! I doubt it!" said Maggie, "Tough as old boots, she is. Besides which, don't let all that Lady Muck nonsense fool you. I knew her when she wasn't no more than plain Patsy Jones. Her mam and dad had an end-of-terrace in Gwyntog Road. Proper dump, it was. At school with her, I was. She had nits. Don't know what Sir Clifford saw in her, I don't. A proper gentleman, he was. Done more for this village than anyone else I know of."

"Sir Clifford put Clogwyn Bach on the map, that's for sure," said Muriel, "You'll no doubt be familiar with his 'Variations on a Welsh Theme'. They are always playing it on the wireless. It attracts the tourists. They hear the music and it makes them want to come here to breathe in the sea air."

"Which is pretty damn' pointless," said Maggie, "Because sea air smells of sea. It don't smell nothing like his music."

"Was he stiff?" Rona said.

"I beg your pardon?" said Ruby.

"Stiff. The corpse. They go stiff after a bit. So when you found him, was he stiff or was he floppy?"

"I don't know. I didn't prod him."

"You missed an opportunity."

"Did I?"

"See, if he was stiff it'd give you a way of estimating the time of death. It takes a few hours for rigor mortis to set in."

"Does it?"

"Oh yeah. Four to six hours usually. Sometimes up to twelve."

"Really? How do you know that?"

Rona shrugged, "It's a hobby. Like with you."

"Like with me *what*?"

"Solving murders. I've read all about you."

Ruby gave a long sigh. She had hoped that nobody in Clogwyn Bach would have heard about her involvement in the so-called Lipstick Poisoner murder case. It had been entirely coincidental that she had happened to make the connection between the lipstick smears on the whisky glass and the person who had poisoned the Ugly Sister. The press had, of course, sensationalised the whole thing to make it sound as though she had single-handedly tracked down the killer.

"I expect the police pathologist will have estimated the time of death," Ruby said, "Not that it really matters, does it?"

"It depends on whether or not you've got an alibi. For the time when he died, I mean."

"Me?" Ruby said, "Why should I need an alibi?"

"Not just you," said Rona, "Everyone." She looked slowly and suspiciously around the pub. Her gaze rested meaningfully upon a woman with an impressive blonde bee-hive hairdo and an equally impressive bust-line who was sitting at a table in the middle of the pub with a middle-aged gent who gave the distinct impression that he worked as a travelling salesman in something slightly disreputable. Ruby narrowed her eyes in the direction of the blonde woman. The woman met Ruby's gaze with a look that could have curdled milk.

"Until we find out who the murderer is," Rona whispered, "everyone is a suspect."

At first, Ruby had supposed that she had been the only person who had wondered if Sir Clifford's death might not have been entirely accidental. But when she had told Max about it, he had immediately leapt to the conclusion that it must have been a case of murder. Rona seemed convinced that someone had thrown Sir Clifford over the cliffs. Ruby might have dismissed Max's and

Rona's suspicions as the result of over-fertile imaginations were it not for the fact that she too felt that there was something very fishy about the old man's death. In fact, looked at dispassionately, everything about his death was suspicious. Why had he been walking alone on the clifftops at the crack of dawn in the first place? By what strange quirk did he end up walking at the very edge? And since everyone knew that the clifftop was unsafe, how did he manage to be so incautious as to slip and plummet to the rocks below?

"Do the police think he was murdered?" Ruby asked.

Rona shrugged, "If they do, they're not saying. But it stands to reason, don't it?"

"Does it? Why?"

"He wouldn't just have gone wandering on the clifftops. Not unless someone lured him there! Or else..."

"Or else *what?*"

"Or else he was bumped off somewhere else then dragged up to the top of the cliff and thrown over."

"Why would anyone do that?"

"To make people think it was an accident. Obviously. I reckon he was bumped off last night, dragged up to the top of the cliff under cover of darkness and then dumped over the edge."

Ruby considered this. She supposed it would take at least two people to drag a body all that way. But surely if they had done that they would have left traces. Footprints and so on. The police cannot have failed to notice footprints, can they?

"I don't suppose no one saw him, did they?" Maggie Pountice asked.

"Up on the cliffs?" said Rona, "I doubt it."

"Matt might have," said Muriel Greenalge, "You know, Matt Jones. Only I was working in my shop late yesterday evening, stock-taking and arranging the chocolate bars. We've got some new walnut choc bars if anyone's interested."

"Put me down for two," said Maggie.

"And anyway, I noticed Matt going past, oh, about nine o'clock it must have been. Him and someone else. He was heading for the road over the headland. The one that goes to Clogwyn Mawr. That would take him right past the cliff path. He might have seen something."

"You think Sir Clifford was killed last night?" said Ruby, "Not this morning?"

"We can rule nothing out," rumbled Muriel, gravely.

"Too early for Matt to have seen anything," Rona said, "It'd still have been light at nine."

"How do we know he didn't get killed when it was light?" Ruby asked.

"There are cars going to and fro on that road all the time," Rona said, "The cliff path runs parallel to the road, only about ten or fifteen yards away. If someone had been there bumping off Sir Clifford or dragging his lifeless corpse through the heather they'd have been seen."

"Well, anyway," Muriel said, "Since I saw Matt drive over there at about nine, I suppose he must have driven back again later on, when it was dark. He might have seen something then."

Ruby did not, at that time, know who Matt Jones was. Nor did she know that he would soon become pivotal to her investigation.

"I suppose Sir Clifford might have gone for a walk this morning," Ruby said, "First thing. When it was light."

Rona thought about that. She shrugged. "If it had been this morning, they'd have had to have been pretty damn' quick to kill him and push him over the edge just in time for you to find the body. Possible, I suppose, but unlikely. If he'd been bumped off this morning, the body wouldn't have been stiff when you found it, Ruby. It's a shame you didn't give him a quick prod. With your experience of murders, I'd have expected you to have thought of that. If you'd prodded him, we'd know for sure whether he'd been done away with yesterday or today."

"What kind of idiot would be out walking at the crack of dawn?" Maggie Pountice said.

"I was!" said Ruby.

"Hmmm," Maggie took a good long sip of her beer while she thought about that. Then she added, "I suppose you can prove that."

"Wait just one minute, are you suggesting…?"

Muriel interrupted: "It was this morning he died, not yesterday." She said with an air of finality.

"How can you be sure?"

"Bronwen told me. And Lady Coot told her. He was at home all night and went out early this morning."

It seemed that Bronwen was the fount of all knowledge. "Well then," said Ruby, "Doesn't that disprove your theory, Rona? That he was killed and dragged up to the clifftops under cover of darkness. He can't have been bumped off last night because he was at home at the time."

"Nah," Rona smiled broadly, "We've only got Bronwen's word for it. That wouldn't stand up in a court of law."

"But surely, if it was Lady Coot who told Bronwen…" Ruby protested.

"Well, she didn't exactly *tell* her," Muriel said, "It was more a case of Bronwen overhearing. She happened to be polishing the silver, you see, when the police were talking talk to Lady Coot."

"She was eavesdropping, you mean?"

"Oh, I wouldn't say that, exactly. It's just that Coot Hall is quite echo-y. Sound carries."

"Ah."

"Anyway, what happened was this," Muriel went on, "Sir Clifford went out very early this morning and Lady Coot assumed he'd gone for a bit of a walk. He often went for a stroll at dawn, she says. He was usually back in time for breakfast. Only today he wasn't."

"I think she's lying," said Rona solemnly, "If you ask me, Lady Coot's hiding something. If you want my opinion, dark deeds were done on the clifftops of Clogwyn Bach!"

"She's right," growled Maggie Pountice, "It was in the cards. I read the cards last night. And I saw death!"

"Did you see Sir Clifford's death or just death in general?" Ruby asked.

"Hard to say for sure. But I saw death. And death means someone dying."

"Do you often see death in your cards?"

Maggie ruminated on that question over a gulp of best bitter. "Pretty often."

"And do people often die the next day?"

"No. Not always the next day. Sometimes months after. Sometimes years. But they always die in the end. The cards don't lie."

"Well, even if you saw death in the cards, that doesn't mean Sir Clifford was murdered, does it?"

"It wasn't a natural death, that's for sure," Maggie Pountice insisted, "The cards foretold evil. And where death and evil go together, that means murder."

Ruby shuddered. All day long she had been trying to convince herself that, eerie as it was to find a body lying on the rocks, there was nothing to be alarmed about. The poor man had fallen from the clifftop. It was a tragic accident and no more. But she had never really believed that explanation.

"Why would anyone want to kill him?" she asked.

"Always the same reasons, isn't it?" Maggie replied, "Love or money. Or both."

"Love? You mean he was having an affair?"

"Keep your voice down," Rona hissed. She glanced again at the woman with the blonde beehive who was, at that moment, pawing the disreputable travelling salesman the way a cat paws a mouse which it is thinking of eating.

"He was sex mad," Maggie said, "One of them philanthropists. No woman was safe when he was around."

So much for not speaking ill of the dead, Ruby thought.

"Mind you," (Ruby noticed that Maggie gave a side-long look at the blonde woman before lowering her voice to a rasping whisper that could have been heard two streets away), "He wasn't short of a few bob. There's some women that loses their heads over a man with money, isn't there?"

"How rich was he, exactly?" Ruby whispered. She was a better whisperer than Maggie.

"You should see Coot Hall!" Muriel said, "It's more like a castle than a house."

"His wife will do all right, that's for sure," Maggie added.

"Maggie!" Ruby was slightly shocked at the impropriety of the suggestion, "You surely don't mean that..."

"Me? I don't mean nothing. All I'm saying is that Lady bleedin' Coot won't be on her uppers, will she?"

"I suppose someone in his position must have made enemies?" Ruby suggested.

"He was a dirty old man, that's what he was," said Rona.

Ruby was beginning to think that her initial impression that Sir Clifford had been a paragon of virtue and loved by everyone might not have been entirely correct.

"He always dressed very smart, though," said Maggie, as though that might be a mitigating factor.

"Why do you say he was a dirty old man?" Ruby asked Rona.

"Let's just say that last year, at the Summer Fayre, he brushed past me *very close* in the beer tent. And he didn't say he was sorry."

"I hardly think that is proof of a dissolute character," said Ruby.

"It's proof enough for me!"

"Maybe it was *you* that killed him," said Maggie.

Rona scowled, "It was *your* cards that foretold his murder. You're batty enough to go and do it just to prove the cards were right! Anyway, I reckon whoever it was, Ruby'll find him. With her experience."

Ruby was about to protest. But she did not want to dwell on the Lipstick Poisoner case. She hoped that most people in the village had never heard of it and that those who had heard of it would soon forget.

"Another bottle of wine?" she said, breezily.

"And another pint of best bitter for me," said Maggie, holding out her empty pint glass.

Ruby had intended to leave the pub early so she was surprised when the landlord called "Time, ladies and gentlemen, please." Looking around, she saw that the pub was almost empty. Chris the art teacher had gone. The blonde woman and her disreputable-looking gentleman friend had gone. Tom Crockley was nowhere to be seen. At the other end of the pub, the small choir had moved on from singing bawdy songs to hymns. When a Welsh choir starts singing hymns in a pub, it is a sure sign that it is getting late.

CHAPTER 8

Ruby's walk home was a nightmare. She kept stumbling on potholes and bumping into spiky-stemmed bushes. Having lived in London for so many years, she had become used to the idea that total darkness was not a feature of the modern world. Most London streets are bathed in the glare of streetlamps. Even the darkest of backstreets is illuminated by the ghostly overspill of the city's lights. A Londoner has no experience of absolute, impenetrable darkness. In London, that kind of darkness simply does not exist.

In the countryside, by contrast, on a moonless, cloudy night the darkness is all enveloping. This was such a night. Ruby had only walked a few yards up Fern Hill before it became imperative to use a torch. Unfortunately, she did not have a torch with her. When she had left the house earlier in the evening it had still been light. She had not anticipated quite how dark it would be on her return journey. Through the network of tree branches that arched over the lane, she could vaguely see the thin crescent of the new moon. When she looked at the lane ahead of her she was able to see nothing. She could not see her own hand when held in front of her face, let alone the raised banks, hedges and trees on either side of the lane.

Silence is another thing that Londoners know nothing about; by night and by day in London there is always noise: the rumble of traffic, people talking and shouting, the clank and rattle of trains, the indefinable reverberations of the ceaseless life of the town.

As she walked up Fern Hill, all Ruby could hear was the sound of her own feet tapping on the worn tarmac and the faint distant swish of the sea rolling in the bay down below. Once, there was a frantic scurrying in a nearby bush. Ruby's heart missed a beat! But it was nothing. Just an animal. A fox maybe? Or a cat? Occasionally she heard the screeching calls of a hunting owl drifting mournfully through the cool night air.

While she was not by nature a particularly nervous person, she was glad when she finally saw the lights shining from the windows of Bessie's cottage and, dimly outlined by the weak moonlight, her own cottage just beyond it. Safety at last!

That was how she thought of her little cottage at that moment – a place of safety. She told herself she was being foolish. She was in no danger. On the other hand, if Sir Clifford Coot really had been murdered, then how could she be certain that his killer was not still at large, lurking and watching in the darkness?

Once indoors, she switched on the hall light and locked the door behind her. Back in her well-lit, cosy cottage, her fears about lurking murderers struck her as ludicrous. She had been letting her imagination get the better of her.

She decided to take a quick shower and then go to bed to see if she could finally get a really good night's sleep. She showered in the bathroom upstairs, then she wrapped a bathrobe around herself and sat in her bedroom to towel-dry her hair.

There was a noise. Downstairs. A rattling sound.

Ruby sat for a few moments, listening. All was silence. She threw down her towel, went out onto the landing and looked down the stairs into the hallway. There was something on the doormat. It looked like a letter. That was the clatter she had heard. Someone had posted it through her letterbox. But who on earth would hand-deliver a letter at that time of night? It was almost midnight and her cottage was well off the beaten track. Unless it had been her neighbour Bessie?

Ruby went down the stairs and picked up the letter. The envelope was made of good quality, cream-tinted paper. There was no name or address written on it but, since it had been hand-delivered and nobody but Ruby lived at Rose Cottage, it was clearly intended for her. She ripped open the envelope and took out a folded sheet of paper in a shade of cream which perfectly matched the envelope. When she unfolded the paper, she saw the following words, written in lilac ink in spidery handwriting: "Stop your snooping or you'll be next!!!" Ruby gasped; the use of three exclamation marks struck her as shockingly excessive.

CHAPTER 9

The following morning Ruby was in her kitchen when the phone in the front room rang. Ruby, who was busy making an upside-down cake at the time, picked up a towel, wiped flour off her hands and went to answer it.

"Hello."

"Mrs Lake?"

"Miss. Who is this?"

"I wonder if you could spare five minutes."

It was voice she did not recognise. A man's voice. Very Welsh. Sing-songy. A voice that rolled the Rs.

"If you are selling anything, I'm not interested."

She was about to put down the phone when the voice said, "It's about the body you found."

She put the receiver back to her ear. "Yes? Who are you exactly?"

"Tegwyn Pritchard. I expect you've heard of me."

Was this some sort of hoax call? Ruby was on the verge of putting the phone down again when the voice continued… "The Clogwyn Clarion? Chief reporter. That's me."

"Ah."

Did she really want to talk to the press? Well, why not? After all, if there had been foul play, maybe her interview would jog someone's memory – or their guilty conscience? Besides which, apart from baking cakes, she had nothing better to do.

"You was out on the beach then, was you?" Tegwyn Pritchard asked.

"I was."

"Walking your dog, I expect?"

"I haven't got a dog."

"Your cat, then?"

"I haven't got a cat either."

"I'll just say you were walking your dog then, shall I?"

"No! certainly not."

"Why not?"

"Because it's not true."

"People like dogs though, don't they. From a human interest angle, I mean. If I was to say you was walking your dog, it would get people on your side, see."

"Why shouldn't people be on my side whether or not I was walking a dog?"

"Ah, that's the mystery of human nature, isn't it. If they thought you was walking with no good reason at that time in the morning, well indeed, you know how people talk..."

"You're saying they would think that I played some part in the man's death?"

"I'm just saying a dog would be better."

"Well, I haven't got a dog!"

"What do you want me to say then? About why you were out there? At the crack of dawn?"

"I couldn't sleep."

"Oh no indeed, you don't want to put that."

"Why ever not?"

"Could be misconstrued, you see. People would be saying you had a guilty conscience."

"Wait just a minute. You're making it sound as though I am a suspect."

"No indeed! Not if you was walking your dog, you wouldn't be."

"I haven't got a bloody dog! Even so, I can assure you, I am not a suspect, Mr Pritchard."

"Who is, then, that's what people will want to know, do you see? Who do you think did it, Mrs Lake?"

"*Miss* Lake! Nobody. I don't think anybody did it. Not that I know anything about the matter one way or another. I mean, if you are suggesting that Sir Clifford was murdered, just about anyone might be a suspect. But *I* am not."

"So if you weren't walking your dog, what shall I say you were doing?"

" I don't know, just say I was out looking for whelks."

"What?"

"Whelks. They are a sort of mollusc. Edible. If you like that sort of thing."

"Ah." Tegwyn did not sound convinced, "So you saw the body, smashed to smithereens I expect. And what happened next?"

"As far as I could see, the body was intact. No smithereens of any description. And what I did next was I phoned the emergency services and..."

"Did you feel faint at all? Scream, did you? Try to give him the kiss of life?"

"Certainly not."

"Not *what*? The kiss of life or the screaming?"

"Not any of them. I didn't feel faint. I didn't scream and I most certainly did not give the body the kiss of life."

"Oh. You are sure of that then, are you?"

"Of course I'm sure."

"Only as it stands there's not really much of a story here is, there? No dog, no screaming, no..."

"The man was dead," snapped Ruby, "In inexplicable circumstances. At the bottom of a cliff. There's your story!"

"You're an actress, I hear."

"Who told you that?"

"I can't reveal my sources, I'm afraid."

"Yes I am... I *was*, I mean, I still am... an actress. What has that to do with anything?"

"Been in anything famous? A film maybe? Or on the telly. Emmerdale, Game Of Thrones, that sort of thing."

"Well, not exactly, no. I have been on television but not in... well, not in leading roles in... Well, actually, I was in Midsomer Murders once. And I've done several...advertisements and..." She was about to mention playing a dancing kitten in the cat food advertisement ("So tasty, they'll eat it to the last miaow") but decided that would lack gravitas in an article about a recently deceased composer – "Oh, well really, I don't think I've appeared in anything that would interest your readers. Look, Mr Pritchard, I don't think there's anything I can tell you. I was out walking. I saw the man's body. Which, as you will appreciate, was quite a surprise. Then I phoned the police and that's really all there is to say. So if you will excuse me, I'm in the middle of baking…"

"Dinner party, is it? For your actor friends."

"That's really none of your business."

"You're not denying it, then?"

"Denying what? I've done nothing worth denying. Look, I am awfully busy so…"

"No problem, no problem at all. You've been very helpful Mrs Lake."

"Miss."

"Keep an eye out for the Clarion next Tuesday. This will be front page news, I can assure you of that."

"Goodbye, Mr Pritchard. I'm sorry I couldn't be more helpful."

CHAPTER 10

Ruby was in her little upstairs office, sitting at her desk upon which stood a big professional-grade, chromium-plated microphone connected to her laptop computer. She clicked a button of the recording software and began reading the opening paragraph of the novel which Max had sent her the previous day:

"Lord Alexander Dalrymple removed his silken shirt and let it fall to the ground, thus exposing his rippling torso to the admiring gaze of Miss Lucinda Deveres, the young and voluptuous Countess of Marlingthorpe. Alexander then unbuttoned his… Oh, my God!"

The exclamation "Oh, my God!" did not appear in the text of the novel. It had been involuntarily interpolated by Ruby when she happened to glance ahead to the next sentence.

She phoned Max. "The book you sent me," she said.

"Yes?"

"It's pornographic."

"No it isn't. It's what is called a Regency Romance. Very popular these days. It's a genre that was popularised by, um, well, Jane Austen and Georgette Heyer."

Ruby had never read any Georgette Heyer novels but she had read Jane Austen's 'Sense and Sensibility' and 'Pride and Prejudice' several times. She was quite certain that the sort of activities in which Lord Alexander Dalrymple and Miss Lucinda Deveres were engaged did not feature in the pages of Jane Austen. She had a strong suspicion that Georgette Heyer too might have blushed at some of the goings on.

"Look, Max, I appreciate your sending me this but I can't help thinking that this sort of book would be better narrated by a man."

Max tutted. "That's a very sexist thing to say," he said, "As a matter of fact, women prefer this sort of book to be narrated by a woman."

Ruby took the opportunity to tut back at Max. "That," she said, "is an astonishingly sexist attitude!"

"It's not an attitude," Max countered, "It's business."

He was right, of course. Max could not have cared less whether or not something was sexist, pornographic or just downright nonsense. All he cared about was the bottom line. Does it make money? Audio books, he assured her, were big business. Easy money for an actress of Ruby's experience. And what's more, he reminded her, she was not, at that moment in time, financially solvent (in fact, once she had received payment for the insurance company and synthetic whipped cream commercials, she would have no source of income of any description). Reading a book into a microphone was, Max insisted, far from an arduous task and would make Ruby a couple of thousand pounds. "Take it or leave it," were his final words. So she took it.

Ruby gritted her teeth and narrated her way through the first three chapters of the Regency buck's passionate adventures, hoping all the while that the teeth-gritting would not sound too obvious in the finished recording. She was ten minutes into the next chapter of "Passions of a Regency Buck" when she was disturbed by a clattering sound. She only heard it because the door of her office was open. Her office was a small room and she felt that keeping the door ajar might help the air to circulate and stop her mouth from drying up quite so quickly. The clattering sound was caused by the flap of the letterbox in her front door. The noise probably would not have been picked up by her microphone but the somewhat colourful expression that Ruby used when she heard it certainly would be, so she pressed 'Stop' on her recording software and went downstairs to see what the post had brought.

It was not a letter in the conventional sense. It was, in fact, no more than a sheet of A4 lined paper, folded into quarters. When she unfolded this she saw these words written on it in capital letters using a ballpoint pen: "IN THE DESK. THE SEECRITS IN THE DESK."

Ruby opened the front door to look outside. There was no sign of anyone. Whoever had delivered the note had scarpered again pretty nippily.

She closed the door, went back up to her office, sat in her chair and looked at the note again. The secret's in the desk. What could that mean? She looked at her desk. It was nothing special – a cheap pine construction with, on the left-hand side, two drawers stacked vertically beneath the desktop. Surely the person who had written the anonymous note could not mean that there was some vital clue secreted in her desk. As far as she could remember, the only person other than Ruby who had even seen that desk was Bronwen, the young woman who did some cleaning for Ruby, and it seemed improbable that she would have posted such an inscrutable note.

Ruby opened the drawers of her desk to see what sort of secrets they might hold. The top drawer contained a jumble of bits of paper, some Post-It notes, half a dozen bent paper clips, a few ballpoint pens and pencils, an eraser, a computer mouse that did not work, some stale mint humbugs, a stapler and assorted balls of fluff.

The drawer beneath that contained a sheaf of A4 paper, a ruler, a copy of an Ed McBain novel ("Oh, so that's where that went to!" Ruby muttered with delight) a pot of turquoise ink which was of no possible use to her since she did not own a fountain pen, and a few more balls of fluff.

Ruby examined the note again. She wondered if the writer had deliberately written it in capital letters to avoid any possibility of having his or her handwriting identified. An alternative possibility was that the writer had never mastered the art of 'joined-up' handwriting which, once upon a time, would have been a sign of an incomplete education but in the present day, when children grew up writing everything on keyboards rather than with pen and paper, might equally be an indication of the author's youth. There was also that egregious misspelling – "seecrits". Surely nobody would accidentally spell "secrets" that way; in fact, there was also a missing apostrophe; it should have been written "secret's". What was she to deduce from that? Perhaps this favoured the theory that the note's author had received little in the way of a formal education. Or perhaps the errors had been deliberately introduced in order to deceive Ruby into making incorrect assumptions about the author's identity.

She wondered if the letter that had been delivered the previous night might have been written by the same person. If so, that person had gone to some lengths to hide the fact. The smart cream-coloured paper of last night's letter in its smart cream-coloured envelope contrasted with the scruffy piece of lined A4 which she was now holding in her hands. The spidery hand-writing of the cream-coloured letter was also quite unlike the blocky ballpoint lettering on the lined A4 paper. And whereas yesterday's letter was a warning, or possibly a threat, today's note gave every indication of being a clue.

Then again, both the letter and the note might just be the work of a crackpot. Or a prankster. "Best to forget all about it," Ruby concluded. She pressed the 'Record' button of her software and started reading where she had left off: "Taking a silken handkerchief from her reticule, Ariadne glanced into Lord Alexander's topaz eyes and sighed. She had never known such ecstasy as she had on that night in the jasmine-perfumed gazebo. But what terrible jealousy might stir in the heart of Countess Lucinda when she discovered that her beau had been unfaithful with a mere serving girl!"

Against her better judgment, Ruby found that she was starting to enjoy narrating this book. There was no doubting the fact that Lord Alexander Dalrymple was a nasty piece of work. Unfaithful, flirtatious, a philanderer, liar and cad. But there was also something quite charming about him. "A bit like Sir Clifford Coot, perhaps?" Ruby thought. Yes, indeed. Sir Clifford seemed to be both loved and hated by an awful lot of people. But who could possibly have hated him enough to kill him?

CHAPTER 11

Later that afternoon, Bessie called around with a bunch of Phlox. Ruby made a joke about sheep which apparently Bessie had heard before so it failed to provoke much in the way of uproarious hilarity. Bessie told Ruby to plant the Phlox in her herbaceous border where it would produce a riot of tiny pink flowers for years to come. Ruby promised she would do so, though she had no idea which bit of her garden was the herbaceous border and she made a mental note to Google it later on.

As the afternoon was sunny, Ruby thought it would be fun to "take tea" in the garden. She and Bessie sat in two saggy old deck chairs that Ruby had found mouldering in a cupboard under the stairs. With the deckchairs facing the bay, they had a wonderful view of the sun-sparkling ocean stretching away from between the wooded slopes whose trees shimmered yellowy-green with early leaf. Ruby brought out a tray bearing her best bone china tea pot, cups, saucers, a jug of milk and a plate on which her upside-down cake reposed solidly.

Ruby cut two slices of the cake, with some difficulty and handed one slice, on a bone china plate, to Bessie. She took the other slice herself and attempted to eat it. The attempt was not successful.

"Perhaps the recipe needs another egg?" Ruby asked.

"Maybe an upside-down cake was a bit ambitious," Bessie suggested, diplomatically, "Perhaps you should try to master a rightway-up cake first?"

Just then a huge black bird swooped down from the sky and landed at Bessie's feet. Ruby's heart missed a beat. She remembered seeing an old newsreel film of Goldie The Eagle which, having escaped from London Zoo sometime in the 1960s, proceeded to attack two small dogs. She felt that, if a Golden Eagle happened to be in a bad mood, it might similarly consider attacking two women sitting in deckchairs. However, the bird to which Bessie was now feeding the remnants of her upside-down cake was not an eagle.

"What is it?" said Ruby, "Is it a raven?"

"A raven?" said Bessie, "No, though it's a mistake that people often make. This is Wenceslas. He's a carrion crow. Tame as a kitten, aren't you, my lovely?"

"What are you doing with a tame carrion crow?"

"A cat attacked him when he was little. I rescued him and nursed him back to health. Ever since then he comes and sees me whenever he feels a bit lonely."

"Ah." Ruby's knowledge of the carrion crow and related corvids was far from extensive. She tried another tack: "Why is he called Wenceslas?"

"Why are you called Ruby?"

"No particular reason. My parents must have liked the name, I suppose."

"There you are, then."

Bessie's version of logic was so obscure that Ruby often could not be sure whether or not it made any sense at all. "You are obsessed with animals," she said, "I've never met anyone as obsessed as you are."

"I wanted to be an explorer, you see. When I was a girl. Never had the opportunities though. So I became a primary school teacher. Didn't you have any wild ambitions when you were a girl?"

Ruby was about to say that she had dreamed of becoming an actress. But whereas Bessie's childhood ambition had remained unfulfilled, Ruby's had not: she did, in fact did become an actress. Just not a very successful one.

"I quite fancied being a ballet dancer," Ruby said, "I was only held back by the fact that I couldn't dance."

"Still, everything's turned out for the best, don't you think?" said Bessie, "I mean, I don't have to go to Africa or Borneo to find nature red in tooth and claw, do I? The battle for survival is just as bloody here in Clogwyn Bach. So I didn't miss out on anything really by not being an explorer. And if you had become a ballet dancer, you might never have moved into Rose Cottage and devoted your life to solving murders."

Ruby spat out a mouthful of cake crumbs when Bessie said that. Wenceslas, deciding that he was not in civilised company, gave a penetrating "caw", opened his great black wings, flapped up into the air and soared down the valley towards the village.

"I hardly think," said Ruby, "that I have devoted my life to solving murders."

Bessie smiled. "No? Well, let's just wait and see, shall we?"

CHAPTER 12

On Saturday, Ruby had planned to sit in her garden to do some sketching but the afternoon turned cloudy, cool and windy so she decided to stay in her living room and work on some landscape watercolours. She had a simple box of watercolour paints and a couple of sable-haired brushes. Her only other equipment was a jam jar filled with water and a stack of A4 paper. It was all quite amateurish. She kept telling herself that she really should buy a proper easel, some better brushes, heavyweight cartridge paper and a decent set of watercolour paints – the sort that come in tubes instead of solid blocks – but she never quite got around to it.

She had already begun a picture of the Old Man of the Rocks, which was the local name for an odd pinnacle of rock that poked out of the sea just beyond the northern end of Clogwyn Bach bay. The painting was based on a photograph she had taken the previous week. She took out her phone and cycled through the pictures to find the one she needed but the screen was far too small to work from.

She had already copied the photograph onto her laptop PC. The computer screen was big enough to display the picture more clearly. There were a few newer photos on her phone too and she thought one or two of them might make the basis of a painting so she would need to copy those onto her computer too. She went upstairs to her little office and brought down her laptop and the cable needed to connect it to her phone. Using the cable, she copied a dozen or so photographs onto the laptop's hard disk by which time she was feeling in urgent need of a cup of tea so she went into the kitchen and made one.

She returned to the table in the living room, tea in hand, and absently flicked through the newly copied photographs on the laptop. There was rather a good one of the sun rising over the sea. There were some out-of-focus photographs of the seagulls paddling at the edge of the surf. There was a picture of a tabby cat sitting under a gorse bush – that was a nice one but she would not paint it because she was not very good at painting cats. Then there were a few boring photographs of the beach and one of the rocks. Why had she bothered to take a photograph of the rocks? Oh, the seal! She had forgotten all about it. In actual fact, it was not a seal, of course. It was the body of Clogwyn Bach's most celebrated resident, Sir Clifford Coot. Not that you could see the body clearly in the photograph. It looked more like a seal.

She clicked the magnification icon on the PC screen to zoom in on the body. But there really was not much to be seen. Just an ill-defined shape lying among the seaweed in the distance. Unless you knew what you were looking for, you would not have noticed anything at all. Just rocks, rock pools, the sheer wall of the cliffs on one side and the sea at low tide on the other. There was a light mist – or maybe it was sea-spray – in the air which did not help matters either. Oh well, that was one photograph she certainly had no intention of keeping.

She was just about to delete the picture when she noticed something else. Something she had not seen before. There was a person. In the far distance. Way beyond the body lying on the rocks. Someone was in the next bay. There were two bays visible from the point where Ruby had been standing when she had taken that photograph. Behind her had been the great expanse of Clogwyn Bach bay. Then there were the rocks of the promontory at the foot of the cliffs where she had found the body. At the other side of the rocks there was another, quite small bay which, if you saw it on a map, would appear as little more than a small 'notch' in the coastline. It was in this bay that the person was standing.

The person's outline was indistinct due to the distance and the mist. Ruby clicked the zoom button to enlarge the picture even more. The image was blurry but it looked to her as though the person in the other bay was wearing some sort of hooded coat, probably an anorak, with something on his back – a rucksack, perhaps? – and he was holding a rod or pole with what looked like a hoop on the end.

"A butterfly net?" Ruby muttered to herself. But that did not make any sense. Nobody would go down to the shore to catch butterflies. A long-handed net for catching fish then? That did not make a great deal more sense. Surely if he had wanted to catch fish he would have taken a fishing rod.

Ruby drank her tea and thought about the person in the photograph. She had the impression that it was a tall person and she assumed it was a man. She had not noticed him when she had been on the beach the previous morning, which was perhaps not surprising given the fact that he was at such a distance.

While it was unusual to see other people out so early in the morning it was not unknown. Sometimes she saw an early-morning dog-walker or a fisherman digging in the sand for things called rag-worms which apparently made good bait. Occasionally she saw someone who, like herself, was out walking for no other reason than that they happened to be awake with nothing better to do.

But in light of her discovery of Sir Clifford Coot's body, the presence of another person on the rocks that morning took on a greater significance. For all Ruby knew, Sir Clifford may have fallen to his death mere minutes before Ruby found him. That is, assuming that he had died that morning rather than the previous evening (as Rona had suggested when they had discussed the matter in the pub). However, all the evidence suggested that he must have died in the morning. According to Muriel, who had heard it from Bronwen, who had heard it from Lady Coot, Sir Clifford had left home early on Thursday morning. It was not much after dawn by the time Ruby had arrived on the beach. Which meant that anyone who had been on the beach before Ruby had arrived might have seen something. Or, indeed, might have *done* something.

Ruby decided that it was a matter of the greatest urgency to find the figure in her photograph. But how could she hope to do that? It was such a blurry photograph that there really was no possibility of identifying the person in it.

She flipped back to the picture she had been using as the basis of her watercolour landscape and continued working on her painting. After half an hour she was so engrossed in her work that she had forgotten all about the distant figure in the photograph.

CHAPTER 13

Sunday morning was cold and bright. At half-past five, the village was asleep. All except for Ruby. She had woken while it was still dark and, not being able to get back to sleep again, she had decided to take a walk down to the bay. She walked down Fern Hill and turned into Harbour Street which was no more than a narrow, cobbled alleyway that some of the older locals still called by its Welsh name, Ffordd Yr Harbwr. At first she had planned to go down to the beach itself and watch the gulls which she often did when sleep eluded her. But when she arrived at the High Street, which was bounded by shops on one side and by the sea wall on the other, she decided to turn to the north and continue walking up the road towards the headland.

To her left the land was grassy, dotted with heather and occasional low-growing, stunted gorse bushes that somehow struggled to survive against the harsh salty winds that scoured the higher land beyond the clifftops. It took her about twenty minutes to walk to the top of the hill, by which time she was out of breath. She paused to look around. At the bottom of the hill up which she had walked, the first signs of life were stirring in Clogwyn Bach. A few early cars were on the roads taking people to their jobs in nearby towns. To her right, in the east, inland fields bounded by wire fencing were being cropped by flocks of sheep. To her left was the wilder landscape of the headland: a heathery, grassy, gorse-covered strip of land crisscrossed by occasional narrow pathways, some of which had been made by ramblers while others had been made by sheep that had escaped from the fields which were intended to contain them.

It was along one of those paths, Ruby assumed, that Sir Clifford Coot had taken his final walk early in the morning just four days ago. Why had he come there? Did he too suffer from insomnia? If so, how long would it have taken him to walk from his home to these bleak headlands? Or perhaps he had gone there for a specific purpose? To meet someone?

Ruby turned down an ill-defined path that was more like a muddy rut bounded by heather and gorse. It was just as well that she was wearing a pair of good walking boots because otherwise her feet would soon have been soaking. In some places the mud was so wet that her boots sank several inches into it. Had she been wearing ordinary shoes they would soon have been filled with mud.

Ordinary shoes. She tried to picture in her mind the body she had found on the rocks. It was an old man wearing a long black overcoat and ordinary brown shoes. Town shoes. Not the sort of shoes you would wear when walking along the churned-up muddy path along those cliff tops.

In a couple of minutes Ruby had arrived at the cliff edge. From that point she was able to look down into two adjoining bays – to her left was the long sandy bay of Clogwyn Bach. To her right was a little inlet – a narrow, sheltered bay which the locals called Rocky Cove. The beach in the cove was no more than an accumulation of pebbles and stones that rose steeply from the margin of the sea towards the cliff that surrounded the bay on three sides. There were several more small bays beyond Rocky Cove, before the much bigger bay at Clogwyn Mawr. Whereas Clogwyn Bach was little more than a sleepy village with a chapel, a few small shops and a couple of pubs, Clogwyn Mawr was a bustling town with supermarkets, schools, restaurants and even a nightclub.

It took Ruby a while to find the place she was looking for, just above the spot where she had found the body. There was a well-trodden path following the contour of the cliff-edge but set back several feet from it. This was the main coast path which ran all the way from Clogwyn Mawr, around Rocky Cove and over the headland towards Clogwyn Bach.

Ruby had always been nervous of heights so it was with some trepidation that she stepped off the path and walked through the tussocky grass towards the very edge of the cliff. From there she could see the rocks at the foot of the cliff where she had found the body of Sir Clifford. There was nothing to show that anything untoward had happened. There were no yellow-and-black crime scene tapes marking off either the clifftop or the rocks below. Ruby could not be certain of the precise position where the body had been lying but, since she recalled that she could see clearly both into Clogwyn Bay and Rocky Cove, she was able to hazard a pretty good guess as to the approximate location. From that approximation she was able to work out which section of the coastal path passed directly above it.

There was not much to see on the path itself apart from mud. In the mud there were footprints but they were so varied and numerous that nothing could be deduced from them other than the obvious fact that many people had walked along the footpath. As for the cliff edge, that was badly eroded and in some places it appeared to be crumbling. Looking hesitantly over the edge, Ruby clearly saw several small heaps of scree showing evidence of recent rock-falls. But there was nothing to indicate that someone had slipped or been pushed. Nowhere were there any signs of a struggle.

"You're a fool, Ruby Lake," she said to herself, "If there had been any evidence of murder the police would have found it."

She was letting her imagination run away with her. Maybe it was due to the insomnia. She was not thinking logically. She had begun to take it for granted that Sir Clifford Coot had been murdered. And yet, there was nothing concrete to indicate that his death had been anything other than a tragic accident. And even if it had been more to it than that, it was clearly preposterous to think that she, Ruby Lake, might be able to solve the mystery when the police had failed to do so.

"You are wasting time trying to solve a crime that probably didn't even occur," she mused.

It was while she was thus musing that her eye was caught by a figure moving over the rocks down below. The figure looked familiar. It was a tallish man wearing a long green anorak. On his back he had a rucksack. In one hand he held a long pole to which was attached a net. It looked rather like a butterfly net. Good Grief! It was the man in the photograph! The man who had been in Stony Cove at exactly the moment when Ruby had found the body on the rocks!

CHAPTER 14

"What?"

"The body," Ruby said between gulping breaths – she had run along the clifftop path leading northwards and then she had run down the steep stone steps leading into Rocky Cove. She was not used to such frenzied exertion and, given the fact that she had to raise her voice to be heard over the noise of the surf swooshing to and fro over the shingle beach, it was hardly to be wondered at that she was short of breath. "I saw you running away. Thursday morning. From the body on the rocks."

"What?" the young man said again.

"The body. Sir Clifford Coot. On the rocks. I saw you."

"Me?"

"You!"

"What?"

"Oh, for heaven's sake, can't you say anything other than 'what?'"

"I probably could if anything you said made any sense. Which it doesn't. First of all, I didn't see any body. And secondly, if you've ever tried running over those rocks, you'll know it's not possible."

"Yes, well, all right," Ruby conceded, "I may have exaggerated slightly when I said you were running. But you were definitely there, moving away from the body, I'd say, in the direction of this cove. What I want to know is what you were doing on the rocks at six o'clock in the morning in the first place."

"I might well ask you the same question. I was looking for gobies, what's your excuse?"

"I couldn't sleep."

"That's not a very convincing excuse."

"Well, neither is looking for gobies!" Ruby retorted, "Whatever they may be. What are they?"

"Fish."

"Ah. Edible?"

"I've never tried. I doubt it. They're only a couple of inches long."

"Why were you looking for inedible fish at six o'clock in the morning?"

"None of your business. Now, if you don't mind, I am trying to find some blennies."

"Let me guess. Fish."

"Of course, fish. What else would they be?"

Ruby was not sure what to make of the man. If he was implicated in Sir Clifford's death he was not showing any obvious signs of guilt. In fact, he was acting as cool as the proverbial cucumber. Then again, she had read somewhere that psychopaths often act cool. They dissociate themselves from their own actions. Whereas you or I, had we bumped someone off, would probably go around the place looking incredibly guilty, a psychopath would be able to deny his crime with complete calmness and confidence.

But surely a psychopathic murderer would have concocted a more convincing alibi than gobies. It might seem a bit simple-minded to go looking for inedible fish in rock pools at six o'clock in the morning but that does not mean that every early-morning goby-hunter is a murderous psychopath. Besides which, this young man had an honest face. Rather an attractive face, as a matter of fact. Yes, all in all, he was a very attractive young man. He was tall and slim with dark, slightly wavy hair – and as for the eyebrows! Ruby was a connoisseur of eyebrows, and this young man's were prize-winners: thick enough to make him moody and interesting without any hint of actual bushiness. Those were not the eyebrows of a murderer.

"Why are you so interested in Sir Clifford, anyway?" asked the young man, "A friend of his, were you?"

"No, but… It was I who found his body?"

"Somebody had to, I suppose. I heard it was an accident. Open and shut case. I don't see what it's got to do with me. Or with you, come to that."

"Let's just say I'm a concerned citizen."

"Oh yes? Very commendable. It's none of *my* concern though, is it?"

"You might have seen something."

"What sort of thing?"

"Someone. On the cliff path. On the rocks. You might have seen the murderer."

"Murderer? I thought you said it was an accident?"

"I didn't say that. You said it."

"You didn't disagree."

"I didn't agree either. What I'm saying is that, just on the off chance that Sir Clifford's death might not have been an accident," here Ruby paused for breath, "You might have seen something. What time did you get down here that morning?"

"First light. About half-past five, I'd say. Why?"

"Well, he must have been… I mean, he must have had his… his accident, when you were down here. We know he left home early in the morning."

"Do we?"

"His wife says so. And he can't have been wandering about in the dark. So he must have fallen – or been pushed – from the cliff path. Quite possibly at around the same time that you were down here."

"Why are you so sure he fell from the cliff path?"

"His body was found at the base of the cliff over there. I found him. I thought he was a seal."

"A seal? Why did you think he was a seal?"

"It's an easy mistake to make. At a distance. He was wearing a long black overcoat, soaking wet. He glistened. The way a seal glistens."

"Seals don't glisten."

"They do if they are wet."

"Where did you say you found him? Over there, was it?" The young man pointed to a spot directly beneath the highest point of the cliff path.

"Precisely."

"He couldn't have been killed that morning then. Completely impossible. Now, if you don't mind, I have work to be getting on with. These blennies won't catch themselves, you know."

And off he went, across the rocks.

Strange chap, Ruby thought. Rather attractive though.

CHAPTER 15

"Alexander gave a lopsided grin and clasped Lucinda in his strong arms. Lucinda's ivory skin trembled beneath Alexander's rough caress.

"'Be gentle with me!' she expostulated, 'For I have never given myself to a man before…' Ha! What utter twaddle. Oh Hell! Now I'll have to do that bit all over again."

Ruby was sitting at the desk in her small study overlooking the garden. She was trying to get the damn' book narration finished. The only problem was that she kept laughing. Often at the most dramatic moments. Whenever Alexander gave his lopsided grin or Lucinda expostulated, it would start Ruby off.

With a click of the mouse, she stopped the recording. Maybe she was not in the mood for passionate romance. If only Max had sent her a murder mystery to narrate, she would have had it finished in no time.

There was a discreet knock at the door of her room.

"Come in!"

The door opened and a plump, rosy-cheeked face popped around the edge of it. "I heard you was very quiet so I thought you might fancy a cup of tea."

"That would be lovely, Bron. I could do with a break from this book."

Bronwen Price was a young woman from the village who came on Monday mornings, to clean and dust Ruby's house. Bronwen was punctual and trustworthy and she did not charge much. Her only deficiency was that she was not very good at cleaning things. She tended to smear dust into artistic patterns rather than actually removing it. But at least she made a good cup of tea. Bronwen entered the room holding a bone china cup and saucer in one hand and a plate of bourbon biscuits in the other. These she placed on Ruby's desk. "You recording something then, are you?" she asked.

Ruby took a long sip of tea and nodded. "Yes. Something."

"A book, is it? A novel, like?"

"It's the latest oeuvre of Miss Cicely P. Tuberose. I don't know if you've heard of her?"

"Heard of her!" Bronwen's eyes lit up, "She's my favourite! You haven't read 'Hot Nights Of Sin In Old Morocco', have you?"

Ruby was forced to confess that, by some curious quirk of fate, she had not.

"Oh, you'd love it! I'll lend it to you if you want."

"Oh no, that's really not…"

"Oh, wait a minute, though, I lent it to Lady Coot. Weeks ago that was, though. She must have finished it by now. I'll ask her, shall I?"

"That's very kind of you, Bron, but really, I don't think I… Wait a minute! Lady Coot, did you say? Of course. You work at her place, don't you? How is the poor woman coping?."

"What? Oh, with Sir Clifford kicking the bucket, you mean?"

Ruby nearly choked on her tea. Bronwen had a good heart but sometimes you would not guess it from the forthright way with which she spoke about sensitive subjects like birth, marriage and death.

"It must have come as an awful shock to her," Ruby said between splutters.

"If it did, you'd never guess it. I was there on Friday. She was out on the veranda drinking gin and tonic and drawing up plans for the party. Half-past ten in the morning that was. Gin and tonic!"

"Grief does strange things," said Ruby, philosophically, "But you say she's throwing a party?"

"Oh yeah. It'll be massive. One of them big marquee tents, wine, beer, tons of food, a band probably. And a disco in the evening, of course."

"A disco?"

"You should come. It'll be fun."

"Oh no. I've never even met Lady Coot. I couldn't possibly intrude."

"Oh, you don't want to wait for an invite. Just turn up. Last year the vicar got plastered and started doing a strip-tease."

"Last year? Someone died last year too?"

"Died? No. No one died last year. Why d'you…? Ohhhh!" A broad smile lit up Bron's face, "You was thinking she was having the party after the funeral, I 'spect."

"She isn't?"

"No. Course she isn't. I mean, I 'spect she'll lay on a few cucumber sandwiches and whatnot. For the mourners."

"But no disco?"

"It's got nothing to do with the funeral the party hasn't. Carnival Week is when the party is. You know, the Summer Fayre. Every year, on the third Saturday of July, Sir Clifford and Lady Coot throw this massive party with a marquee tent and wine and beer…"

"And a stripping vicar?"

"Up at Coot Hall. The party's in the evening but they have stuff going on all day. There's the choir, of course. Sometimes a magician or a mind reader. They had a juggler last year and a man on stilts. It's great. All free too. You don't have to pay for nothing."

"Oh well, that sounds, um, fascinating."

When Bronwen had taken away the empty tea-cup and the untouched plate of bourbon biscuits, Ruby stared malevolently at the text of the novel on her laptop screen. She was trying to will herself to read, enthusiastically and without so much as the hint of a snigger, all the details of Alexander's lopsided grin and Lucinda's trembling ivory skin.

She was afraid she had made a bit of a fool of herself, thinking that the party that Lady Coot was planning was to be in celebration of her husband's death.

She clicked the mouse on the 'record' button of the software and started reading Chapter 5 all over again…

"Alexander gave a lopsided grin and clasped Lucinda in his strong arms. Lucinda's ivory skin trembled beneath Alexander's rough caress.

"'Be gentle with me!' she expostulated, 'For I have never given myself to a man before and I fear that if my father heard of this there would be trouble!'

"Funny thing to be arranging a party a few days after your husband has been found dead. Oh, bother!"

Ruby clicked the button to stop the recording. Her attention had wandered and she had spoken her thoughts aloud before she had realised what she was doing.

But it really was a funny thing to do. Sir Clifford Coot's body had been found on the rocks in Clogwyn Bach Bay on Thursday morning. And, according to Bronwen, the very next day his widow was sitting on the balcony guzzling gin and tonic and planning a party. Either she was remarkably good at controlling her grief or else there was no grief for her to control.

Lady Coot might be a pretty cold fish but that did not mean she was a murderer. Ruby knew several married couples who put on a thin pretence of mutual adoration but who, in reality, hated one another's guts. But they did not kill one another.

Lady Coot interested her. To be sitting on the veranda drinking gin and tonic and planning a party the day after her husband's death showed a certain sort of British stiff upper-lip that bordered on the pathological.

From downstairs, Ruby could hear the sounds of Bronwen slopping mucky water around the kitchen floor with the aid of a mop while making a low wailing noise which Ruby assumed to be Bronwen's nearest approximation to singing. On an impulse, she ran down the stairs to the kitchen.

"Bron," she said, "When did you say the Summer Fayre is? The thing with the stripping vicars in a marquee at Coot Hall? July, wasn't it?"

"That's it. Third Saturday. You coming, then?"

"Possibly. You said there were events. Music, magicians, that sort of thing?"

"Singing, dancing, face-painting for the kids. All sorts of stuff. You'll have a whale of a time. Nothing to do and plenty of time to do it in, if you know what I mean?"

"Do they have plays?"

"Plays? How d'you mean?"

"Plays. Theatrical productions. Hamlet, Hedda Gabler, The Caucasian Chalk Circle, er… Charley's Aunt, that kind of thing."

Bronwen stopped sloshing water about and leaned on the handle of her mop to have a good think. Having thought, she told Ruby that, to the best of her knowledge, there had never been any plays performed at the Summer Fayre, probably because there was nobody in the village who knew how to act.

Ruby gave a look of triumph – "There will be soon. I shall teach them!"

"You?"

"Me!"

"What sort of play will you being doing, then? I like a good murder mystery myself."

Ruby thought about that. "Given the circumstances, I hardly think that would be the most sensitive choice. Perhaps a comedy. Or… well, we don't need to decide right away. The choice of play can wait until we have some actors. And, er, well, of course, we'll need Lady Coot's permission. If we are to present the play in the garden of Coot Hall or in one of her marquees. Do you think she would be enthusiastic?"

"Don't know. She watches Coronation Street on the telly, I know that. Not sure about plays as such though."

"I shall have to broach the subject to her. When would be a good time, do you think?"

"Give her a ring. Go and have a chat to her. She'll be around most days. Except the day of the funeral, I suppose."

"When is that, by the way?"

Bronwen shrugged. "Not sure. They have to wait for the post-mortem, so I heard."

"Oh, there's a post-mortem, is there?"

"Just a formality, Lady Coot reckons. They've already brought back his effects, though."

"His effects?"

"His wallet, his wedding ring, some music, things like that. A bit morbid, really, I thought. Ransacking a dead body."

"Music, did you say?"

"Yeah. In the pocket of his jacket, apparently. He was always jotting down bits of music, Sir Clifford was. I said to Lady Coot, 'You should get someone to play it'. I was thinking, you know, it might have been the last piece of music he ever wrote. But she didn't seem bothered one way or the other. I don't think Lady Coot is all that interested in music, really."

"Isn't she, indeed? How fascinating."

CHAPTER 16

"Oh, so you are an actress. It must be so lonely for you here after all the bright lights of London, I should imagine!"

Lady Coot had one of those affected voices which afflict some Welsh people who are determined to sound posher than their background. The long, flat "o" of her natural accent had become sharpened into an uncomfortable "oh!" so that it sounded as though she was constantly surprising herself – "It must be soh! loh!-nely…"

"Acting is not quite as gregarious a profession as people suppose," Ruby said, "I'm quite used to working alone. Learning scripts and so forth."

"Ah yes, I suppose so. I'm afraid I know nothing about 'show business'," (she said the words "show business" with an emphatic hesitancy as though afraid her lips might be soiled by uttering them), "My husband and I did go to Stratford from time to time, however. Were you with the Royal Shakespeare Company at all?"

"No, not at all. Not even the slightest bit."

Ruby grimaced at the phone in her hand. She had phoned Lady Coot with the intention of ingratiating herself, so it probably was not a good idea to be sarcastic; but she could not help herself. There was something about her ladyship that made Ruby want to shout at her. However, Ruby need not have worried. Lady Coot had a very literal way of thinking and she appeared to have detected not the slightest hint of irony in Ruby's remarks.

"So what sort of play would you have in mind?" Lady Coot asked.

"Something light, I thought. Something jolly."

"Good idea. We don't want anything gloomy for the Summer Fayre, do we? A Whitehall Farce perhaps? One of those things the late Brian Rix used to do. You know, people running in and out of doors and occasionally someone's trousers would fall down. They were most entertaining, I always thought, didn't you?"

"Oh yes! Terribly funny." As far as Ruby could recall, she had never seen a Whitehall Farce with or without the late Brian Rix but if Lady Coot thought they were entertaining then it would be good diplomacy for Ruby to think they were entertaining too. "Of course, the choice of play would all depend on who is in the cast."

"Ah, yes. I hadn't thought of that. Mr Crockley from Craigwen Farm has done some acting, I believe. He'd be a very good choice, don't you think. If you need a romantic lead, that is."

A horrible vision of the naked Tom Crockley sprawling his considerable bulk over a chair in the art class came unbidden to Ruby's mind. Ruby tried to imagine what sort of romantic lead he might play. Somehow Romeo did not seem quite up his street.

"Tom Crockley?" Ruby said, "Well, I suppose, if the part is right..."

On the other end of the phone line, Lady Coot was laughing. "Good Heavens no! Not old Tom! Frankly, my dear, I am astonished that you think him suitable to take the romantic lead in anything. I had in mind his son, Frank. He has that dark, brooding look about him which some women find so attractive."

The "some women" including, first and foremost, Lady Coot herself, Ruby thought. She wondered whether there might be a touch of the Lady Chatterley about Lady Coot. Lady Chatterley took a fancy to a gamekeeper. Might Lady Coot have taken a fancy to a farmer's son?

"At any rate..." Ruby felt that since she had not yet recruited a single member of the cast, nor had she chosen a play to perform, it was somewhat premature to be discussing who would play what; it was time to get to the nub of the matter "I thought I might call round to see you?"

"See me? Whatever for?"

"I would need to see where the Fayre will be held. To work out how we would arrange the scenery. And the props. I wonder if perhaps there might be somewhere we could use as a dressing room? That sort of thing."

"Oh, very well. I am rather busy at the moment. I expect you've heard. My husband, Sir Clifford..." Lady Coot sniffed most affectingly. However, she was clearly a woman who was not going to let a little thing like her husband's death stand in the way of such an important matter as the Summer Fayre. In this respect, she had much in common with the Carthaginian general, Hannibal. When the insuperable barrier of the Alps confronted Hannibal, he did not succumb to a fit of gloom, turn to his assembled army, and say, "Well, boys, that's the end of it for us, we may as well give up and go back home." No, what he said was, "We need elephants!"

Lady Patricia Coot evinced a similar stoutness of spirit when, after producing two or three more heart-wrenching sniffs, she threw off her melancholia and exclaimed "The show must go on! Call around at half past three this afternoon. I'll get Cook to lay on some sandwiches."

Ruby agreed to the arrangements and added, seemingly as an afterthought, that she would be bringing an associate, "The producer, you know."

"Quite. Quite. The more the merrier. I'll tell Cook to bake some fairy cakes."

So that was that. All Ruby had to do now was to go and explain how things stood to the show's producer. The show's producer did not yet realise that she was the show's producer, so that would have to be explained too.

*

"You want me to produce a play? What do I know about plays?"

"You were a teacher. You must have put on plays at school."

"I taught the infants. We did a few Nativity Plays. One year we did Jack and the Beanstalk. Is that the sort of thing you have in mind?"

"Well, actually, I was thinking more along the lines of Waiting For Godot."

"I hope you are kidding!"

"The thing is, Bessie, the play doesn't matter. What matters is that you can come with me this afternoon to meet Lady Coot. That way, you can keep her talking while I go looking."

"Looking? What for?"

"Clues, of course!"

CHAPTER 17

Coot Hall is a magnificently ugly monstrosity set in twenty acres of grass and woodland on the western fringes of Clogwyn Bach. It is approached via a long avenue that curves majestically through great rambling clumps of mighty oak and beech trees which hide the building from view until, at the very last moment, the visitor is struck full in the face by the sight of its sprawling wings and crenelated towers.

The Hall was built in the late nineteenth century by Horatio Eukleides Coot, an English mine-owner who, having discovered the remnants of a Norman castle in the middle of a field a mile or so inland of the village, had decided that he would build a more magnificent castle in the gothic manner upon the site. When neither his finances nor his architect's ability extended to the heights of Horatio's ambitions, a more modest house was eventually constructed, albeit with many more tall embrasures, stained-glass windows, archways and turrets than are customary in the typical family home.

Ruby, who did not own a car and had never bothered learning to drive, gladly accepted a lift in Bessie's antique Mini Minor – a rusty and creaking vehicle painted in an improbably lurid tone of yellow ("Speed Yellow", Bessie informed her). The interior of the car was notable for a pair of dangling furry dice in the front window, a toy nodding dog in the back window and a pervasive stink of antique fish and chip wrappers comingled with synthetic orange air freshener.

"So there it is," Bessie said, as the car emerged from the avenue onto the gravel crescent leading to the turreted entrance of the house, "Castle Dracula in all its glory."

A piercing scream tore through the air.

"My God! What was that?"

The answer to that question presented itself in a shimmer of tail feathers as the source of the screaming strode nonchalantly in front of the car.

"She likes peacocks," said Bessie, "Personally, I think chickens would be more practical. But chickens are too common for the likes of her."

Ruby got out of the car, took a breath of fresh air in an attempt to cleanse the smell of the car from her nostrils and had a good, long ogle at the rustic scenery that sprawled all around her. She could not resist comparing it with her own modest garden. Her garden did not fare well from the comparison. Coot Hall boasted several acres of well-tended lawns surrounded by another few acres of trees which presented a most attractive view spoilt only by the repulsive house plonked right in the middle of it all.

"How snotty-nosed little Patricia Jones managed to inveigle her way into this stately heap I'll never know," muttered Bessie, "Oh, and talk of the devil…."

Standing at the top of the steps leading up to the mighty oaken doors in the turreted porch of the house stood a well-upholstered woman wearing a blue-and-pink floral dress of a hideousness which perfectly complemented her surroundings.

"Bessie," Lady Coot gushed, "How splendid to see you. It's been such a long time. I had no idea you were a dilettante of amateur histrionics."

"She gets the fancy words from the Reader's Digest," Bessie muttered to Ruby, "She doesn't have a clue what they mean," and then, stepping briskly forward like a galleon in full sail, Bessie gushed back at Lady Coot, "Patricia, love. Sorry to hear about your terrible loss. You inherit everything, I suppose?"

"Oh, most certainly!" Suddenly realising that her cheerful tone might be misconstrued, Lady Coot pulled a frilly handkerchief from its resting place in a flowery sleeve and dabbed aesthetically at the corners of her eyes, intoning mournfully, "'What is life but full of care, with lots of time to stand and stare,' as the poet Keats so aptly phrased it."

"Davies," said Bessie.

"I beg your pardon?"

"Not Keats but Davies. William Henry Davies. A Welsh poet who wrote in English. You slightly misquoted him, I fear. His poem begins: 'What is this life if, full of care, we have no time to stand and stare.'"

"Ah!" There was something about the way in which she raised her eyebrows and the piercing tone in which she said "Ah!" that led Ruby to believe that this might not be the first time that Lady Coot and Bessie had disagreed upon something. In fact, she got the distinct impression that there was a bit of a history between them.

"And you, my dear," Lady Coot turned her attentions to Ruby, "You must be our famous actress." Ruby could not help but smile at the compliment. "What did you say your name was?" The smile froze into a grimace. "Well, never mind, follow me through to the loggia. I'll get Cook to bring some tea and nibbles, shall I?"

In order to get to the loggia, they had to walk through the central hall, which was an echoing cavern whose walls were lined with dismal pictures of gloomy men with overabundant sideburns and horse-faced women who looked like extras from a cheap Jane Austen dramatization. Most of the pictures were faded, covered by the yellowing patina of time and grime. One alone shone out in pristine colours. It was an almost life-sized portrait of Lady Coot. She was standing by the trunk of an artistically gnarled tree in an improbably perfect landscape rendered in a chocolate-box imitation of the 18th century painter, Thomas Gainsborough. Wearing a crimson satin dress, she gazed from the portrait with an inscrutable smile hovering over her lips. The painted version of Lady Coot appeared to be twenty years younger and twenty pounds lighter than her real-life counterpart.

"Nice painting," Ruby commented, "Done recently?"

"Last year."

Whoever had painted it was either short-sighted or else had been paid to flatter. Cynically, Ruby thought the latter was more likely.

At the centre of the hall there was a magnificent, if rather grubby-looking, marble staircase leading to the upper floors; big mahogany doors led into rooms on the left and right of the hall itself.

"Most interesting house you have," Ruby observed, "Do you do all the dusting yourself?"

The smile froze on Lady Coot's face. "If only I had the time!" she said, adding just a hint of carefree laughter to indicate that the very concept of dusting was so unfamiliar to her as to be humorous, "But, alas, I have so many other things to do."

"Planning the Summer Fayre, you mean?" Ruby said.

"And your husband's funeral," Bessie added.

Lady Coot either did not hear the remarks or else she chose to ignore them. "As the weather is so clement I thought it would be a shame to take tea indoors. Besides, the Italian Garden is such a picture at this time of year."

How very posh, thought Ruby, she has so many gardens that she has to give them names.

The loggia, it turned out, was a paved patio at the back of the house. The grandly-named Italian Garden that lay beyond it was a scrap of lawn with, at its centre, a fountain surrounded by a crumbling wall. The fountain took the form of a naked man (of more classical proportions than old Tom Crockley, Ruby was pleased to see) who was for some inexplicable reason, holding a large fish from the mouth of which water gushed.

"What a bucolic scene!" Ruby cooed.

Lady Coot opened her mouth to respond, thought better of it, then picked up a small hand bell from a white cast-iron table and tinkled it gently. From this behaviour Ruby ungraciously, but entirely accurately, deduced that "bucolic" was not a word which had thus far cropped up in Lady Coot's studies of the Reader's Digest.

"Please take a seat," Lady Coot said, "Cook will be along presently with refreshments."

"First," said Ruby, "let me say how appreciative I am of your agreeing to see us today at what must be a very difficult time for you."

Lady Coot waved a magnanimous hand. "Life must go on. And so must the Clogwyn Bach Summer Fayre. Oh, here's Cook with our tea. Put it down on the table, would you. We shall serve ourselves."

"Very good ma'am."

For some reason, Ruby had expecting the cook to be a jolly, fat, red-cheeked, grey-haired woman of mature years. That was how cooks in large country houses are generally portrayed on television. In fact, Lady Coot's cook was a slim, young, dark-haired woman who… Ruby knew her! It was Rona, the girl she had met at the art class. If Ruby was surprised to see Rona, the feeling was mutual. When Rona caught sight of Ruby, she gave a little gasp. Then she smiled and winked.

By the time Rona had departed from the loggia, Lady Coot was already pouring tea into three small, bone-china cups. "Do help yourself to sandwiches," she said, indicating a mound of dinky little triangular-cut sandwiches arranged in a pyramid. There are fairy cakes too. They are Cook's speciality.

"You are lucky to have such a capable cook," Ruby said, "Where did you find her?"

"Oh, a local girl. We've always tried to help those less fortunate than ourselves."

They sat and ate sandwiches and fairy cakes for the next ten minutes while Ruby discussed the practicalities of putting on a play for the Summer Fayre.

"We'll need a dressing room."

"You can use the Cook's scullery."

"What time slots are available?"

"Evening would be best, I should think. Just before the disco."

And so on and so forth. Ruby's mind during all this chatter was elsewhere. She wanted to know more about Sir Clifford Coot. Had he and his wife had any arguments? Had he been having an affair? Had *she* been having an affair? Why did he go out so early in the morning? Had he said anything before he left which might provide a clue as to his reasons for going?

But somehow the conversation never seemed to provide an opportunity to slip in a question on any of those topics. It was Bessie who finally broke the ice. She was not to be hidebound by social convention. When she wanted a question answered she came right out with it. And so she did on this occasion.

"When's the funeral?"

"I beg your pardon?"

"Your husband's funeral. He must be having one, I suppose?"

"Oh yes. Of course. We are hoping for May the 25th. There's the little matter of the post-mortem but I am assured that won't hold up arrangements."

"Post-mortem?" Bessie could hardly have said this with a more astonished tone had Lady Coot said "There's the little matter of the human sacrifice."

Lady Coot smiled benignly. "It's quite normal in cases of accidental death. Nothing sinister about it, if that is what you were thinking."

Ruby was struck by how totally unruffled Lady Coot appeared to be. Other than the odd sniffle for the sake of decorum, there was nothing of the grieving widow about her.

Ruby said quite suddenly, "To think, if I had been on the beach just minutes earlier…" She allowed her voice to trail off. She was, in fact, not at all sure what she might have seen or done had she arrived a few minutes before she chanced upon Sir Clifford's body.

"Ah yes, it was you who discovered…" Lady Coot gave a theatrical sigh, "So very tragic."

"What time did he leave that morning, if you don't mind my asking?"

"Oh, quite early. It was still dark. I was asleep but I heard him rummaging about in his office and then shortly after that the front door banged as he left. That," (here she took her lace-edged hanky and sniffed into it) "was the last I heard of him."

"Darling, have you seen my…?" The smooth masculine voice came from behind Ruby. She turned to see a tall, elegant man wearing a light tweed jacket. He was one of those men who look as though they have spent their lives preparing to blossom into middle age. He was slim, square jawed, had dark auburn hair, greying tastefully at the temples and he wore the sort of neat, clipped moustache that had gone out of fashion with Errol Flynn.

"Ah, Ronald!" Lady Coot stood, her calm exterior unruffled, "Let me introduce you. This is my old school friend, Bessie Morgan and this is a newcomer to the village, Ruby, er?"

"Lake," Ruby said.

"Quite. Ruby Lake. An actress. You may have seen her in, er…?"

"Oh, all over the place," Ruby said, waving a hand as though to indicate she really did not want to show off.

"Charmed to meet you," said the man.

"Oh, and this is Ronald Masters. A friend of the family. He's helping me with the arrangements."

"For the Summer Fayre?" said Ruby.

"I wish it were," said Ronald suavely, "The dashed funeral, alas. Awfully complicated things to arrange. The solicitor, the vicar, the headstone, the undertaker, the light buffet for the guests."

"Mourners," Lady Coot corrected.

"Ha! Yes, quite. Dashed lot of stuff to get sorted, at any rate."

"Not to mention the deceased's effects," said Ruby.

"Ha! You've heard about those, have you!" Ronald chuckled, "Pretty rummy that music, I thought."

"Music?" said Ruby as though this was the first she had heard of it.

"Yes. Most odd. He had nothing on him except his wallet and a photocopied page of music. Strange, don't you think?"

"Oh, not really," Lady Coot interjected, "People were always sending him their blasted music. Or, at least, they sent the damn' stuff to Cindy."

"Cindy?"

"His agent. I told him, he should instruct Cindy to throw the damn' stuff away. But Clifford always feared that something of real merit might be accidentally destroyed in that way. In any case, these days it's all done by email, isn't it. I suppose you get your scripts the same way, my dear?"

"And books," said Ruby.

"Books?"

"Audio-books. Narration, you know."

"Ah. And do people send you unsolicited manuscripts too?"

"Well, no. People send scripts to my agent, of course."

"And he or she no doubt throws them away. Or presses the Delete button or however it is done? Very wise. You would not believe how many amateur composers think that they have written a masterpiece and that my husband might be instrumental in making them successful."

Ronald snorted with laughter. "Instrumental. Damn' good, that!"

Nobody else was laughing. Ronald explained the joke – "Music, don't you see? Instrumental. Musical instruments! Ha! Ha!"

Still nobody laughed.

"Let me show you the grand lawn where we have the marquee," said Lady Coot, rising gracefully from her chair and wafting towards the large area of lawn at the side of the house.

Ruby was not interested in the lawn. Or the marquee. She felt there were secrets to be learnt and the lawn was not the place to learn them.

"Oh, do excuse me, Lady Coot, but after all that tea. I wonder if…" She left the sentence unfinished since it would certainly be impolite to be more specific in such refined company.

"Oh, of course," Lady Coot replied, "Past the loggia, down the hallway, on the left just under the stairs."

CHAPTER 18

Ruby scurried back into the house with not the slightest interest in finding the door under the stairs. She could hear the rhythmical sounds of electronic music emanating from a lower level. Not being an aficionado of electronic music, Ruby was unsure if the sounds she was hearing were typical of the genre. If so, she thought, there really could be no accounting for taste. The music comprised a reverberating bass beat that went *Boom-boom!* Followed immediately by a sound, *splat!*, like a sock full of blancmange being struck with a cricket bat.

Next to the door under the stairs there was another door which opened onto a short staircase leading to the basement. That was where Ruby headed. She had a feeling that the only person in Coot Hall who would be likely to listen to electronic music would be a certain dark-haired young woman employed as the cook. When she pushed open the big, oak door at the bottom of the stairs, Ruby found that her instincts had been correct. There was Rona, standing alone in the middle of a huge, gloomy Victorian kitchen, whacking an octopus against the floor in time to the electronic beat of the music. Time after time, Rona lifted the octopus over her head and brought it down with a squelchy splat on the red ceramic floor tiles: *Boom-boom-splat! Boom-boom-splat! Boom-boom-splat!*

"What on earth are you…?"

Rona looked up. She could not hear what Ruby was saying due the music so she went over to the radio on the window ledge and turned it off.

"What are you doing with that octopus?" Ruby said.

"Banging it on the floor," said Rona.

"Well, I can see that, but…"

"Don't worry. It's dead. It won't feel a thing."

Ruby was unconcerned about dead octopuses. It was the sheet music that had been found on Sir Clifford's body that occupied her thoughts. It had been, Ronald had said, a photocopied sheet of music.

"Look, Rona. I need your help. Do you know where Lady Coot keeps a photocopier?"

"Hmm. Don't think she's got one."

"Oh, really!" Ruby was crestfallen. She had thought she might be on to something. But if there was no photocopier in the house, she appeared to have run into a dead end.

"Oh, wait a minute though," Rona said, "He's got a scanner."

"A what?"

"You know. It's like a photocopier only it's attached to a computer."

"Would it photocopy a sheet of paper? A sheet of music, say?"

"I suppose so."

"Where is it?"

"In his office. Come on, I'll show you."

Casually throwing the ill-abused octopus into the large ceramic kitchen sink, Rona wiped her hands on a tea towel and scampered briskly out of the kitchen and up the stairs which Ruby had just descended. Back on the ground floor of the house, Rona pointed to a dark mahogany door in the left-hand wall. "There you are. That's it. You have a theory, then?"

"I beg your…?"

"You've worked out who killed him and now you've come to gather evidence?"

"Well, no, not exactly. There was just a small detail I wanted to check on. Is the door open?"

Rona grasped the door knob and turned it. The door creaked quite loudly as it swung inward on its hinges.

"I'll come with you," said Rona, "I can show you where he kept everything."

But just then, from the direction of the loggia, a little hand bell could be heard tinkling.

"Oh, nuts!" said Rona, "That's her ladyship. She'll be wanting tea or biscuits or something now. I'll have to be going. Don't leave fingerprints anywhere."

"Fingerprints?"

"In case the police find them, think it was you who did away with Sir Clifford and then bang you up for murder." And off she trotted back through the house towards the loggia.

"Fingerprints?" Ruby mused. Surely the police would not be dusting for fingerprints. That was a ludicrous idea. Even so, she took out a handkerchief and carefully wiped the knob of the door. After all, better be safe than sorry. As she was so doing she became aware of a slobbering, panting sound such as an asthmatic St. Bernard dog might be expected to make and, turning to discover the source of the sound, she saw a small, fat, bewhiskered, exceptionally dirty man wearing muddy Wellington boots, plodding towards her across the elegant Carrara marble tiles of the hallway. The man had a pipe stuck into the corner of his mouth from which issued clouds of pungent smoke while in his hands he carried a large plant pot, decorated with Chinese dragons, containing a plant that appeared to comprise nothing more than a cluster of three-foot tall, spiky, leathery leaves.

Catching sight of Ruby, the man issued an exclamation which may or may not have been in English (so thick was his accent) and which ended with "You're her what solves murders, 'n-you? Well, then, Missus, I got something for you!"

"Miss," Ruby corrected automatically. Then, wondering what on earth such a strange and filthy man might have for her, she asked him – "What? What have you got?"

Just then there was a sharp tapping of feet across the marble tiles and who should appear around the bottom balustrade of the steps but Bronwen Price! Until that moment, Ruby had completely forgotten that Bronwen did housework for Lady Coot.

"Maldwyn Placket!" she screeched, aiming her screech in the direction of the little man, "How many times have I told you not to come into the house wearing those bloody Wellington boots? I cleaned this floor only this morning and now I'm going to have to clean it all over again."

"Oh, aye. Well, you know how it is," said Maldwyn, with little conviction.

"There's muddy footprints all the way from… oh! Mrs Lake!" She had only that moment noticed Ruby standing by the partly open study door, "You've come to see her ladyship, then? I wasn't expecting to see you here so soon."

"Yes, yes. I phoned Lady Coot just after you left this morning. She was so keen on getting me to put on a play that I came over without delay."

"If it's the toilets you're looking for, they're down that corridor, downstairs." Turning her attention back to Maldwyn, Bronwen added, "And *you* can come with me."

"Oh, just a moment," said Ruby, "Mr Placket had something for me."

Maldwyn Placket blushed under the grime and whiskers that covered his face. "Here," he said, and handed the potted plant to Ruby.

"What's this?" said Ruby.

"Aspidistra," said Maldwyn. He was a man of few words.

Once Bronwen had escorted Maldwyn from the scene, Ruby pushed open the door and went into the study. She felt sure that the thing that Maldwyn had wanted to give her was not the aspidistra. She was convinced he had a clue to Sir Clifford's death but did not want to impart it while Bronwen was there. Ruby would have to find some occasion to speak to the man in private. However, that was a problem for another time. For the moment, Sir Clifford's study was the sole object of her attention.

Having entered the room, she closed the door behind her and, cradling the potted aspidistra under her left arm, she once again wiped the doorknob with the handkerchief in her right hand. She had expected Sir Clifford's study to be a small room. In fact, the room in which she stood was huge. At first sight, it looked like a moderately-sized library. Three walls were lined with bookshelves that extended from the floor to the high ceiling. A folded wooden stepladder, which would be needed to get to the books on the uppermost shelves, rested against the wall next to the room's only window. In front of the window there was a grand piano. To the right of the grand piano there stood an artist's easel with a cloth draped over it. At the centre of the room there was a vast, ornate mahogany desk. On the desk stood a computer, with its huge flat monitor facing the leather upholstered chair at the other side of the desk. The empty expanse of the desk seemed to cry out for a potted aspidistra and, by good fortune, Ruby was in possession of one which she carefully placed upon the desk next to the computer.

On the floor, to the right of the desk, there was a wooden trolley with two shelves. On its bottom shelf there was a laser printer. On its top shelf was a flat oblong device which Ruby assumed must be the scanner that Rona had mentioned. She went around to the working side of the desk, where the leather chair was. There were some pens and pencils scattered around on the top of the desk. Apart from that, there was nothing other than the computer. The desk had several drawers. Holding her handkerchief over her fingers, she pulled out the drawers at the side of the desk but they contained little of interest – papers, paperclips and more pencils and pens. There was a much larger drawer running horizontally beneath the desktop. She pulled its handle. The drawer did not move. There was a keyhole in the drawer. It was clearly locked.

Then Ruby looked at the printer and the scanner. There was nothing out of the ordinary about the printer. The lid of the scanner, which was somewhat larger than an A4 sheet of paper, was hinged at one edge. She opened the lid and saw that there was a piece of paper lying face-down on the sheet of glass beneath it. She picked this up, closed the scanner lid, and turned the paper over. It was a sheet of music. Ruby was unable read music so the notation meant nothing to her. It looked as though the music had been hand-written with a fountain pen. She wondered if she might be holding the manuscript of an original, and as yet unperformed, piece of music written by Sir Clifford Coot? If so, she supposed it might be valuable. She was just about to put the paper back inside the scanner when her attention was caught by the draped easel.

While the presence of the grand piano was explicable by the fact that Sir Clifford was a composer, the presence of the easel was more mysterious. She had never heard it said that Sir Clifford was an artist. She picked up the corner of the cloth that covered the easel and peered beneath it. There was a canvas. Upon the canvas there was a painting of an austere looking man with collar-length grey hair. He was pictured in this very study, sitting on the great mahogany desk. In one hand, he held a musical score. The other hand, palm upwards, was held out towards the viewer of the picture. It occurred to Ruby that this must be a portrait of Sir

Clifford himself and that the curious gesture was supposed to suggest that he was exhorting an unseen orchestra to a musical and spiritual crescendo. It was not a bad painting, on the whole, thought Ruby though some parts of it appeared incomplete.

There was a creak of the door. Then a voice: "Rotten likeness, don't you think?"

Ruby spun around in shock, letting the drape fall back over the painting as she did so. It was Lady Coot's friend, Ronald. Ruby tried to act innocent. She was not very good at acting innocent. She was top-notch at acting a vicar's housekeeper or a villain, but acting innocent was not one of her preeminent talents – particularly when she was at that moment holding incriminating evidence of her activities: namely, a sheet of music which she had purloined from the scanner. Fortunately, the aspidistra which she had placed upon the desk was at that moment directly in front of her, its large pot conveniently hiding the paper in her hands from Ronald's view.

Having entered the study, Ronald now proceeded to walk towards Ruby. At any moment, the paper clutched in her hands would present itself clearly to his view. Ruby picked up the potted aspidistra. Her fingers clutched the pot while her thumbs pressed the sheet of paper against that side of the pot which was facing towards her. She pulled the pot closer to her body, thus squeezing the paper between pot and bosom. This has the desirable effect of making it impossible for Ronald to see the paper. It also had the undesirable effect of making it impossible for Ruby to relinquish the potted aspidistra. Only by continuing to clutch the pot to her bosom could she be certain to hide the paper from view.

"I'm afraid I am not the best person to judge how good a likeness the portrait is," Ruby said, "I never met Sir Clifford."

"Ah, I was given to understand that it was you who found his lifeless body sprawling on the rocks."

"Well, yes, but…"

"He wasn't looking at his best, huh?" Ronald chuckled. He seemed to think he had made a splendid joke, "Believe me, if you didn't know the old codger in life, you didn't miss much. By the way, if you don't mind my asking, what on earth are you doing with that plant?"

"Maldwyn gave it to me."

"The gardener? Gave you a plant? What, as a present? He hasn't taken a fancy to you, has he? I know he has a certain reputation in that regard. If I were you, I should be hesitant of accepting unsolicited aspidistras from the old goat. You never know where it may lead."

"I was just about to take it out to the loggia. To give it some sun."

"Do they like sun? I had the impression that they thrived in dark corners where they can accumulate a healthy layer of dust and cobwebs. Here, give it to me. I'll take it for you."

"Oh no!" Ruby stepped back briskly as though she had unexpectedly encountered the business end of an electric cattle-prod.

"Yes, well," Ronald smiled, "if you are that fond of the plant, let me not come between you and it. What are you doing in the old boy's study anyway?"

"I got lost."

"Lost?"

"I was looking for the, er, ladies, er…"

"The facilities, huh? Well, you won't find them in here. This is Sir Clifford's Inner Sanctum, as you might say, and it is not well furnished with ladies' facilities."

"You knew him well?" Ruby asked, "Sir Clifford, I mean."

"Oh, we rubbed shoulders at cocktail parties, you know."

"You are a friend of the family?"

"I say, haven't I seen you on television?"

Ruby tried to look modest, hoping that he was about to comment favourably on her role in the episode of Downton Abbey in which she had spoken two small but pivotal lines: "His lordship is in the drawing room, m'lady," and "Shall you be requiring the best silver, m'lady?" But no, it was not that role which had sprung into Ronald's mind. "I know!" he said, "The dancing kittens. You were the grey one with the white paws that stroked its whiskers and said 'So tasty, they'll eat it to the last miaow.' Ha! That always makes me chortle! Such a clever line, I really don't know how those scriptwriter chaps think of them!"

Being recognised as a dancing kitten was the bane of Ruby's life. When she had performed in the advertisement, she had hoped that the makeup and whiskers would have made her unrecognisable to the viewing public. Unfortunately, such was not the case. However, it was beneath her dignity to accept a compliment for her portrayal of a dancing kitten. She looked sternly at Ronald and said, "You probably remember me from my role in the BBC adaptation of Dickens's 'Bleak House'." She did not explain that the role in question was that of an itinerant match-seller with no scripted lines (though she had ad libbed, "Buy me matches, guv," which is just about audible if you listen very closely).

"Ah, Dickens?" It was clear from the baffled look on his face that Ronald had either never heard of Dickens or, if he had, he had long ago concluded that he would rather watch a shipping forecast for the Outer Hebrides than settle down in front of the TV set to binge-watch a ten-hour dramatization of one of Mr Dickens's gloomier novels.

Ruby waved a deprecating hand, "In the acting profession these days, one has to be versatile."

"Quite. Are you sure you don't need any help with that aspidistra? It looks rather heavy."

"No. No, I am quite all right."

"Well, then, I am on my way to the loggia myself, as a matter of fact. We can go together. Unless you are concerned that our arrival together might cause a scandal!"

Ruby smiled. "I am prepared to take that risk."

CHAPTER 19

In the car on the drive back, Bessie said, "She did it. I'm convinced. Patsy Coot has been having an affair with that seedy bloke."

"Ronald, you mean?"

"It's obvious, isn't it? He's all over her like a rash."

"Didn't she say he was a friend of the family?"

"Friend of the family, my foot! You only had to take a look at that moustache. He's her fancy man."

"Because of his moustache?"

Bessie nodded gravely. "I've had prior experience of men with moustaches just like that one."

"Ah."

"Believe me. I've known Patsy since she was a snotty-nosed little girl. She used to show boys her knickers for a penny."

"I doubt if she still does that."

"You're probably right. Her charges will have gone up. If you want my opinion, I'd say they plotted it all out between the two of them. The perfect crime. Get rid of her husband then embark upon a new life on the Costa del Sol."

"The Costa del Sol?"

"Or Rio de Janeiro. Somewhere far away from Clogwyn Bach at any rate. She'll be rich now, you see. She'll inherit the house and the money. And then there's all the royalties from his music. That'll come to a tidy sum! Before the year is out, greasy Ronald and slimy Patsy will be living the high life on Sir Clifford's money, you mark my words. That's been her dream ever since she was a showgirl."

"A showgirl? Lady Coot?"

"Oh, yes. Didn't you know? She left the village as a teenager to seek fame and fortune. Patsy Jones she was then. She ended up as a chorus girl in one of the less glamorous musicals in the West End of London. I don't know how she managed to get the job but it wasn't through native talent since she can neither sing nor dance nor act. There are, I gather, other ways of getting into show business."

"I hope you are not suggesting that *I* got into the theatre via the casting couch, Bessie!"

Bessie laughed. "You are not pushy enough. Not like Patsy."

"That's odd though," Ruby said, "Lady Coot told me that she knew nothing about show business. She said it with a sort of sneer as though she looked down upon the profession."

"That's because she's a pathological liar," Bessie said, "You can't take anything she says at face value."

"So she could have killed her husband and then immediately started acting the part of the grieving widow. But if she killed him, that means she would have had to have persuaded Sir Clifford to go out walking with her on the clifftop path first thing in the morning. And then she'd have had to push him off. How would she have done that?"

Bessie swerved the car wildly to avoid a cat that was languidly crossing the road down which she was at that moment driving at a speed which would have been unexceptional at the Brands Hatch racing circuit but which seemed to Ruby unnecessarily daring in a narrow, pot-holed lane on the outskirts of a sleepy Welsh village.

"How she bumped him off," Bessie said, "is a minor detail. The fact that she *did* is what matters."

Ruby, whose heart had accelerated to an uncomfortable degree thanks to Bessie's reckless driving, took a few long, deep breaths before speaking. "I suppose," she said between gasps, "that Ronald might have…"

"That's it!" exclaimed Bessie, "You see, I knew you'd work it out. Her fancy man, Ronald, was the one who did it. He tied up Sir Clifford with ropes, bundled him into the back of a car, took him up to the cliff path, untied him, and pushed him over the edge."

"Yes," said Ruby, "I suppose that's a possibility." But she was far from convinced. "Oh, by the way, I meant to ask you... who's the strange little man with the aspidistra?"

"Aspidistra?"

"I was in Sir Clifford's study and he suddenly appeared. Grey stubbly whiskers, red, wrinkly face, muddy Wellington boots, an accent so thick you could spread it on toast."

"Oh, that'll be Maldwyn Placket," Bessie said, "Her ladyship's gardener."

"I have a feeling I've seen him before but I can't quite place him. In town, I suppose. Down the pub maybe? I think he was going to tell me something. But then Bronwen came along and he clammed up. Gave me a potted aspidistra instead."

"Why would Maldwyn Placket want to tell you something?"

"Hmmm. You're right. It's probably nothing. The thing we need to concentrate on is this." She unfolded the sheet of music that she had found in Sir Clifford's scanner. "There is something about this music that's significant. I'm sure of it. But I can't for the life of me think what it could be."

If only she had been able to read music, it might have made more sense.

CHAPTER 20

On Tuesday morning, Ruby was pottering about in the wasteland that she called her garden when she heard a loud knocking at her front door. For the last five minutes she had been considering a small yellow flower growing beneath her window and debating with herself whether the best course of action to take would be to apply some high potash fertilizer which she had bought online or to spray it with weed-killer. The decision would have to be deferred until later. For the time being, the small yellow flower was reprieved.

Ruby stripped off her blue rubber gardening gloves, which were still pristine due to the fact that she had not yet done any actual gardening, and strode purposefully through the kitchen and down the hallway towards the front door. She was hoping it would be someone delivering the gardening book she had ordered. The ultimate fate of the small yellow flower would be decided once Ruby had made a positive identification.

"Bessie!" exclaimed Ruby when, upon opening the front door, she was confronted by the sight of her next door neighbour, red in the face and hopping from one foot to another while waving a newspaper in the air.

"You've seen this, have you?" said Bessie.

"Have I seen *what*, exactly?"

"If there was ever any doubt that he was murdered, there's no doubt any more."

"You'd better come in for a cup of tea, Bessie. I haven't got the foggiest idea of what you are going on about."

Once in the kitchen, Bessie placed the newspaper upon the table. "There!" she said, "What do you make of that?"

It was that morning's issue of The Clogwyn Clarion. The front page showed a photograph of a distinguished-looking, white-haired gentleman whom Ruby recognised as the same man portrayed in the portrait in Sir Clifford Coot's study. Ruby sat down with a groan. It was not the photograph which had caused her to groan but the headline which ran above it:

"Celebrity Actress Finds Composer's Corpse!"

Underneath this, in bold text inside a box were the words: "'I am not a suspect,' insists Ruby Lake."

Ruby groaned again.

"Are you all right?" said Bessie.

"I feel in great need of some tea," Ruby replied, "In fact, I wouldn't object to something a bit stronger. But I suppose it's a bit early in the day…"

Once the tea had been made, Ruby sat down to read the entire article, "Special Report by Clogwyn Clarion Chief Crime Reporter, Tegwyn Pritchard". The report gave a highly dramatized account of Ruby's discovery of Sir Clifford Coot's body with words emboldened at random and exclamation marks put where no self-respecting exclamation mark belonged.

"The morning of Thursday the 13th of May dawned, **cold and dreary**, when local celebrity TV actress, Ruby Lake (48)…" ("That's not my age," Ruby protested) "…found herself alone on the eerily forbidding rocks of the bleak northern promontory of Clogwyn Bach Bay! Alone **but for the body** of Sir Clifford Coot!

"Miss Lake, whose starring roles include appearances in numerous **top-rated TV shows** and who was one of the dancing kittens in a popular cat-food commercial…" ("Oh, bollocks!" moaned Ruby, "How did he find out about that?") "…stumbled over the dead body of the famous composer while she was out **collecting whelks**!"

"Whelks?" said Bessie.

"He wanted to know if I was walking a dog. I told him no, I was collecting whelks. It was meant to be a joke."

"You told a joke to a journalist?" Bessie shook her heard in dumb astonishment.

The article went on: "Prior to moving from her fashionable London home to a remote cottage in Clogwyn Bach, Ruby Lake had made national headlines in the case of the **Lipstick Poisoner!** Readers may recall the notorious murder of Mr Alfie Gruttock, a popular TV comedian, who was playing the part of an Ugly Sister in a pantomime in Suffolk. The details of that case are too well known to merit repetition here.

"When this reporter asked Miss Lake whether she suspected that Sir Clifford's death might be in any way suspicious, she said, 'Just about **anyone might be a suspect! But I am not!'**"

"You said that to him?" said Bessie.

"No! I mean, well, I might have used those words. But not in that order. Anyway, he's quoting me out of context."

Bessie shook her head again. "He's a journalist. Haven't you ever come across journalists before?"

"But this is ghastly!" Ruby flung the newspaper down onto the table and stood in order to pace around the kitchen, "It makes me sound like some eccentric, out-of-work actress who goes around solving murders!"

"Well," Bessie took a meditative sip of her tea, "maybe there is some truth in that?"

"Truth? Of course there's no truth in it. The damned poisoned lipstick case was purely accidental. The evidence was there for anyone to see. It was just my misfortune that I was that person."

"And the murder of Sir Clifford?"

"Oh, now, Bessie, don't you start. There's not a shred of evidence that he was murdered. If there were, the police would be on the case by now."

"But *I* thought that *you* thought..."

"I don't think anything! Not about the murder. If there *was* a murder. The fact that Sir Clifford was murdered. Or not. As the case may be. I really don't have any opinions on that matter."

"No?"

"No. Well, yes, I do have an opinion. It is my opinion that, in spite of the high regard that everyone in the village claimed to have for him, there are some people who might not be entirely unhappy to see him go. But that's not at all the same thing as accusing anyone of murder. Not at all! The established fact of the matter is that Sir Clifford left his house at the crack of dawn on Thursday morning, went for a walk along the clifftops and fell off. Anything else is surmise."

Bessie took another long sip of tea. Through the kitchen window she saw the great expanse of Clogwyn Bach Bay, looking picturesquely innocent with the waves of the sea making silvery sparkles in the sunlight. "I wouldn't be too sure that anything is 'established fact'," Bessie said at last, "If you think it is established fact that he fell off the clifftop on Thursday morning, you might want to think again."

"What do you mean?" Ruby stopped pacing long enough to aim a particularly baleful glare in Bessie's direction.

"If you would just sit down for a minute and finish reading the front page of the Clogwyn Clarion you'd see what I mean."

So Ruby sat. And she read. What she read was the final paragraph of Tegwyn Pritchard's article.

"The Coroner has stated that, following a post-mortem examination, it has been determined that the cause of death was drowning. South Wales Police said the death is being treated as unexplained but is not believed to be suspicious. An inquest has been adjourned until the 5th of July."

Ruby stared, wide-eyed at the paragraph.

"That can't be right," she said, "He can't have drowned. The sea was way out. That's how I was able to climb over the rocks. If it had been a high tide the rocks would have been underwater. There was no high tide that morning. So how could he possibly have drowned?"

"The sea can go out very quick around here," Bessie suggested.

Ruby shook her head, "Not that quick. There's more to this than meets the eye. I don't know what it is. But I do know someone who might."

Ruby told Bessie about the young man she had happened to photograph in the distance on the morning when she had found Sir Clifford's body and of how she had subsequently met that man while he had been (so he claimed) looking for gobies and blennies in Rocky Cove.

"The thing is," said Ruby, "he was absolutely insistent that Sir Clifford couldn't have died in the morning."

"But," interrupted Bessie, "if Lady Coot is to be believed, he can't have died before then because she says he was at home all night. He went out that morning and never came back again."

"I think you've put your finger on it there, Bessie – 'If Lady Coot is to be believed…'"

"You don't believe her?"

"The young man I met in the bay," Ruby said, "insisted that it was completely impossible that Sir Clifford had died that morning."

"You think he knows something that we don't?"

"I'm sure of it. We need to speak to him. The only problem is, I have no idea who he is. I know nothing about him, in fact. Not even his name."

"I may be able to help," said Bessie, "He wouldn't be about six foot tall, slim, dark hair, late twenties…"

"With fascinating eyebrows," Ruby added.

"What?"

Ruby blushed slightly. "Sorry, it's just something I noticed."

"His name," said Bessie, "is Matt Jones. And he'll be here at half-past one."

"Here?"

"Well, not here. Not in Rose Cottage. He'll be next door in my cottage."

"Why would he be in your cottage at half-past one?"

"Semicolons," Bessie said, inscrutably.

"Semicolons?"

"And gobies, of course."

"Oh. Of course."

CHAPTER 21

At half past one precisely there was the sound of knocking on Bessie's door. "It's open!" Bessie bellowed, "Come on in!" In a more conversational tone she told Ruby, "One thing I'll give him credit for – he's always on time."

Matt strolled into the kitchen and saw Ruby sitting at the table.

"Oh!" was all that Matt had to say.

Bessie made the introductions. "Matt, this is Ruby. Ruby, this is Matt."

"We've already met," they said in unison.

"Now then, Matt love, sit down and take your coat off, there's a good boy. I'm in the middle of baking Welsh cakes and they won't be interrupted. Not even for a murder."

Bessie was standing by the gas stove. Over the middle gas ring sat her bakestone – a heavy circle of cast iron – and on the bakestone there were half a dozen flat, round, current-dotted Welsh cakes. Bessie was holding a fish slice and, from time to time, she used the slice to lift up a corner of a Welsh cake to see if the side in contact with the bakestone had turned brown and, if it had, she flipped it over to cook the other side.

"They are nearly finished," she said, "Then we can have a couple of them with a cup of tea. There's nothing quite so nice as a freshly-baked Welsh cake, warm from the bakestone."

Ruby was desperate to ask Matt why he thought Sir Clifford had died the night before Ruby had found his body. But nothing would come between Bessie and her Welsh cakes. The interrogation would have to wait.

"Nice weather," Ruby said.

"Yes," said Matt.

"Do you live nearby?"

"In the village."

"Ah." That was the full extent of the small talk that Ruby could come up with. She waited until the last Welsh cake had been flipped off the bakestone and onto a wire rack standing on the worktop between the stove and the sink. Then Bessie put on the kettle, made the tea and the three of them sat at the table with a mug in one hand and a Welsh cake in the other while Bessie made the formal introductions. She gave Matt an exaggerated version of Ruby's career which made her sound as if she was one of the most sought-after actresses in Hollywood. Then she turned her attentions to Matt who, she said, was quite a well-known writer (though Ruby had never heard of him). He had written several books all about escaping from the hurly-burly existence of the modern world and getting back to the simple pleasures of life in the heart of nature.

Matt's breakthrough book had been called "Inner Peace In Wildest Wales". It purported to tell the unembellished true story of a London-based advertising executive who had put his high-pressure lifestyle behind him and had given up commuting, tablet computers and mobile phones in order to find peace and happiness in a lonely, rundown shack in a remote corner of coastal Wales. It was a funny, heart-warming story that found a ready audience among all those people with high-pressure lifestyles which they wanted to put behind them. They read Matt's book, while commuting, on their tablet computers and mobile phones.

According to Bessie, the book was a work of fiction from start to finish. Matt had spent three months selling classified advertisements for a local newspaper in North London (which was the nearest he came to being an "advertising executive") before quitting to come back home to Wales. He had grown up in the Merthyr Tydfil but did not want to return there due to his large number of relatives, most of whom he disliked with a passion, so he had rented a cheap room from Clogwyn Bach's local psychic, Maggie Pountice. In his book, he was rather vague about the details of his accommodation but he gave the impression that it might be an old fisherman's cabin in an isolated bay rather than the upstairs room of a comfortable terraced house in the High Street. His readers lapped it up. They thought that Matt had stumbled upon the secret of inner contentment. What he had actually stumbled upon was the secret of a regular income.

There was just one problem: punctuation. Matt was good with words but not so good with commas, full stops, colons and semicolons. He relied on Bessie to insert those. Being a retired teacher of the traditional sort, Bessie was pretty hot on punctuation. The subtleties of Oxford and Parenthetical Commas held no terrors for her. She knew how to wield an ellipsis like a weapon of war; and she was fearless in her exploitation of the humorous potential of the semicolon. Currently she was striving to turn Matt's latest book, "Meditations Upon Life In A Rock Pool", into something that bore a passing resemblance to the English language.

"Every Tuesday," Matt said morosely in answer to Ruby's question about the frequency of his visits to Bessie.

Matt was very good at being morose. It came naturally to him. Ruby had a weakness for sultry men, especially those with attractive eyebrows. Sadly, sultry men with attractive eyebrows had never had a weakness for Ruby. Besides which, she reminded herself, Matt Jones must be half her age so it would be most indecorous to give the slightest indication of flirtatiousness. She therefore adopted a brisk, business-like manner and devoted herself to the serious business of Sir Clifford Coot's drowning.

"So let's get to the crunch, young man," said Ruby, "The last time we met you informed me with absolute confidence that Sir Clifford Coot cannot have been killed on the morning of his discovery, by which I mean Thursday morning when I had the misfortunate of chancing upon his body. It now appears that the Coroner agrees with you. What I want to know is how you had foreknowledge of this fact."

"The moon."

"I beg your pardon?"

"The moon. The thing that whizzes around the earth once a month, or actually, more like once every twenty-seven days."

"Yes," Ruby conceded, "I've noticed it. But what's that got to do with Sir Clifford's death?"

"Thursday was a New Moon. Well, actually, it was a waxing crescent but as near to a New Moon as makes no difference, which is why, if you've been out walking at night, you'll have noticed that it's been pretty damn' dark."

Ruby had indeed been out walking at night. She had walked back from the art class on Thursday evening and she had barely been able to see anything.

"And the fact that it was dark means that he can't have been killed in the morning?"

"No, it doesn't mean that at all." Matt gave her a look that implied an unspoken 'tut'. "The fact that it was a New Moon means that it was a spring tide. That is, a tide that comes very high up the shore twice each day and also recedes very low down the shore twice each day."

"And that means?"

"It means that since it was low tide when you and I were on the shore on Thursday morning it must have been about six hours since it was high tide. But you said yourself that the body you found was soaking wet."

"I did?"

"You did. When you accosted me on the beach a couple of days ago while I was out looking for blennies. You said his overcoat was soaking wet. You thought it made him glisten like a seal."

"Ah."

"Well, it wasn't raining so that meant he must have got wet from the sea. But as it was low tide that meant that the sea can't have been that far up shore for about six hours. And that meant that he can't have been in the sea that morning. He must have been…"

"…bumped off the night before," Ruby said, "Matt, you are brilliant. So that means that Lady Coot was lying when she said Sir Clifford had been at home all night and left in the early morning. By heck, I think we have our murderer."

Matt was staring blankly at Ruby. "Who?" he said at last.

"Isn't it obvious? Lady Coot. She thinks she's covered her tracks with some cock-and-bull story about Sir Clifford going out for an early morning walk. Well, she may have fooled the police, but they probably haven't realised the significance of the New Moon."

Bessie sniffed dubiously. "Before you get too excited, love," she said, "You are forgetting about the Coroner, aren't you?"

"What do you mean?"

"It was the Coroner who said he had drowned. Now, I'm not saying the police might not sometimes make a mistake, they might overlook some vital piece of evidence that the likes of you, me and Matt might not…"

"They certainly overlooked a vital piece of evidence in the case of the Lipstick Poisoner," Ruby reminded her.

"Yes, but even so, I think they probably did notice that it was low tide when they came to examine the body on Thursday. I have a feeling that when the post-mortem showed that he had drowned, even our slow-witted bobbies might have thought, well, that's a bit funny. So what I'm saying is that just because he drowned on Wednesday night instead of fell off a cliff on Thursday morning, that's not proof that he was murdered."

"Yes it is!"

"The police don't think so, do they? Otherwise they'd be all over the place by now looking for the murderer."

"But she lied, Bessie. Lady Coot lied. And the only conceivable reason for her to lie would be to cover her tracks so that she can inherit her late husband's wealth and shack up with her fancy man."

"Fancy man?" said Matt.

"I'll explain later," said Ruby.

"But why would Sir Clifford have gone walking on the cliff path at night?" Bessie asked.

"To meet his murderer," Ruby said, "He must have been enticed there. Which means the murderer must have been someone he knew. Now if only someone had seen him…" Ruby suddenly remembered what Muriel Greenalge had told her when they had been talking down in the pub after Thursday's art class. Muriel had been working in her shop when she had noticed Matt driving his car in the direction of the headland, quite near the cliff path. "By heck! You were up there on Wednesday evening!"

"Me? I wasn't…"

"You drove there in your car. Someone mentioned seeing you."

"Oh, I… I went out for the evening. To Clogwyn Mawr. I wasn't near the cliff path. I didn't see anything."

"What time did you drive back? Did you see anything then? Anyone around? A torch beam in the darkness?"

"No, I didn't see anything."

Bessie stuck her little finger into her mouth and sucked on it. This was an odd and, arguably, unhygienic habit she had when she wanted to think deeply. "There's more to this than meets the eye, I can't help thinking."

"The sheet of music, you mean?" said Matt, "The one that was in the dead man's jacket pocket."

"How do you know about that?" Ruby snapped, "Only the police and Lady Coot are supposed to be aware of the items found upon the body."

"*You* know about them," Matt protested.

"Yes, well… let's just say that I heard about them from a reliable source."

"So did I."

"Bronwen," said Bessie, "The whole village will know by now."

"Well, then," Ruby said, addressing Matt, "What you don't know is that I also found a sheet of music in Sir Clifford's study."

"In a photocopier," said Bessie.

"A scanner, actually. But it amounts to much the same thing. You don't suppose the sheet of music in his pocket and the sheet of music in his scanner might be one and the same? Or anyway, that one might be a copy of the other?"

"What's the music you found?" Matt asked.

"Who knows? You don't read music, by any chance, do you, Matt?"

He shook his head. "No. But I know someone who does."

"Elfyd!" said Bessie.

"You're not a Methodist, I suppose?" Matt asked Ruby.

She shook her head. "Does it matter?"

"Probably not. But if you want to know about that music you should go to the chapel."

CHAPTER 22

Later that afternoon, Ruby walked down to the village to buy a few things from "Food'n'News", the shop run by Muriel Greenalge and her husband Emrys. The weather was mild but breezy. She watched the gulls circling overhead, buffeted by the wind. The sea was choppy and she was surprised to see a couple of people swimming some way offshore.

She commented on the swimmers while she was buying the few things she needed. Muriel said that anyone swimming in the bay must be nuts. Emrys agreed with her.

"The sea's so cold at this time of year," Muriel commented.

"This time of year," Emrys agreed, "The sea's cold."

Emrys was a small, wiry man with the sort of face that merged seamlessly into any crowd. His life centred around his small shop and his wife. He gave every appearance of being entirely contented with that arrangement.

The shop itself was the closest thing Clogwyn Bach had to a supermarket. It sold tins of soup and tins vegetables, packets of washing powder and packets of cornflakes. It had a small fridge and a smaller freezer in which could be found such delicacies as sausages, fish-fingers and ice cream. If you wanted anything more exotic you would be out of luck. Ask for a jar of lime pickle or a packet of Formosa Jada Oolong Tea and you would be met with a blank stare. Ask, on the other hand, for a box of teabags and you would be presented with two choices: a big box or a little box. Ruby asked for a little box and Muriel took one down from the shelves behind the counter.

"It's not just cold, either," said Muriel, "It's dangerous."

"Cold and dangerous," Emrys confirmed.

"This time of year," Muriel repeated in the apparent assumption that Ruby may have lost the thread of the conversation, "the sea round here is cold and it's dangerous."

Emrys nodded sagely. "It is. Cold and dangerous."

"All sorts of undercurrents in that sea. Rip currents and I don't know what else. There's an offer on the biscuits if you're interested. Buy one packet of chocolate bourbons and get another packet free."

"The second packet's free," Emrys explained.

"I don't need any biscuits at the moment," said Ruby, "I just baked a cherry cake. What are rip currents?"

"Oh, don't ask me! I'm not a swimmer. It's just what I've heard people saying."

"Something to do with the shape of the bay," Emrys said, "and the rocks and the seaweed."

Muriel nodded, "The rocks and the seaweed. That's what's behind it all. If you're not careful you can get swept out to sea and then swept back in again."

"Onto the rocks," said Emrys.

"Whenever we get tourists I warn them it's dangerous but do you think they pay any attention?"

Emrys shook his head, "They don't pay any attention. We warn them, don't we Muriel?"

"We do."

"But do you think they take us seriously?"

"No," said Muriel, "They do not. The butter's on offer too. Ten pence off. This week only."

"I'll take two packets of butter then and some demerara sugar."

"Have we got demerara, Emrys?"

"We've got molasses."

"Is that the same as demerara, Emrys?"

"Similar."

"I'll take molasses," said Ruby who had no idea if it was similar to demerara until she saw the packet and decided that it was not. She took it anyway. "Do people ever get drowned?" she asked.

"Apart from Sir Clifford, you mean? I've never heard of anyone. Have you, Emrys?"

"I haven't, Muriel. Not drowned. There've been a few narrow escapes, though."

"There have," Muriel confirmed, "A few narrow escapes there've been."

"Has anyone ever been swept onto the rocks?" Ruby asked.

Muriel looked at Emrys. "I've never heard of anyone being swept onto the rocks. Have you, Emrys?"

"Not onto the rocks, no. But I suppose they might be. If they were unlucky."

"Oh yes," Muriel said, "If they were unlucky, I suppose they might be. We get a lot of flotsam and jetsam on those rocks. Plastic bags, bits of rope, rubber ducks, old boxes."

"A lot of old boxes get washed up," said Emrys, "I'm not sure where so many old boxes come from."

"Ships, I expect," said Muriel.

"You don't get flotsam and jetsam on the beach though?" said Ruby.

"We get some," Muriel said.

"Not much though," added Emrys.

"Emrys is right. It mostly ends up on the rocks."

"There are rip currents and undercurrents, you see," Emrys explained.

Muriel nodded, "All sorts of currents we get here. Whenever we get tourists round here I warn them it's dangerous but do you think they pay any attention?"

"They pay no attention," Emrys said.

"Hmmm," said Ruby, "That's most interesting."

Muriel's eyes suddenly grew wide. "You've got a theory, haven't you!"

"What?"

"It's a clue, isn't it? The currents, I mean."

"A clue?" Ruby assayed a light laugh. Back in the days when she had been acting in a small theatre in Balham, she had been noted for her light laugh. She had used it to good effect in several Restoration Comedies. She was, sadly, out of practice and it came out more as a maniacal cackle.

"There!" Muriel said, "I knew it! You've solved the murder, haven't you! Go on, tell us. Who did it? And why?"

Ruby waited for Emrys to say something. He said nothing. Ruby felt disoriented as though she were playing a scene and an actor had failed to pick up his cue.

"Oh, really, Muriel!" she said, "I haven't solved anything."

"You haven't?"

"No."

"But you've got an idea, though?"

"Well…"

"You have, haven't you!"

Just then the bell tinkled as someone opened the door to the shop. Ruby glanced around and saw a very large, muscular young man whom she had never seen before. He had one of those impressively rectangular physiques that are the speciality of Welsh rugby players.

"Good evening," said Ruby.

"How be," returned the man.

"I'll be with you in just a minute," said Muriel.

"I'm almost finished," said Ruby, "I'll just take a packet of plain flour. Oh, and do you happen to have a beach ball?"

"A beach ball?"

"An inflatable beach ball."

"Well, yes, but…"

"I'll take one of those too."

Just then there was the sound of shrieking from the street directly outside the shop. Startled, Ruby turned and looked through the window. A statuesque woman wearing a long fawn coat over a red silk blouse was advancing aggressively towards an unseen opponent. As she did so, she was jabbing her finger and yelling imprecations with such violence that her platinum blonde beehive hairdo trembled with each jab and yell.

"Oh dear," said Emrys, "Gwendolyn's on the warpath again."

"Oh dear, dear," Muriel added, "What's it about this time, I wonder?"

Muriel recognised the blonde woman. She had seen her down the pub in the company of a disreputable-looking travelling salesman. "Who's Gwendolyn, exactly?" she asked.

"Gwendolyn Gormly," said Muriel.

"Gormly," Emrys echoed.

"You haven't visited Gwendolyn's Grotto, I take it?" said Muriel.

"It's her shop," Emrys explained, "New Age. Crystals and cannabis."

"Cannabis?" Ruby raised an astonished eyebrow.

"Emrys means joss sticks," Muriel explained. She lowered her voice and added, "Gwendolyn's a bit notorious, if you know what I mean."

"Bit of a hussy," Emrys said.

"Here's your change," said Muriel, "You sure you don't want any chocolate bourbons? Buy one packet and get another packet free."

Ruby assured Muriel that she was already more than adequately supplied with chocolate bourbons which, as a matter of fact, was a blatant lie. At that moment, Ruby's interest was less focussed upon biscuits than upon the rumpus in the street outside.

CHAPTER 23

"Don't you call me a tart, you raddled old bag!" Gwendolyn was screeching as she advanced upon the target of her wrath, "Everyone knows what you were like. The good time that was had by all, back in the days when you still had a figure worth looking at!"

"Oh yes, well, we've all had a good look at your figure, haven't we!" a gravelly voice returned, "If that blouse wasn't no tighter it'd be a tourniquet. Not that it wouldn't stay on none too long if there wasn't any men around." To her horror, Ruby saw that the speaker was Maggie Pountice. She had hitherto assumed Maggie to be a quiet, unassuming person. At that present moment, she was a raging dragon. For every step that Gwendolyn took towards Maggie, Maggie took two steps towards Gwendolyn. But for a couple of beefy men restraining Maggie and a couple of even beefier men restraining Gwendolyn, the two women would have been grappling one another like professional wrestlers by now; from the looks on their faces, it would be a no-holds-barred match with the possibility of a knockout but no submissions.

Now there was another man standing between Maggie and Gwendolyn. It was the tall, muscular man who had entered Muriel's shop a few minutes earlier. He looked the sort of person you would not want to get on the wrong side of. "Now, now, ladies, let's be calm about this, shall we?"

"Who's he?" Ruby whispered to Muriel who had come from her shop to get closer to the action.

"Frank Crockley," Muriel said, "Tom Crockley's son."

The vision of the sprawling expanse of Tom Crockley's naked body flashed upon Ruby's mind. "But he's nothing like his father."

"That has been commented on before," Muriel replied enigmatically.

Frank Crockley interposed himself between the two combatants, gave them a friendly smile and, in the next moment, let out a piercing shriek of pain. Gwendolyn's arms might be restrained but her legs were not. She had aimed a powerful kick to Frank's shin with the steel-toed point of a stiletto shoe. It had struck the bone and brought tears to Frank's eyes.

"You keep out of this, Frank Crockley!" Gwendolyn yelled, "This is a matter between me and Maggie and it won't be sorted until I get her sorted out myself."

"You?" yelled Maggie, "I'd like to see you try." She turned to the men who were holding her arms and grumbled, "Let me at her, can't you? It's about time that someone wiped that smile off her over made-up face!"

Three young boys, attracted by the noise, were hopping from foot to foot at the edge of the crowd and shouting, "Go on, Missus, kick him again!" and (to Maggie) "Wallop her with your handbag, Missus!"

Frank Crockley, hobbling slightly due to the pain in his shin, once more entered the fray, being sure to keep well out of kicking range. "Come on, ladies. This isn't the way to behave on the streets. I don't know what the argument's about but…"

"I'll tell you what it's about," said Gwendolyn, "This old ratbag called me a name that I wouldn't even sully my lips with."

"Trollop!" Maggie interjected, "I called her a trollop and I'm not afraid to call her a trollop again."

"Ladies, Ladies…" said Frank.

"Fight! Fight! Fight!" shouted the three young boys, hopefully.

"If anyone's a trollop," Gwendolyn screeched, "it's her! Oh yes, she's all very high and mighty, prim and proper, butter wouldn't melt in her mouth now, isn't she. But anyone who knew her twenty years ago when her husband was…"

"'Ere!" cried Maggie, indignantly, "You leave my Stan out of this!"

"Oh yes. Hit a sore spot, have I? You say I put it about a bit. Not half as much as your Stan did, and that's a fact!"

"Wash your bloody mouth out, you brazen…"

"Ladies, ladies," begged Frank, "If you have private things you want to discuss this isn't the place to do it."

"Fight! Fight! Fight!" chanted the three boys.

"Couldn't satisfy your husband yourself, could you? You shrivelled up, chapel mouse!" screeched Gwendolyn.

"Wash your damn' mouth out."

"Which is why he came to me!"

"I swear to God I'll take a swing for you. The filth that comes out of your mouth! When my poor Stan's been in his grave these five years and more."

"And what put him there? The booze. Drank himself to death, didn't he? And why did he drink so much? Because of you, you miserable old bag. He drank to forget he was married to you."

"Let me at her! Let me at her!" There was real rage in Maggie's face now. She was straining to be free of the grip of the men who were holding her.

Frank Crockley, who had appointed himself as the unofficial peacemaker, was calling for calm again. "Ladies! Ladies! If you don't calm down and go home now I will have to call for the police."

"The *what*?" screamed Maggie, "You mean you'd call the bobbies on us?"

"No one's arresting *me*, sonny boy," said Gwendolyn, "It's *her* what should be arrested. For… for… incitement to violence. Public affray. For being a foul-mouthed nasty old witch who'd be better behind bars."

But in spite of her words, the harshness was going out of her voice. As Gwendolyn looked around and saw the crowd and the chanting boys, she began to appreciate the spectacle she had made of herself. In a moment, as though a switch had been flipped, her anger drained away. As for Maggie – Muriel and Emrys were with her, talking to her quietly. Muriel hugged her. There were tears streaming down Maggie's face.

"Yes, well, young man," Gwendolyn said, addressing Frank Crockley, "Maybe my temper did get the better of me. All I'm saying is, I had good cause." She turned to one of the men who had been holding her back. "It's all right, Alf," she said, "You needn't worry that I'll be getting into a fight. Not with someone like that. Ha! Not worth it, she isn't." She turned to the other man who had also been holding her and said, "How about you walk me home, Bill?"

When the men had released their grip on her, Gwendolyn pulled her coat and her dignity around herself, gave a supercilious toss of her beehive, turned around and strode away with majestic hauteur, her six-inch heels clattering like castanets on the pavement.

CHAPTER 24

"What was all that about?"

Ruby and Maggie Pountice were sitting at a table outside the Cat and Ferret pub. It was late afternoon, the sun was shining and there was a slight breeze. Maggie, feeling that it was too early in the day for serious drinking, had decided on a pint of mild ale. Ruby had settled for a large gin and tonic.

"She's a nasty piece of work, that Gwendolyn Gormly," Maggie said, "Man mad. Money mad too. There's nothing she wouldn't do to get her claws into a man with money."

"So what's that got to do with you, Maggie? You two were going at it hammer and tongs just now. If you hadn't been held back you'd have been tearing chunks out of one another."

Maggie took a long, meditative slurp of beer. "Don't you believe it. She wouldn't tear no chunks out of me! All mouth and no knickers, that Gwendolyn Gormly is. Screaming and threatening is what she's good at. When it comes to the crunch, she'd no more get into a fight with me than she'd run a four-minute mile."

"Do I take it then," said Ruby, "that this is not the first time that you and Gwendolyn have…?"

"The first time! You have got to be kidding! I can't abide her and she can't abide me."

"Yes, I did get that impression."

"Believe you me, that Gwendolyn Gormly's a lowdown, good-for-nothing hussy. Leads men astray is what she does. Well, you seen how she packages herself. Wrapped up like an oven-ready turkey. She's been the cause of more strife between man and wife in Clogwyn Bach than… than I don't know what!"

Ruby sensed that she would need to pick her words carefully. "Gwendolyn has caused you some, er…"

"Strife? Too bloody right she has. Went after my Stan like a terrier after a rat she did. But if she was thinking I'd let a toe-rag like her come between me and my Stan she was very much bloody mistaken."

"So she and your late husband…?"

"Got her claws into him at a weak moment she did. By rights there's no way my Stan would have fallen for no dolled-up trollop like Gwendolyn Gormly. Only had eyes for me, my Stan did, not for the likes of her."

"I'm sure he did," said Ruby. She felt uncomfortable listening to Maggie pouring out her heart. As a rule, Maggie came across as gruff, tough and armour-plated against the world. In fact, she was more sensitive than she appeared. Which just goes to show, thought Ruby, how little we truly know about our friends and neighbours.

Ruby and Maggie sat in silence for a while. Beyond the small lawn that divided the pub's outdoor seating from the low sea wall a great expanse of sand ran between the northern and southern headlands of the bay. In the distance, towards the northern end of the bay, someone was throwing a ball for a black and white collie dog which scampered over the sand and into the surf to fetch the ball and return it to its owner. Ruby could not help thinking about the undercurrents and rip currents that Muriel had mentioned. She hoped the dog's owner would not be foolish enough to throw the ball far enough into the sea to encourage the dog to swim out to get it.

"But there you are. My Stan's gone now," Maggie said mournfully, "Heart attack. Only fifty-seven he was. Still, I got my Gwilym. That's a comfort, at least."

"Gwilym?"

"My son. Lives in Birmingham. You should see the home he's got! Beautiful it is. I went there once. Sandra, that's his wife, well, she's a nice enough girl. A bit house-proud but she means well. A daughter they got too. Riverdance. She calls me granny. But what sort of name is Riverdance for a girl? I told Gwilym they should have given her a good Welsh name. Ceridwen maybe. Or Arwenna. But they were set on Riverdance and once Gwilym's set on something, there's no arguing with him. Mind you, he's got a good job. Top man he is. In engineering. I thought that meant he was on the trains but it doesn't. He did try to explain once but it's all above my head. You should see the 'stificates he's got. Paper a wall with all them 'stificates, you could."

Ruby was still at a loss to understand why Maggie and Gwendolyn had been arguing with such ferocity. As gently as she could, she tried to get Maggie to tell her what it had been about. "Gwendolyn said you called her a name. Did you?"

Maggie laughed. "I called her more than one. A thieving, lying trollop is one of the things I called her. She stole my shop, see."

"Shop? I didn't know you had a shop."

"Not now I haven't. I used to, though. Maggie's Mystic Emporium. Tarot cards and runes and crystals. Only, see, with a shop like that, you never can tell from one month to the next how you'll make out. Raking in the money you can be one month. And then the next month nothing. Going through a lean patch I was, that's all. My Stan hadn't long passed away and I was struggling to make a go of it on my own. I got a couple of months in arrears with the rent. In another six months I'd have been back on my feet. But do you think Ken Collop would listen to reason? Oh no, not him!"

"I'm sorry," Ruby said, "You've lost me. Who's Ken Collop?"

"My landlord, that's who Ken Collop was. Rented the shop from him I did. Nasty bugger he was too. But then that's the sort of man Gwendolyn attracts."

"Ken Collop and Gwendolyn were…"

"Caught him in her snares she did. Sex mad the both of them. At it like rabbits they were. Ken was well off, see. Rented out a couple of shops. Made a packet. And he owned the bingo hall in Clogwyn Mawr. Rolling in money he was."

"So Ken Collop threw you out. And you blame Gwendolyn."

"Oh aye. She was behind it, there's not no doubt about that. She didn't never like me. And I didn't never liked her neither. No sooner was I out of my shop than she goes and opens her own shop, Gwendolyn's Grotto. Which should, by rights, be *my* shop."

Given their history, Ruby could understand why there was so much animosity between Maggie and Gwendolyn. What she could not understand was why it had all boiled over so vigorously on the street that afternoon. She asked Maggie.

"She provoked me. Walking along minding my own business I was when out of the blue, up she totters on her high heels and tells me she's going to open another shop in Clogwyn Mawr. Got plans to open a chain of New Age shops she says. New Age, my foot! Cheap tat is what she sells. So, being nice and friendly like, I asks her where she's going to get the money from because one thing's for sure, Gwendolyn's Grotto isn't no big money-spinner. So she gives me one of her nasty, smirky little looks from under her false eyelashes and she says, 'Let's just say I've come into a bit of money.' A bit of money? More like blackmail, I reckon. Ken Collop left her my shop in his will when he died. And now Sir Clifford Coot has left her enough money in his will to go opening up even more shops."

It took a few moments for the implications to sink in. Then Ruby said, "You really think Sir Clifford left Gwendolyn an inheritance?"

"Sure to have. It wasn't no secret that he'd been seeing her on the sly. Gwendolyn was on the make. She was all over Sir Clifford like a rash. She must have had something on him, I reckon, some dark secret. Maybe she knew something about him, had some photographs, if you know what I mean." Maggie winked and tapped the side of her nose with a forefinger. "Anyway, one way or another, she got herself written into his will."

Thinking aloud, Ruby said, "Which means that Gwendolyn might have had a motive to kill him?"

"That's what I think too," said Maggie.

Ruby opened her mouth to say something more then closed it again. A horrible thought had just occurred to her. Maggie was not the most circumspect of people. The arts of diplomacy were unknown to her. But surely not even Maggie could have... well, could she?

"You didn't," said Ruby, hesitantly, "You didn't actually *accuse* Gwendolyn of…?"

"Doing away with Sir Clifford? Of course I didn't bloody accuse her. I'm not stupid."

Ruby breathed a long sigh of relief.

"But I did drop a few hints."

"Maggie! What did you say?"

"I reminded her that the cause of Ken Collop's death has always been a mystery. Just fell down dead one morning, he did.

Not long after Gwendolyn had stolen my shop. The official cause was some brain thing. But I didn't never believe that. Too bloody convenient that was. First she gets him to give her my shop, then he drops down dead. She poisoned him, that's what I reckon."

"But you didn't say that to her in the street, did you?"

"I may have mentioned it in passing."

"Oh, Maggie…"

But Ruby was not really very interested in the unexplained demise of Ken Collop, whether due to natural or unnatural causes. She was, however, very interested indeed in Maggie's assertion that Gwendolyn Gormly was a beneficiary of Sir Clifford Coot's will.

Chapter 25

After finishing her pint of mild ale, Maggie strode off briskly down the High Street towards her house and Ruby walked along the sea wall until she came to some steps descending to the bay. She strolled along the beach towards the headlands at the southern extremity. As at the northern end of the bay, there were rock pools here but these were fewer and the rocks were less extensive.

Ruby walked over the rocks towards the sea margin. Once there she took from her jacket pocket the uninflated beach ball which she had bought in Muriel Greenalge's shop, she popped open the rubber stopper on its little air tube, put the tube to her mouth and began blowing. It took a few minutes to inflate the ball completely, by which time Ruby was feeling slightly dizzy. She sealed the air tube with the rubber stopper and threw the beach ball as far out over the water as she could manage which, to be frank, was not very far. The ball floated where it landed, bobbing about on the waves with no obvious movement either towards or away from the shore. Looking at it sitting there, brilliantly coloured and aimless, Ruby wondered what become of it? Would it bob up and down on the waves all night? Would the currents swirl it away out to sea? Or was it possible that it might eventually be transported from the southern end of the beach to the northern – quite near, perhaps, to the location where Ruby had discovered the body of Sir Clifford Coot?

She would come looking for it in the morning.

*

The alarm rang at 6 o'clock. Ruby yawned, rubbed her eyes, stretched and reluctantly got out of bed. She had been sound asleep. She would, in fact, have been perfectly content to sleep on for another four hours. But she had a job to do. She washed quickly, splashing her face with cold water to try to drive away the tiredness, then dressed and walked briskly down to the bay. She headed immediately for the northern rocks. The tide was still coming in but only slowly. This was not a spring tide so the sea did not come up the full extent of the shoreline. She walked over the rocks looking for any sign of the beach ball. She glanced out to sea in case it was at that moment being swept ashore by the tide. But there was no sign of it. Then she walked back along the beach to the southern rocks. Once again, there was no sign of the beach ball either on the water or on the shore. Oh well, she thought, it was a long-shot but it had been worth a try. Maybe the beach ball had burst or sprung a leak and sunk? Or maybe it had floated across the Irish sea and was at that very moment being washed up in Ballycotton or Ballycroneen. In the meantime, she had another line of investigation to follow. One that involved penetrating into the determinedly masculine world of a Welsh male-voice choir.

CHAPTER 26

The Methodist Chapel was a big, solid, building at the end of a narrow, dark street at the northern end of the village. It was built from quarried stone on a colossal scale, three storeys high surmounted by a tiled pitched roof. There were two steps leading up to massive double-doors at the front of the chapel. Above the doors, set into the wall, was a stone plaque stating "Capel Ezeciel, AD 1862". Judging by its monumental size it looked as though the residents of Clogwyn Bach must have been far more enthusiastic chapel-goers in 1862 than they are now.

As she approached the chapel Ruby heard the magnificent swell of a church organ accompanied by the soaring voices of a superb male-voice choir. They were singing one of the great Welsh hymns ending with an earth-rumbling "Amen". There was a big cast iron ring on the door. It was one of those rings that you have to turn in order to release a latch. As the thundering "Amen" rose to its mighty climax, Ruby grasped the ring, turned it, opened the door, strode into the chapel and clapped heartily. The six elderly men standing around the elaborately carved, dust-covered pulpit at the far end of the hall stared at her blankly.

"Can I help you?" said a tall, willowy, white-haired man.

"I was admiring your singing," Ruby said, weakly, "I heard you as I was coming up the street. I had thought, well… it sounded as though there were more of you."

"Oh, that was not us," said the white-haired man, "That was the Morriston Orpheus Choir," he nodded towards the stereo speakers on either side of the pulpit, "We were listening to them, you see, by way of inspiration."

"Oh, Mrs Lake! You've come to hear us, I suppose?" That was a familiar voice. The speaker was Elfyd Davies, the local doctor, whom she had met at the previous week's art class. From his attendance at both the art class and the choir rehearsal, Ruby deduced that he must be a man with plenty of leisure time, so either the residents of Clogwyn Bach were healthy by nature or else Doctor Davies had already cured them of their ailments.

"Well, I certainly haven't come to join you," replied Ruby, "what with this being a specifically 'male voice' choir."

"Oh, we could always squeeze in a woman, I suppose. Move with the times, isn't it? You're not alto, by any chance, are you?"

"Does a St Bernard dog growl in the alto register? My music teacher at drama school once compared my singing voice to the aforementioned canine."

"Ah. Possibly baritone, then. To what do we owe the honour of your presence here, dear lady?"

Ruby glanced across at the small group of men gathered around the pulpit. Her first impression had been wrong. They were not all elderly. One of them was positively young – early twenties, perhaps. Doctor Davies was probably in his mid-50s. But the other four were distinctly far removed from their first flush of youth.

"Look, I don't want to disturb your rehearsals," Ruby said, "Maybe when you've finished, I might…"

"Oh, but we are finished. There's not much for us to rehearse, you see. Given our reduced numbers, most of the traditional male voice choir repertoire is cut off from us. The soaring splendour of Verdi's 'Chorus of the Hebrew Slaves' is beyond our vocal means. Unlike the massed voices of the Pendyrus or Treorchy choirs our renditions of 'Ar Hyd Y Nos' and 'Cwm Rhondda' do not make the earth tremble. We do what we can but the plain fact of the matter is that we struggle. We need more singers, do you see. To fill a space like this."

Ruby glanced around the vast interior of the old building. A few dim lights suspended from the ceiling provided scant illumination and pools of darkness filled the little rooms and archways leading from the main body of the chapel. Everywhere were the signs of its lost magnificence. The walls were damp and the paint was flaking but the great oak-balustraded gallery that ran around three sides facing towards the huge, neglected and cobwebbed pipe-organ that was ranged across the wall behind the pulpit at the far end, gave the impression of stately permanence as though the old chapel was only waiting for the day when the pews would once again be filled with a devout and enthusiastic congregation.

Just then, the young man whom Ruby had noticed moments earlier detached himself from the geriatric barbershop quartet huddled around the pulpit and began walking in the general direction of Ruby and Doctor Davies. The young man was rather good-looking, Ruby thought, in a typically Welsh sort of way: short and stocky with dark, curly hair and a ruggedly square jaw. Had Ruby been twenty years younger she would have been inclined to give the young man a 'come hither' look. But then again, what are a mere twenty years? She gave him a 'come hither' look anyway. The young man came hither. Ruby flattered herself that she still had It, whatever It might be.

"Miss Lake," the young man said, smiling. He had a nice smile that showed lots of improbably white and even teeth. At least he had called her "Miss". Most people called her "Mrs", assuming that a woman of her age could not have committed the unpardonable transgression of remaining single.

"Do I know you?" Ruby asked.

"We met on Thursday."

"Did we?" Ruby tried to think what she had been doing on Thursday. "Oh, at the art class?"

"On the rocks."

"The rocks?"

"You probably don't recognise me out of uniform."

"Uniform?" What sort of uniform was he talking about? The Royal Navy? The Grenadier Guards? She tried to imagine him dressed in a red tunic with a big furry bearskin hat. Then it suddenly came to her – "The policeman!"

"That's me. Police Constable Ian Tucker." He put out a hand and for want of anything better to do, Ruby shook it.

"Pleased to meet you. Again. Police Constable Tucker."

"You can call me Ian."

"Only if you call me Ruby."

"Agreed."

"You are obviously a man of many talents," Ruby said, "A police officer and a singer."

"Oh, some police officers can do as many as three different things," he replied.

"I'm sorry, I didn't mean to suggest..."

"It's all right. It's just that I get used to people assuming that because I'm a policeman I can't possibly do anything else. It's as if they think I was born in uniform and once I take it off I don't exist."

"I know exactly how you feel," Ruby said.

"You do?"

"People think the same about middle-aged women. Especially unmarried ones."

Ian flashed that gleaming smile of his again. "Except, of course, you don't wear a uniform."

"Ha! Don't you believe it. Grey wool-mix skirt, low-heeled brown shoes, sensible pullover. They can tell us a mile off."

"I think you are making fun of me," Ian said.

"You deserve it," Ruby replied.

She had decided that she rather liked PC Ian Tucker. She also had a feeling that it might be very useful to be chummy with a police officer. Very useful indeed.

CHAPTER 27

The Cat and Ferret was quiet when they arrived. Ruby sat at a table with Ian Tucker and Elfyd Davies. Ian and Elfyd were drinking beer. Ruby had a glass of white wine.

"I put the decline in the choir down to the decline in religion," Elfyd said.

"Can't atheists sing?" Ruby asked.

"What I mean is, when the chapels were full there was a ready-made choir. They went to the chapels, they listened to a few hell-fire sermons and then they sang the hymns. That's where the Welsh choirs all came from. The chapels."

"How many go to the chapel now?"

"Nobody. Well, not regularly anyway. The preacher only comes once a month. Someone has to fetch him from Abercwmtwrch. And that's forty miles away. Even then, he's lucky to get a congregation of more than half a dozen. The old chapel's falling to wrack and ruin. We keep trying to raise money to fix the roof, re-plaster the walls and whatnot. My dream is to restore the organ but that would cost a small fortune. If it hadn't been for Sir Clifford's patronage, both the chapel and the choir would have been as dead as dust years ago."

"He financed the choir?" Ruby said, "Do you know if he left you anything in his will."

"He did, as a matter of fact. But only a small amount. His executor phoned me today with the details."

"Oh, really? Who is the executor of his will, if you don't mind my asking."

"Not at all. It's no secret. It's a chap called Masters. Ronald Masters."

"Ronald? Oh, you mean Lady Coot's friend who's staying with her at the hall?"

"That's the one. Don't ask me who he is or where he came from. All I know is that he was appointed the executor of Sir Clifford's will. We are very grateful for the small amount he's left us, of course, but there's no way that can make up for the loss of his music. We did the first performances of a few of his compositions, you see. They kept us afloat, you might say. So we were able to do concerts now and again. Mostly local. We did a concert in Cardiff last year as well. BBC Wales broadcast a bit of it."

"An entire concert with just the six of you?"

"Oh, well, we had to join forces with the Clogwyn Mawr choir," Elfyd explained, "But the posters said 'Clogwyn Bach and Clogwyn Mawr Male Voice Choirs'. With us listed first, see. That's Sir Clifford's influence. We're rehearsing a new piece now. The last new Clifford Coot composition we'll ever have to learn, I suppose. This weekend we're going to Clogwyn Mawr to rehearse it with the choir there. At least we'll be able to give him a good send off."

"A new piece?"

"Welsh Requiem it's called. It's the last thing he ever wrote. One of his best, too. We were planning to sing it at the Summer Fayre. Its world premiere, you see. Get some TV people round. But now we're going to do it at his funeral. Well, anyway, we're singing the Dies Irae which is one part of it."

"Dies Irae, the Day of Wrath," Ruby said.

"Oh, you know Latin?"

Ruby smiled, "Alas, no. But I am familiar with Verdi's Requiem."

"I'm not sure the Coot Requiem is quite up to Verdi's," Elfyd said, "But even so, it's the best thing Sir Clifford has written in years. Better than Ouverture Celtique by a long way."

"Ouverture Celtique was his most popular piece, wasn't it? If the Welsh Requiem is better than that then it must be quite something. I look forward to hearing it."

"It's sad, really. It's almost as though Sir Clifford had a premonition of what was going to happen."

"What do you mean?"

"Well," said Elfyd, "The title of the piece, do you see. 'Welsh Requiem'. The requiem is the mass for the dead. Ironic that it should be the last piece he ever wrote, don't you think?"

CHAPTER 28

There is a long tradition in Wales that when the local male voice choir finishes a rehearsal it migrates, *en masse*, to the local pub. The Clogwyn Bach choir believed firmly in tradition and so, even though their dwindled numbers could not muster much of a *masse* to migrate *en*, the half dozen of them, plus Ruby, briskly tottered down the old cobbled street in the direction of The Cat and Ferret. The cosy, friendly pub, with its thatched roof, stone floor and dark oak beams, was warm and welcoming. At one end of the pub, an informal concert was in full swing. In a high-backed wooden settle sat a woman and two men playing jigs and reels on a fiddle, a mandolin and a penny whistle.

Four members of the choir decided that the instruments would be improved by a vocal accompaniment and so, having ordered their beers, they went off to that end of the bar and began a spirited rendition of the traditional Welsh song 'Sospan Fach' which tells the moving tale of a little saucepan boiling on the fire while a baby cries in a cradle and the cat scratches little Johnny. The general consensus is that it sounds considerably better when sung in Welsh than in English.

Ruby meanwhile went to sit at a table at the other, quieter, end of the pub with Elfyd and Ian. It was time, she felt, to broach the subject which had brought her out that night. From an inside pocket of her coat she took a folded sheet of paper.

"Why is there an inquest?" Ruby had decided that, if anyone could shed light on the police's latest theories about Sir Clifford's death, it was a policeman. Having a policeman readily to hand was too good an opportunity to miss.

"It's standard procedure," Ian said, "when death is not from natural causes."

"Not natural, eh? So you think there was malice aforethought?"

"What? Oh, you mean, do I think his death wasn't an accident? Nobody thinks that, do they? But as far as the law is concerned, an accident is not a natural cause. A heart attack or a stroke is a natural cause. Falling off a cliff or falling under a bus isn't. The inquest is a formality."

"It won't hold up the funeral?"

"No. Not at all. Why are you asking? Do you know something the police don't?"

Ruby shrugged off the question. Then Ian and Elfyd started talking about some fund-raising plans for the restoration of the chapel. Ruby was not very interested in chapel-related matters so she listened to the music wafting across from the other end of the pub. When she tuned back into the conversation she found that they were discussing a forthcoming rehearsal of 'Welsh Requiem' with the combined forces of the Clogwyn Bach and Clogwyn Mawr choirs.

"We'd better get some copies of the score for the Clogwyn Mawr lot," Ian said.

"Best thing is to send them a scan by email," said Elfyd, "Then they can print out as many copies as they want."

This provided the perfect opportunity for Ruby to broach the subject of the score that she had pilfered.

"That reminds me…" she said, as she unfolded the paper and smoothed it out on the table-top.

"What's that?" said Elfyd, "Been writing some music, have you?"

"Ah no. That's the problem, you see, I neither write nor read music. The blobs on this paper might just as well be squashed flies for all they mean to me. I was wondering if they meant anything to you."

Elfyd reached into his jacket, took out a pair of reading glasses and put them on. Meanwhile, Ian had been craning for a look at the music. "Those opening bars look familiar," Ian said.

"Let me see." Elfyd held the paper at arm's length to focus on it. He began making little "pom-pom-pom" noises, singing the tune under his breath. "Oh, yes," he said at last, "Yes, I know that one all right. Where did you get this?"

"Oh," Ruby hoped they would not see her blushing in the dim pub lighting, "Someone gave it to me. You know the piece, then?"

"Oh yes. It's what really started it all off for Sir Clifford."

"Really? What do you mean?"

Elfyd handed the sheet of music to Ian. "There's a few mistakes though," Ian said, "Look, the third bar. That shouldn't be C-Sharp. And here, there's a quaver missing. But on the whole, yes, there's no doubt about it." Ian handed the paper back to Elfyd.

"No doubt about what?"

"It's the 'Ouverture Celtique'," Elfyd said, "Well, the opening part anyway. That was Sir Clifford's first big hit, as you might say. It was what got him into the classical music charts. It looks like someone's copied it out here, or transcribed it by ear maybe, which is why there are one or two mistakes. But apart from that, there's no doubt about it. It's the first page of the score all right."

"And when did Sir Clifford compose that?"

"Oh, Lord, a while ago. Do you remember when it was, Ian?"

"It was before he moved back to live in Clogwyn Bach, that much I know. So it must have been ten, twelve years ago. Something like that."

"He moved back? Where was he before that?"

"He was teaching music in Oxford, I think. Or Cambridge. One of the two. His father was living in Coot Hall in those days. But the old man was fragile towards the end so the family decided it would be better if he went into a nursing home."

"The family? Sir Clifford had brothers and sisters?"

"A sister, but she lives in Australia. She didn't want to come back to live in the Hall so Sir Clifford moved in. Who's Eve?"

"I beg your pardon?"

"Look, here at the top corner of the score, the page of music you just gave me, someone has written 'Eve G'. Probably the name of the person who made the copy of the music, I should think."

"Yes, probably," Ruby said, as though it was a matter of no interest to her.

"Coo-eee!" The penetrating baritone voice of Maggie Pountice easily cut through the rising swell of the violin, mandolin, penny whistle and singers at the other end of the bar.

Maggie was approaching Ruby's table, pint in hand, accompanied by Rona who was clutching a half-pint of something fizzy which Ruby, with distaste, suspected of being cider.

Maggie made an exaggerated mime of looking for a space at Ruby's table. Elfyd and Ian took the hint. Standing, Elfyd said, "We were just off to add our voices to the choir, ladies. Please, take our seats."

"Call that a choir?" growled Maggie, "A couple of cats and a Yorkshire terrier would sound better than that bunch of old scarecrows."

Elfyd smiled through gritted dentures. Maggie's social graces, or lack thereof, were not unfamiliar to him and, since Maggie gave every impression of being able to handle herself well in a fist-fight, he thought it safer to smile than to start an argument.

As soon as Maggie and Rona took the two vacated seats, they were all of a flutter to know the latest developments in Ruby's sleuthing. Ruby showed them the sheet of music, explained where she had found it and pointed out the mysterious signature.

"Eve?" said Maggie, "One of his music students, do you think?"

Rona shook her head. "I never heard of him teaching anyone. Not around here. He used to teach music at a university once upon a time. But not here."

Ruby told them that Elfyd had identified the music as an extract from The Ouverture Celtique. "But why," she asked, "would he have a copy of an old piece of music in his scanner?"

"You can't trust Elfyd," Maggie said.

"Why ever not?"

"Him and Sir Clifford never hit it off. Elfyd was jealous, that's what it was. The choir was always singing Sir Clifford's stuff. Elfyd gets them to sing stuff he's written too sometimes…"

"Elfyd's a composer?" Ruby said.

Maggie chortled. "Of sorts. Bloody dirges is all he writes. No one wants to listen to them."

"So there may have been some professional jealousy," mused Ruby.

"Do you think it was Elfyd who killed him?" Rona asked.

Ruby ignored the question. "There's another peculiarity," she said, "Elfyd believes that the music here isn't quite right. There are some mistakes."

"What does it matter?" said Maggie, "I can't see how a sheet of bloody music can't have nothing to do with him being murdered."

"I don't know," Ruby said, "I have a feeling it's important. I think he scanned this and then put a copy of it into his jacket pocket which is why a sheet of music was found on his body."

"It doesn't make sense," said Rona.

"That's why I think it's important. It doesn't make sense that he would scan and print his own music in a version containing mistakes, and then put it into his pocket before going off and meeting the person who killed him. It's such a peculiar thing to do that it must be significant."

"Did you find anything else while you was snooping?" asked Maggie.

The word "snooping" reminded Ruby of something. She could not think quite what.

"Actually, there were a couple of other things of interest in his study too," Ruby said, "For one thing. His desk. All the drawers were unlocked except for one. What was so important that he kept it in a locked drawer?"

"Money," said Maggie.

"Or drugs?" suggested Rona.

"Love letters," said Maggie.

"Or pornography?" said Rona.

"You don't know where he kept his keys, I suppose?" Ruby asked.

"You're not thinking of rummaging in his private places, I hope!" Maggie said, disapprovingly.

"He's dead," Ruby said, "I don't think it matters to him any more."

"He had a keyring," said Rona, "He always carried a bunch of keys around with him – his car key, the front door key, all that sort of thing. He kept the keyring on a little chain clipped to the belt of his trousers."

"That would have been returned with his effects, then, I suppose?" said Ruby, "The possessions he had on him when the body was found."

"I never heard about any keys," Rona said, "I'll ask Bronwen. She'll probably know. I mean, she sees and hears more than I do. I'm stuck in the kitchen most of the time but Bron cleans all over the house. In the study. In the living room. In Sir Clifford's bedroom. In Lady Coot's bedroom."

Ruby was startled. "They had separate bedrooms?"

"Oh yeah. A house that big, they have loads of rooms. They didn't have to share a bedroom like common people. Plus, they didn't much like one another anyway."

"He sowed his oats elsewhere," rumbled Maggie.

"The blonde woman, you mean, what's her name, Gwendolyn?" Ruby recalled Maggie's argument with Gwendolyn and her belief that Sir Clifford had left her a bequest in his will.

"Gwendolyn Gormly for one," Maggie said, "But there was plenty of others too."

"He was sneaky," Rona added, "He had to travel away quite a bit, see. To Cardiff, to London. Abroad. That gave him loads of opportunities, didn't it? He tried it on with me a few times too. Didn't get anywhere, though. He was a dirty old man, if you want my opinion."

"What about Lady Coot? Did she have any…?"

Maggie butted in – "She'll have anything that moves. Always been like that, she has. Even when she was a teenager."

"Who's the friend she has staying with her?"

"Greasy Ronald?" Rona said, "Probably her bit on the side."

"Have you ever seen him before?"

"He's visited the Hall a few times. But he never stayed before. This is the first time."

"It was Lady Muck and Greasy Ronald that bumped Sir Clifford off, that's for sure," said Maggie.

"I have to admit," Ruby said, "that they do seem like the prime suspects. But why would they lure him away to the clifftops? And why would Sir Clifford agree to go? And why would Lady Coot fabricate the story that her husband had left the house on the morning of his murder when the post-mortem showed that he had drowned? And, since the tide was way out the morning I found his body, that must mean he had drowned the previous night."

"Maybe because she's a bit dim," said Maggie, "Patsy Coot was always a bit on the thick side."

"If you want to know his movements, Lady Coot would be the last person to ask," Rona said, "Sir Clifford often kept himself locked away in his study. Working. Sometimes I don't think they saw one another for days on end."

"I can't help wondering if Sir Clifford had some secret that we don't know about," said Ruby, "Maybe he was being blackmailed? There was never any gossip, I suppose?"

"If there was," said Rona, "Rod's the bloke who'd know about it. Who's been cheating on who, what they did, where they did it and what equipment they used. Rod would know all the details."

"Rod? I don't think I know him."

"The hairdressers," Maggie said, "All the best gossip round here can be heard from under them hair-dryers."

"Plus Rod has what you'd call a busy social life," Rona added, "If you know what I mean."

Ruby raised an eyebrow. She had no idea what Rona meant. Maggie filled in the gaps – "Pubs, clubs and parties. *Swingers'* parties."

"In Clogwyn Bach?" Ruby found the idea hard to imagine.

"In Clogwyn Mawr too," Rona said.

"*Especially* in Clogwyn Mawr," Maggie added with a stern air of disapproval.

"There was another odd thing in his study," Ruby said, "A painting. A portrait of Sir Clifford. In oils. Standing on an easel. It seemed to be only half done."

"Oh that old picture," said Rona, "Chris hated it. It was so bloody pompous looking. But that's how Sir Clifford wanted it done."

"Chris. The art teacher? He's been to see the painting?"

"Seen it? It's Chris who's painting it!"

"Really!" said Ruby, "I had no idea that Chris even knew Sir Clifford. I suppose if he was doing a portrait, Chris must have spent quite some time alone with Sir Clifford in his study?"

"Not recently," said Rona, "They had an argument. Chris stormed off. I haven't seen him at the Hall since a week or so before Sir Clifford died."

"Aha!" said Ruby.

"Have you solved the murder?" Maggie asked.

Ruby shook her head. "Sadly not."

"Then why did you say 'Aha!'?"

"I'm not sure. It seemed like a good thing to say at the time. Do you know what was the cause of Chris and Sir Clifford's argument?"

"Money probably," said Rona, "Isn't that the cause of most arguments?"

"Or an artistic disagreement?" Ruby suggested, "Artists are notoriously temperamental. There's something important in all this. The portrait, the locked drawer, the key chain, the printout of a sheet of music. It must all mean something."

"It means," said Rona, "that Sir Clifford was having his portrait painted, kept the drawer of his desk locked, kept his keys on a chain and printed out a sheet of music."

"There's something in that locked drawer, I bet!" said Maggie, "It's a shame you wasn't able to do no proper snooping in there!"

There was that word again – "snooping". Where had Ruby heard it used before? Ah, yes, the letters! She had intended to show them to Rona and Maggie but it had slipped her mind.

"Here take a look at these." Ruby took the cream envelope and the piece of lined A4 paper from the inside pocket of her jacket. "Someone popped these through my letterbox last week. This one came Thursday night."

"The day you found the body?" said Maggie.

"Yes. That evening I came to the art class. When I went home, someone popped that letter through my letterbox."

Maggie opened the envelope and took out the single sheet of paper on which was written: "Stop your snooping or you'll be next!!!"

"What's that supposed to mean?"

"I take it as a threat," said Ruby, "But the odd thing is that I hadn't even done any snooping last Thursday night."

"We talked about it though," said Rona, "Here. In the pub. Don't you remember? You said you thought he'd been murdered."

"Did I?" Ruby's recollection was somewhat different from Rona's.

"You did," Maggie said, "And Rona said that you'd be sure to track down the killer on account of your previous experience at that sort of thing."

"The letter-writer must have been in the pub at the time," Rona said, "overheard what you were saying and decided to put the frighteners on you."

"You think I'm in danger?"

"Nah. She's all bluster."

"Who is?"

"Gwendolyn Gormly."

"Gwendolyn? What has she got to do with…?"

"It's her who wrote that," Rona said, "I've seen her handwriting before. And I've seen the paper and envelopes she uses."

"You have? When?"

"A few months ago. After I started working up at Coot Hall. Gwendolyn sent me an anonymous message. Told me to stop 'flaunting my body' as she put it 'or I'd soon regret it'. She thought I was having it away with Sir Clifford."

"And were you?" asked Maggie.

"No, I was not! Not that he'd have objected. He was a randy old bugger. Gwendolyn was always on the lookout for anyone she thought might be flirting with Sir Clifford. As far as she was concerned, he was hers by rights."

"But why would Gwendolyn threaten me?" said Ruby, "I never flirted with Sir Clifford. And anyway, even if I had, it's a bit late in the day to be bothered about that now, I should think."

"Gwendolyn Gormly's a nasty piece of work," Maggie rumbled, "I wouldn't turn my back on her, not if I was you, in case she sticks a knife in it!"

"That's not a comforting thought," said Ruby, "But here's another odd thing: Another note was delivered the following morning. See if you can make any sense of this one."

She smoothed out the lined A4 paper on the table top. Maggie and Rona peered at the words printed in ballpoint pen: "IN THE DESK. THE SEECRITS IN THE DESK."

"What secret's that?" said Maggie.

Ruby shrugged. "It must be referring to something in Sir Clifford's desk, I suppose."

"You'll have to do some more snooping," said Maggie.

"Mine's a dry cider," said Rona, "and make it a pint."

As it turned out, the meaning of the message written on the A4 sheet of paper would not require any more snooping on Ruby's part because she was about to meet its author.

CHAPTER 29

A broad sliver of moon was visible in the sky as Ruby walked up Fern Hill towards her cottage. The night was silent but for the distant background surge of the tide washing over the sand of the bay and the occasional hooting of an owl or barking of a fox. Far below in the village someone shouted "Goodnight" and someone else shouted "See you tomorrow". Apart from that, all that Ruby could hear was the sound of her own breath and her footsteps tapping and crunching over the worn, mud-crusted tarmac. At least she had remembered to bring a torch with her this time. By its beam, she saw the spiky outlines of hawthorn and beech hedges at the sides of the lane and the leaf-heavy branches of the trees arching overhead.

There was another sound. Behind her. Footsteps. No, surely she was mistaken. Nobody else would be walking up Fern Hill at that time of night. She stopped and listened. Yes, they were footsteps, sure enough. Heavy footsteps. Following her. She turned and shone the torch back down the lane.

A haggard face with deep, shadowy, wildly-staring eyes was illuminated by the beam of light. Ruby gasped! "What do you want?" she cried.

"You!" came the answer.

"Me?" Ruby glanced around in panic. It was a ten minute walk up the hill before she would come to the first inhabited dwelling – Bessie's cottage. To go back down the hill towards the village would mean she would have to push past the man who stood in her way. "What do you want with me?"

The man took a couple of paces towards her. "The murder. You knows about the murder."

Ruby felt her heartbeat accelerating. Could this be the murderer standing just feet away from here? Was this the man who had killed Sir Clifford Coot?

"I don't know what…" Ruby gasped, "Wait a minute, haven't I've seen you somewhere before?"

"'Course you seen me before. That's why you been doing all this detectivating stuff, innit?"

"What?"

"On account of the clues I been giving you, like."

"Clues?"

"You seen me note didn't you? Hand-delivered it meself, I did."

"You? You sent me that note?"

"I seen you down the pub, see. You probably didn't notice me, you being in the lounge, like, and me being in the snug. I thought to myself, if anyone can figure out the secret, it'll be you. I knows it's in there. I was thinking you'd be wanting to have a good nose about and find what the secret is. You didn't find it though, did you?"

Now that the man was close to her, Ruby was able to see his face more clearly by the light of her torch. It was what, in the acting profession, might be called a 'characterful' face. It was not the face of a romantic lead. Nor the face of a solid and dependable bank manager or company director. It was a lived-in face, a face of the outdoors, a rough, unshaven face, the sort of face which central casting might assign to the role of a dosser, a petty-thief or a pirate; or, Ruby thought with a shudder, a serial murderer.

"Coot Hall!" Ruby exclaimed, "I saw you at Coot Hall. You were carrying an aspidistra!"

The crabbed and hairy face illuminated by the beam of Ruby's torch belonged to Lady Coot's gardener, Maldwyn Placket.

"I was hoping to tell you, see. To look in his desk, like. In case you forgot. Only Bronwen turned up so I never had the chance. The secret, see, that's where it is. In the desk. Very cagey about that desk, old Sir Clifford was. Nobody knows what he kept in it. Only I know it was a secret."

"Why are you so sure?"

"I goes in his study one day, see…"

"With an aspidistra?"

"With a pot of jasmine. Very partial to smelly plants was old Sir Clifford. And this day I catches him unawares, like. He had something on his desk. He didn't hear me coming in, see. Well, when he caught sight of me, he says 'What the hell are you doing in here, Maldwyn?' – 'scuse the language only that's what he says – and so I says 'I'm bringing the flowers like what you asked is what I'm doing,' and he says 'You must knock, Maldwyn. I've told you a hundred times, you must knock before entering,' and I says 'I didn't know you was in here, or else I would have knocked,' and he says 'That is the point of knocking, Maldwyn, to establish if I'm in here or not' and I says, 'So where shall I put the flowers?' and he says…"

Ruby felt that Maldwyn's narration was tending to stray from the point. "The desk," she said, "You were telling me about something he kept in his desk drawer."

"Oh aye. Papers, I think they was. Secret papers. And a letter. There was definitely a letter. When he seen me that day, holding that pot of jasmine, he shoves his secret papers back in the drawer before I even gets a chance to see what they is. But I'm thinking to myself, 'Them papers is a guilty secret if ever I seen one. Hidden away like that in a locked drawer'. He always kept that drawer locked, you see. None of the other drawers. Just that one. And then a week after that he's found dead at the bottom of the cliffs. And I'm thinking to myself, 'If it wasn't for whatever he's got in that drawer, he'd be alive today.'"

"So let me make sure I understand what you are telling me, Maldwyn. You think Sir Clifford kept something so secret in his desk drawer that it was worth killing him for?"

"Aye, that I do."

"You said you thought there was a letter in the drawer. Why do you think that?"

"I heard him screeching at someone, a few days before he was killed. He was in his study and he was shouting, real mad like, 'For God's sake! I've got the letter!'"

"Who was he shouting at?"

"That I don't know. I daredn't go in his study when he was in one of his moods."

"So you wrote me a note to tell me about it."

"Aye, that I did."

"And then, when I came to Coot Hall, you again tried to draw my attention to Sir Clifford's desk."

"Aye, I did that too. Everyone knows you are after his murderer, see."

"They do?"

"Oh aye. You must be, mustn't you. Well, we all know how you solved the murder of that actor fella. The case of the Lipstick Poisoner, they was calling it." Ruby groaned. "So it stands to reason that you'd be after the killer of Clogwyn Bach, don't it?"

Ruby had thought she was being so discreet that nobody would have had the remotest suspicion that she might be doing a few private investigations into Sir Clifford's untimely demise. But if even Lady Coot's gardener knew, then she would have to assume that the whole of the village knew too. And that, presumably, included the murderer.

CHAPTER 30

Ruby was wakened by her alarm clock ringing at half past five the next morning. She would happily have spent five more hours in bed but the time was crucial. She had consulted the tide tables online the previous day and low tide was due at 06:18 in the morning.

Quickly, she washed, dressed and made her way down Fern Hill towards the beach. She walked up to the northern shore and clambered, with difficulty, over the slippery seaweed-covered rocks. The tide was on its way out which was why the rocks on the upper part of the shore were so wet. The air was cool and misty. Nobody was out on the beach, not even Matt, not even dog walkers. There was just Ruby and the seagulls. She glanced up toward the cliff path. Everybody believed that Sir Clifford had fallen from there onto the rocks below. Ruby had hoped that the beach ball would provide an alternative hypothesis. But she was beginning to think that she had been letting her imagination run away with her. Every time she had tried to imagine how Sir Clifford might have been murdered, she had run up against the problem of how and why he had been walking along the clifftop path in the dark. When Muriel Greenalge had told her about the treacherous currents in the bay, Ruby had considered the possibility that Sir Clifford might have been killed in some other location and his body had washed up beneath the cliffs. And yet, the absence of the beach ball gave her cause for doubt. Maybe the simple explanation was correct, after all. Maybe Sir Clifford really did decide to go for a walk on the clifftops late at night and had slipped to his death. Maybe it was just an accident.

And maybe that red, blue and yellow thing lying amongst the seaweed further down the shore was exactly the thing that Ruby was looking for. She moved with caution over the uneven rocks. The further she moved down the rocky shore towards the receding tide, the harder it became to keep her balance because of the greater quantity of wet seaweed. The object she was looking for was almost totally obscured by a great mass of bladder wrack – a slippery, slimy, brown seaweed covered with inflated swellings that looked like blisters. But for its bright colours, Ruby would never have spotted it. When she pulled back the heavy fronds of weed, it was clear that she had found what she was looking for. Punctured and deflated now, it was nonetheless the same beach ball that she had set adrift the night before last – at the other end of the bay. The tide had carried the ball out from the southern promontory and brought it back in again at the northern one.

"That's it! I know how it was done!" she cried.

A seagull cried mournfully above her and wheeled off into the mist.

CHAPTER 31

"Uncle Ted is in the funeral parlour," said the woman with the tight perm.

"In the funeral parlour?" said the woman wearing curlers, "Is he dead, then?"

"I should hope so," said the woman with the tight perm.

"They say the weather'll be brightening up later," said Karen, the proprietor of Karenz Kutz, the hairdressing salon on the High Street, "That'll bring the flies out, I expect."

"That's the way it is these days," said the woman wearing curlers, "It's all funeral parlours and rest homes. Not like the old days. In the front parlour, that's where they used to put them in the old days. But who's got front parlours now?"

"We haven't, anyway," said the woman with the tight perm, "Had it knocked through years ago. When they put in the kitchenette."

"We decided against a kitchenette. A kitchenette attracts vermin."

"Last Friday it was."

"What was?"

"Uncle Ted. That's when he went. Next door neighbour found him in the passageway. You know who I mean? Elsie Evans. Used to serve bar down the Cat and Ferret till that business with the sailor from Aberystwyth. Well, apparently he'd been eating a cheese and pickle sandwich at the moment of death."

"The sailor from Aberystwyth?"

"No. Uncle Ted."

"You can get compensated for that," said the woman wearing curlers, "Write to the cheese company. You could get a tidy sum."

"I doubt it," said the woman with the tight perm, "The cheese wasn't implicated."

"The pickle, then."

"His neck was broken."

"It's the horse flies I can't stand," Karen said, teasing a curl on the head of the woman with a tight perm, "A horse fly only has to take one look at me and the next thing you know it's sinking its teeth into my arm. My hubbie says I have particularly succulent arms where flies are concerned."

"Fell down the stairs," said the woman with a tight perm, "His neck snapped like a twig. It's the linoleum I blame. If they hadn't polished the linoleum on the landing, he'd be alive now."

The woman wearing curlers took a slurp of tea from the cup which Rod, the assistant stylist had just handed her. "Where these pickle companies are concerned," she said, "the more fuss you kick up, the more you are likely to be compensated. I saw a programme on the telly. These pickle companies are rolling in it, believe you me."

"How would you like the sides? Brushed back or curling under in a pageboy style?" Rod asked Ruby.

Ruby was sitting at the back of the salon. She'd opted for a simple shampoo and cut. She had not really needed her hair done at all but she wanted an excuse to get out and listen to some village gossip. In case it helped with her enquiries. But nobody seemed to have anything to say about Sir Clifford. The only death she had heard mentioned was that of somebody's uncle Ted. It was starting to feel like a wasted trip.

"What's a pageboy style?" said Ruby.

Rod looked aghast. "You've never had a pageboy? Oh, you should! It would make you look like Barbara Stanwyck in 'Double Indemnity'."

"Who?"

"Barbara Stanwyck. You're not telling me you don't know Barbara Stanwyck!"

"That's exactly what I'm telling you."

"No! You're pulling my leg. The actress. One of my absolute favourites. Then again there's Veronica Lake. Ooo, that's your name, Lake, isn't it! You're not related, are you?"

"Not to my knowledge."

"Well, I could do you a Veronica Lake peekaboo hairstyle. That would be most elegant."

"How old are you, Rod?"

Rod stopped brushing and looked at himself in the mirror on the wall directly in front of Ruby. The light was not at its most flattering so he turned his head slightly which caused the light from the front window to cast a shadow that showed off his cheek bones to good effect – "Go on, guess."

"Thirty."

The shriek that proceeded from Rod's mouth startled some seagulls that had been fighting over a discarded sandwich on the pavement outside the shop. They flew off emitting squawks in the same shrill tone as Rod – "Noooo! Me!! Thirty!!! You are kidding, I hope."

Ruby had not been kidding but since Rod was holding the scissors and was quite capable of doing significant damage to her hair, she thought diplomacy was called for. "Ha!" she said, "Of course I was."

"Go on, then," said Rod, "How old do you think I am, really? Go on. Be honest. How old do you think?"

She had never been good at guessing people's ages and she was not entirely certain whether she had previously under- or over-estimated Rod's age. She glanced at Rod in the mirror. He was sucking in his cheeks and pouting. Ruby guessed that was intended to make him look younger. "Twenty-three," she said.

Rod broke into a broad smile. "There, you see, people always think I'm younger than I am. I have good bone structure. And I look after my skin. You'd never believe it, I know, but I'm twenty-six. Why did you ask?"

"Ask what?" Ruby had completely forgotten how the conversation had started.

"You asked me how old I was."

"Oh, yes. Well, you keep wanting to cut my hair to look like Hollywood actresses who died in the middle of the last century. Either you are a lot older than you look or else you have an unhealthy obsession with dead actresses."

"There, you see," Rod had started curling the damp ends of Ruby's hair around a brush and using a hairdryer to blow them dry, "you did know who Barbara Stanwyck was all along, didn't you? You were just teasing."

"You caught me out, there, Rod. I have seen one or two of her films on the telly. I must confess that I do rather like the style of some of those old actresses. Dietrich…"

"Oh!" Rod's eyelids fluttered in ecstasy.

"Bacall."

"The divine Bacall."

"Garbo."

"Oh! Greta Garbo was the most beautiful woman who ever lived." Rod's knees seemed to quiver slightly. For a moment Ruby was afraid he might fall to the ground in a swoon but, after a few seconds he pulled himself together and continued drying her hair.

"I'm surprised you find old actresses attractive," Ruby said, "I mean, I should have thought a young man of your generation would be more interested in, oh, I don't know, whoever the sex symbols are these days."

"Sex symbols!" Rod laughed, "Oh, you are a scream. You don't think I find Greta Garbo and Marlene Dietrich sexy, do you?"

"Don't you?"

"Oh no. Ramon Navarro and Rudolph Valentino are more my cup of tea."

"Oh, I see. Even so. Ramon Navarro and Rudolph Valentino died long before you were born. They died before even *I* was born, so that really was a long time ago. Isn't there anyone more contemporary that takes your fancy?"

"Oh, James Dean wasn't bad, I suppose."

"How about someone who is still alive?"

"A film star, you mean? Oh no. They are all teeth and muscles these days. I prefer a man with style. Cary Grant maybe. Or Robert Donat."

"And in real life?"

"I don't think they exist in real life."

"You've never found the right man, you mean?"

"Oh, I've found the right man lots of times. But none of them wanted to be found by me."

"Ha! Join the club," said Ruby, "That's the story of my life."

"There, how does that look?"

Ruby glanced at her hair in the mirror. It looked impossibly perfect. She knew that it would remain perfect for all of two minutes, if she was lucky. It would only take the slightest breeze to return it to its usual disordered mess.

"I look," she said, "like Barbara Stanwyck."

"Yes," Rod smiled, "You really do."

Ruby glanced at the clock on the wall. It was five to one.

"What time do you go for lunch, Rod?"

"Oh, any minute now. You're my last booking until two."

"Let me treat you."

"If you are after my firm young body, I have bad news for you."

"Fear not," said Ruby, "It's your mind I'm after."

CHAPTER 32

The cream cheese and smoked salmon bagels in the Little Cloggy Caff were much better than Ruby has been anticipating. So was the coffee. Made with dark-roasted, freshly ground Arabica beans given the high pressure treatment of a proper Italian-style espresso machine that hissed and rumbled on the counter.

"I never even guessed this place existed," Ruby enthused, between creamy mouthfuls of bagel, "I mean, I've passed it dozens of times but I never expected it to be like this."

"It is good, isn't it. Of course, we had nothing like this ten years ago. If it wasn't for the tourist trade a café like this would never be able to survive. Most of the locals would be just as happy with a cup of instant and some beans on toast. So that's something we can thank Sir Clifford for. Things really picked up once he moved here."

"The tourist trade, you mean?"

"Mmmmph." This, with a mouthful of bagel, was the nearest Rod could get to saying "Yes."

Rod swallowed and washed it down with a slurp of coffee. "Here, have you heard about that wine bar that's opening at the end of the month?"

Ruby recalled reading something on the subject in The Clogwyn Clarion.

"Ace that'll be," said Rod, "Let's face it, we only got two manky old pubs in this village."

"Two?" said Ruby, "I know the Cat and Ferret. I didn't know there was another one."

"You don't want to neither," said Rod, "The Smuggler's Itch is a real dive. Anyway, what I'm saying is, a wine bar has to be better than them manky old pubs, surely."

"Perhaps," said Ruby. In fact, she was supremely indifferent to the forthcoming wine bar. There was just one topic on her mind: "I suppose, Rod, that you must have known Sir Clifford?"

Rod took a moment to gulp down another mouthful of bagel before answering. "Knew *of* him. I don't think anyone really knew him much. He didn't mingle with us common folk. Chris knew him as well as anyone, I suppose. You know Chris? The chap that teaches art? He was painting a portrait, I believe."

"So I had heard."

"He did a portrait of Lady Coot too. Chris was a professional artist in London before he came here."

"Oh, really? How long ago was that?"

"When did Chris arrive? Oh, a ages ago. Not long after Sir Clifford, I'd say."

"How interesting. He just turned up out of the blue. An odd place to choose for someone who'd been living in London, wouldn't you say?"

"A bit like you then?" said Rod.

"Um, yes…" Ruby sipped her coffee and glanced around at the other people in the café. At one table there was a harried looking woman with a little girl sitting on her lap. The girl was smearing an elaborate ice cream concoction over her dress and giggling while she did so. At another table, a teenage boy was having a frantic, whispered conversation with a teenage girl ("Ah, the mysteries of young love!" thought Ruby). At the counter, a thin young man wearing a dark suit several sizes too big for him was ordering a takeaway sandwich ("An estate agent," Ruby surmised).

"…everybody likes him."

"Sorry? I was daydreaming."

"I was saying," said Rod, "that everybody likes Chris. He's talented, he's always cheerful. And he's also not at all bad looking. Wouldn't you say?"

Ruby decided it would be diplomatic to avoid answering that question. "He must have spent quite a while up in Coot Hall, I suppose? If he was painting two portraits."

"Oh, he was always there! He must have been six months just doing the picture of Lady Coot. She was always pestering him for sittings. That's what they call it, you see – a sitting – even though she was standing in the picture."

Several thoughts went through Ruby's mind in quick succession: 1) As Rod had observed, Chris is rather good-looking, 2) Maggie Pountice was of the impression that Lady Coot was man-mad, 3) All those sittings for her portrait must have meant that Lady Coot had been alone with Chris on a frequent basis. What could Ruby conjecture from that collection of facts? Surely there could be only one conclusion…

"How well do you know Chris?" Ruby asked.

"Oh, pretty well. Why?"

"I was just wondering if he had ever mentioned anything about, well… how can I put this? Do you think that he and Lady Coot might have had, um, an, well, you know…?"

"Was he shagging her, do you mean?"

Ruby felt herself blush. "You could put it that way."

Rod hooted with laughter. "Oh no, my dear, you have got quite the wrong end of the stick. That's not the way Chris swings, if you get my meaning."

"Isn't it?"

"He is not what you'd call a lady's man *at* all."

"Ah." Ruby did a quick mental recalibration. "Then what about Sir Clifford?"

"You think him and Chris was having it away? Oh, you have got a filthy mind! That's why I like you. No, Sir Clifford fancied women. And the more the merrier, if all the rumours are true. Notorious for it, he was."

CHAPTER 33

After lunch, Rod went back to work while Ruby took a walk along the sea front. Just opposite Karenz Kutz stood a little shop in the window of which there was a higgledy-piggledy jumble of glittering rocks and crystals, tarot cards, wind chimes, rune stones, pendulums, beads, incense and tiny glass bottles containing herb extracts, unguents, attar of roses and patchouli oil.

"Looking for something?"

Ruby had not noticed the woman leaning against the open door of the shop. It was Gwendolyn Gormly, wearing a tight leopard-spotted miniskirt and diaphanous pink blouse with ruffles around the plunging neckline. She was smoking a pungent cigarette which Ruby assumed to be herbal though she was not entirely sure on which side of the law the herbs might be.

"I was admiring the, er, rocks," Ruby said.

"Which rocks?" Gwendolyn took a long drag on her cigarette and blew a stream of smoke in Ruby's direction, "The amethyst cluster or the blue howlite tumblestone?"

"The, um, the purple one. Very attractive."

"I'd have thought a crystal ball was more in your line," Gwendolyn commented acerbically, "Very helpful in the snooping business, I'm told."

"Now just a minute!" said Ruby, "You might be able to get away with picking fights with Maggie Pountice. But pick a fight with me and you may live to regret it."

"Ha!" Gwendolyn blew out some more smoke, "Is that a threat?"

"I seem to recall it was *you* who threatened *me*," said Ruby.

"Me! I don't know what you're on about. I never said a damn' word to you."

"No, you didn't say it to my face. You didn't have the damn' well nerve. But you wrote it in lilac ink, posted it through my letterbox and ran away again, as fast as your stilettos would carry you."

"Oh, someone's been talking, have they? Spreading rumours. Typical of people round here, that is. Always poking their noses into other people's business. Well, so what if I did write it? No harm in that."

"You threatened me."

"I did not."

"'Stop your snooping or you'll be next' – that's what the letter said. If that's not a threat, what is it?"

"It was a bit of friendly advice, that's what that was. Just warning you that people round here can take umbrage against someone poking their noses in where it's not wanted. I heard you down the pub, see. Asking questions. Making insinuations. Too many damn' questions. Probing into people's private lives. Well, it's none of your bloody business and I don't mind who hears me say so!"

"Look," said Ruby, "I'm not looking for an argument. I just want to say that you've got the wrong end of the stick. I'm not interested in your private life." But she was speaking to nothing but thin air and a cloud of pungent smoke. Gwendolyn Gormly had gone back into her shop. Her parting gesture to Ruby involved two fingers and it did not mean 'V For Victory'.

Chapter 34

"I'm getting the impression that nobody really liked Sir Clifford but I can't think of anyone who had both the motive and the means of doing away with him."

Ruby was sitting in Bessie's kitchen, a cup of tea in her hands and a slice of Bessie's freshly baked teisen lap, a traditional Welsh fruit cake, on a plate in front of her.

"Then it's back to square one," said Bessie, "Maybe it was just an accident after all?"

"No. I can't believe that. As far as I can see, Lady Coot must be the prime suspect. Presumably she inherits everything. Well, almost. Apparently Sir Clifford bequeathed a small amount to the choir, and Maggie Pountice reckons he left some money to Gwendolyn Gormly too."

"Gwendolyn! I'd heard the rumours about her and Sir Clifford but that was all supposed to be very hush-hush. I'm surprised he left her some money. That would be a public acknowledgement of their affair, I should say."

"I don't suppose that bothers him now he's dead."

"I expect it bothers Lady Coot though."

"If so, it's the only thing that does bother her about his death. As far as I can see she hasn't shed a tear for him and she's already shacked up with a fancy man called Ronald whose moustache alone makes me suspect him of dark deeds. Lady Coot definitely has to be my number one suspect. But how would she have persuaded him to go walking on the cliff path late at night?"

"She could have employed a third party, I suppose?"

"What do you mean?"

"Everyone knew Sir Clifford was a lothario. He had a taste for young women. Suppose that someone set him up? Maybe they fooled him to make an assignation with a young woman ?"

"Or with a not-so-young woman," said Ruby, "Gwendolyn Gormly, for example. If she knew about her inheritance, she could have done away with him. The clifftop path is dark and secluded. So if you wanted to be far away from prying eyes, you could hardly choose a better location. On the other hand, it's also cold, wet, muddy and covered with spiky gorse bushes. Not the most comfortable place for a romantic triste."

"Frankly," said Bessie, "the idea that a man of Sir Clifford's age could be lured out to the clifftops at the dead of night on the promise of a bit of slap and tickle is a non-starter, in my opinion."

"Mine too," said Ruby, "Which is why I think he was done away with somewhere else. Not on the clifftops."

Ruby's experiment with the beach ball had convinced her that a body deposited at some other location might have been washed up on the rocks beneath the northern cliffs. But she had no conclusive evidence for that conjecture nor did she have any plausible theory to explain where, why or how Sir Clifford's body might have been thrown into the sea.

Ruby nibbled a corner from her slice of fruit cake. "If only I could work out what that sheet of music meant. I wonder…?

"Bessie, I have an idea. Max, my agent, sent me a book. I'm recording an audio book, did I mention? No? Well, it doesn't matter. The thing is, he sent the text of the book attached to an email message. Now when you scan something, you can save a copy onto your computer's disk and then you can attach that copy to an email message. So maybe he was planning to send a copy of the music to…? Well, someone."

"His agent?" suggested Bessie.

Ruby thought about that. Actors have agents. Writers have agents. Do composers have agents? Yes, she thought, they damn' well do. Or, at any rate, Sir Clifford did because when she and Bessie had visited Coot Hall, Lady Coot had said that amateur composers kept sending their scores to Sir Clifford's agent who emailed them to Sir Clifford. So was the page of music in the scanner part of a score that had been sent to him? If so, it had not been sent by email because it was written by hand, on paper, in ink. And what is more, if Elfyd Davies, the choir master, was to be believed, the music was part of a piece that had been composed by Sir Clifford himself.

"A thought occurs to me!" said Ruby with a smile.

"I'm not sure I like the mad gleam in your eye," Bessie commented, "The last time I saw that, I ended up going to Lady Coot's with you so that you could go thieving which, I should imagine, is a highly criminal activity."

"The thought that occurs to me is that the only logical explanation for the mistakes in the music is that they are not mistakes at all."

"No?"

"No. Are you familiar with Led Zeppelin?"

"The rock group? I am. Though I am more of a Deep Purple fan myself. But one thing I can tell you is that Sir Clifford's music is nothing like Led Zeppelin."

"That's not the point. Do you know a group called Spirit?"

"Nope. Never heard of them."

"Well, a band called Spirit wrote a song called Taurus. This would have been in the late sixties, I think."

"So what?"

"A few years after Spirit recorded Taurus, Led Zeppelin recorded Stairway To Heaven."

"I've heard of that one."

"I should damn' well hope so. But the thing is, Spirit reckoned that Stairway To Heaven sounded more than a little similar to their song, Taurus. Now, given the fact that Stairway To Heaven had earned millions and millions of dollars, whereas Taurus hadn't…"

"I follow your drift. Spirit claimed that their copyright had been infringed and they wanted a goodly heap of Led Zeppelin's dollars for themselves."

"Exactly. There was a big court case but eventually it was decided that while the Led Zeppelin song and the Spirit song were similar, it was likely that they had both been inspired by some other, older, tunes rather than Led Zeppelin deliberately copying Spirit."

"And the moral of the story is what?"

"I think the music I found in the scanner was written by someone else. It's very similar to a piece that Sir Clifford wrote but it's not identical. Maybe his agent had been alerted to the similarities in this other composer's composition and so they sent the music to Sir Clifford for his opinion. Maybe, at the time of his death, he was already in the process of taking legal action against this other composer."

"Which means that this other composer would be pretty upset with Sir Clifford. Upset enough to kill him?"

"Salieri and Mozart."

"Eh?"

"Didn't you see the film, 'Amadeus'? The great composer Salieri was so vexed by the greater composer, Mozart, that he poisoned him."

"Hmm. I'm not sure that's historically accurate."

"Nevertheless, it's possible, isn't it."

"Well, the only composer around here is our local doctor, Elfyd Davies."

"So I've been told," said Ruby, "But is he our Salieri?"

"He's a doctor!" Bessie said, "He wouldn't kill anyone."

"No, perhaps you are right," But Ruby was thinking of Doctors Crippen and Shipman, neither of whom had had any such qualms, "Now how would I find out who Sir Clifford's agent is? I could phone Lady Coot and ask her but that might arouse her suspicions, don't you think?"

"Google it," said Bessie.

So that's what Ruby did. She did an internet search for "Sir Clifford' Coot's agent" and there it was: Cindy Bridforth Associates "a friendly agency specialising in the representation of composers and songwriters for concerts, film, TV, new media and theatre."

CHAPTER 35

"Hello. Could I speak to Cindy Bridforth please."

"I'm sorry. Cindy isn't available at the moment."

"I'll hang on."

"It'll be a long wait. She's having a baby. Should be back in the office in about three weeks."

"Ah. I wonder if you could tell me who's dealing with Sir Clifford Coot's affairs."

"Hang on. I'll put you through to Vincent. Who's calling?"

"Ruby Lake. I'm working with Lady Coot."

Well, that was not a lie exactly. Ruby and Lady Coot were working together, in a sense, on the Summer Fayre.

Click. Clunk. A blast of Vivaldi, The Four Seasons: Winter. Clunk.

"Hi, Ruby. Vinnie here. You're working with Patsy on something?"

"Lady Coot. I'm working with…"

"Lady Patricia Coot, yeah, right. Sorry, bit informal. We call her Patsy."

"Oh. Quite. We are having a Summer Fayre here."

"Yeah? Cool. That's in that place in Wales, right?"

"Right. We were thinking of doing the Celtic Overture."

"Ouverture Celtique? Yeah. Great, isn't it! Well, everyone loves it, don't they."

"Do they? Oh, I mean, yes, of course, everyone, um, adores it."

"You said it! So how can I help? Worried about performing rights, I guess? That's no problem, Ruby. Leave it with me…"

"Actually, I was worried about, well, another version."

"Another version of what?"

"There's a different version, I think, of the music. With, you know, some different notes. In different places."

"Hmm. An arrangement, you mean? Can't say I've heard of it. Hang on, Ruby, love, let me check…"

("Mumble, mumble.... Ouverture Celtique... some old biddy on the line reckons there's another... I don't know, an arrangement... mumble, what? ...really? When? Oh...Ah...Right...Yeah. OK")

"Hi, Ruby. Apparently there was a score, a sheet of music, anyhow, with a few differences. Is that what you mean?"

"Someone sent it to you?"

"Sir Cliff. Yeah. He emailed it to us."

"Sir Clifford? He emailed you the score? But had someone sent you a copy of the music prior to that?"

"I'm not sure I understand."

"Well, I'm assuming that someone sent you the music, the one with the misplaced notes. I don't know, maybe someone tried to pass it off as their own work? And someone wanted to bring it to your attention?"

"Bring it to our attention?"

"And I'm further assuming that you then sent that piece of music to Sir Clifford for his expert opinion."

"Hang on, Ruby, love."

("Mumble... she wants to know if someone sent it... Sir Cliff... what? ...said what?...mumble, mumble... never seen it before? No? ... Nah, I don't know what she's rabbiting on about either.")

"Sorry about that, Ruby, love. I just checked with a colleague. You've got it the wrong way around, darling. It was Sir Cliff who sent the music to us. Not us who sent it to him."

"That was the first time you saw it?"

"Absolutely."

"And how many pages did he send?"

"Just the first page, apparently. It's a bit of a mystery, to be honest. No title on it, even. We weren't sure what he wanted us to do with it. He sent a scan of the page and a note saying that we should hang onto it. If things turned out badly, he was going to send us a copy of a letter that would explain everything."

"A letter? What letter would that be?"

"Your guess is as good as mine, love. We never got it, of course. For obvious reasons. I was wondering if you might have any idea what he meant?"

"Me? No. No, I... When did he send the email to you? What was the date, I mean?"

"I can tell you the date and the time, my love. It's on the email. Tuesday May 11th, 21: 37."

"Two days before he died," Ruby said, "Or rather, two days before I found his body."

"You did what…?"

"It's a long story."

*

"Hi, Bron here."

"Bronwen, sorry to phone out of the blue. It's Ruby. Are you alone?"

"Alone as I ever am. I'm mopping the kitchen floor."

"You're at home?"

"Nah. My kitchen floor can stay dirty for all I care. Up at Coot Hall."

"Is anyone with you? In hearing distance, I mean."

"Rona's here. She's peeling potatoes. Does that matter?"

Ruby thought about that. On the one hand, Rona knew that Ruby was digging into the circumstances of Sir Clifford's death so it surely couldn't matter if she overheard Bronwen talking about that. On the other hand, Ruby could not be absolutely sure that Rona was not implicated in some way. Then again, she could not be sure that Bronwen was not implicated either. Oh, what the heck, Bronwen would be sure to tell Rona all about their conversation anyway.

"No," Ruby said, "It doesn't matter. I was wondering if you could do something for me?"

"What sort of something?"

"Look for clues."

"Oh, yeah! Just say the word."

"Well, the thing is, I have reason to believe that there might be a clue in the top drawer of the desk in Sir Clifford's study."

"Yeah?"

"Yeah. I mean, yes. But the drawer is kept locked."

"You want me to get a crowbar and break it open?"

"Yes. No."

"You said yes."

"I meant no. No, absolutely not. No crowbars. No breaking things. That's not what I intended at all. Apart from anything else, it would cause a noise. It would also be criminal damage. We must not do anything criminal, under any circumstances."

"You stole that sheet of music, though. That's criminal, isn't it?"

"I didn't steal it. I borrowed it."

"So if you don't want me to break into the drawer, what *do* you want?"

"I want you find the key."

"To the drawer."

"Exactly."

"Where is it?"

"I don't know. That's why I want you to find it."

"Where shall I look?"

"I don't know. Where did he keep his keys?"

"In his pocket, I think. His trouser pocket. Or his jacket pocket. I'm not sure."

"Maybe you can have a look?"

"I'll see what I can do. I'll ring you back."

*

"Ruby?"

"Bron? Did you have any luck?"

"I had a good rummage around in his study. But then Ronald came in. You know, Lady Coot's, er…"

"Friend of the family?" Ruby suggested.

"I was going to say 'bit on the side'."

"Did he see you up to anything?"

"Only cleaning. That's what I do anyway so nothing suspicious there, is there?"

"Who is Ronald, anyway? He seems a bit of a mystery man."

"He's an estate agent. Lives in Clogwyn Mawr. He's a bit dodgy. I seen him going into the Hellfire Club once."

"What on earth is the Hellfire Club?"

"Don't know, really. It's just an end-of-terrace house in Clogwyn Mawr. What I do know is that it's got a bit of a reputation."

"Really? What sort of reputation?"

"People say that things go on there." The way she said the word "things" suggested unspeakable debauchery and depravity.

"Oh! Well, each to his own, I suppose. Anyway, I take it you found nothing in Sir Clifford's study?"

"Not a thing. So then I went up to his bedroom. To do the cleaning, hoovering and stuff. I had a look in his wardrobe. He had lots of jackets and suits and… anyway, it took me a while."

"Any luck?"

"Nope. So then I had a word with Lady Coot."

"You did what?"

"Don't have conniptions. I didn't give the game away. I said I was cleaning out his study and I wanted to wax his desk but the drawer was locked. Did she know where the key was? She said she didn't. I said maybe it was on the same keyring that Sir Clifford used for his house keys and his car key. She said it might be. I said did she know where the keyring was? She said it was probably in one of his jackets. I said I'd been cleaning out his wardrobe and I couldn't find it. So she said it must be somewhere else then but not to worry as it would show up in due course."

"He probably had the keys in his pocket on the night he was killed."

"I suppose so."

"But, wait a minute, didn't you say that his possessions has been returned after the post-mortem?"

"That's right. They brought back his wallet and that piece of music."

"No keys?"

"No."

"So either the keys are lost or…"

"Or what?"

"Did the funeral director take any of Sir Clifford's clothes?"

"I don't know. Why would he?"

"Where is the body now?"

"They took him to the funeral parlour in Clogwyn Mawr."

"That's it!"

"What? Well, once they lay out the body, they like to make them look as smart as possible. They obviously can't dress him in the clothes he was wearing when he died. They were soaking wet.

Probably torn too, I should think. The rocks are covered in barnacles. Very sharp things, barnacles. The undertaker will no doubt have asked Lady Coot to find another suit. To dress the body in. Which means that if the keys aren't in the suits in his wardrobe and they weren't among the items found on the body, they must be in the clothes he's wearing now."

"In the funeral parlour?"

"I have to get those keys!"

"How are you going to do that?"

"I suppose I shall have to steal them."

CHAPTER 36

That evening, being a Thursday, Ruby went once more to the art class. She was relieved to find that the subject that night was a vase of carnations. She was no prude and she had no objections to sketching the naked male body. But, from a purely practical point of view, a small vase of carnations took a lot less sketching than Tom Crockley's considerable expanse of flesh.

Tom Crockley was sitting at the desk to Ruby's right while Maggie Pountice sat at the desk to her left. To her surprise, Ruby saw that Tom was quite an accomplished artist. His drawing was actually recognisable as a vase of carnations whereas Ruby's looked more like some wilted dandelions in a jam jar. Maggie Pountice appeared to be experimenting with surrealism; her drawing bore a close resemblance to a dancing elephant.

As they sketched, they occasionally made small talk to one another. Ruby told Tom that she would be holding auditions for a play to be put on at the Summer Fayre. Tom said his son, Frank, was the actor in the family because "He played the dormouse in Alice In Wonderland once." Ruby said that sounded like an admirable qualification and she would certainly bear him in mind for a part.

"What play you going to be putting on, then?" Maggie Pountice wanted to know.

"I was thinking of A Midsummer Night's Dream but that would require a very large cast which might be difficult to assemble."

"Shakespeare!" Maggie made the name sound like a swear word, "Nobody wouldn't go to see that. Something with a few laughs is what you want."

"One of the early Pinter plays, perhaps?" said Ruby.

In reality, Ruby was hoping that the play would never be produced. She had only concocted the idea as an excuse to go and have a look around Coot Hall. If Lady Coot turned out to be implicated in her husband's death, the Summer Fayre would surely be cancelled and Ruby would be able to forget all about the play, which would be for the best, in her opinion.

Conversation dwindled after Ruby mention Pinter since neither Tom nor Maggie had the slightest idea what Ruby was talking about. Silence might well have reigned had not Maggie decided to take off her shoes in order to relieve her bunions. That reminded Tom about the problems his prize ram was having with his foot. The ram's foot had an abscess on it which was producing quantities of smelly grey pus which was all down to the fact that it had been grazing where it should not have been grazing. Ruby asked where the ram should have been grazing and Tom said that it should have been grazing in the old Hog's Back field and Ruby asked where might that be and why had the ram failed to graze there. Tom said the field was next to the Coot Estate and by rights the old Hog's Back field belonged to the Crockley family but Sir Clifford had stolen it and that is why the ram could not graze there. At that, Ruby's ears pricked up. "He stole your field?" she asked, in what she hoped sounded a casual and disinterested tone of voice, "How did that happen?"

"Solicitors is how that happened," said Tom with barely suppressed anger, "They reckoned I didn't own the old Hog's Back field according to the law. I said, I don't know what the law says but that old field has been in the Crockley family ever since my granddad's day. But you know what them solicitor fellas are like. They can argue black is white and up is down and before you know where you are they've tied you all up in knots and stolen your own land right from under your nose."

"I don't understand. How did Sir Clifford steal it?"

"Ah, well that's the clever thing, isn't it. He reckoned it was his land all along and I was squatting on it. His granddad, Francis Gwydion Coot, sold that land to my granddad, Roderick Llewelyn Crockley, for three bales of hay and a goose. It was all done fair and square on a shake of the hand. Everyone knew they was my two acres by rights. But Sir Clifford decides he wants them two acres for an apple orchard and he gets his solicitor to write me a letter telling me that I could like it or lump it. He says that if my granddad and his granddad never signed any papers then the Hog's Back field isn't ours. Ach! Don't talk to me about solicitors. Bloody crooks the lot of them. Mind you, it was Sir Clifford who was behind it all. It was him that put his solicitors onto me. So it was Sir Clifford that stole my field. He was a mean old bugger, there's no getting away from that."

"You didn't like him, then?"

"Like him? I was never so happy than when I heard he was dead!"

"Oh, really?"

Ruby added some shading to her drawing of the carnations to try make them look a little less diseased but that had the effect of making them look as though they had died and were in an advanced state of decay. Her mind was not fully engaged with her art. She was more interested in the ferocity of hatred that Tom Crockley evinced for Sir Clifford Coot. Would somebody be prepared to commit murder in revenge for a disputed piece of land, she wondered? Looking at the way Tom Crockley was grinding his teeth, she thought it a distinct possibility that they would.

As soon as the art class was at an end, everybody once again migrated, with the unerring instinct of a herd of wildebeest stampeding across the Serengeti plains, to the public bar of the Cat and Ferret.

"That was very interesting," Ruby said, as she was about to sit at a table in one corner of the pub, "What you were saying about chiaroscuro." She was addressing the art teacher, Chris, who had been on the verge of moving towards a table at the other end of the pub. Once installed in the pub, the art class had a tendency to separate itself into a group of men at one end and a group of woman at the other, an arrangement which did not suit Ruby's plans at all.

"Oh, yes?" Chris replied, "In what respect?"

"The light, the dark, the contrast…" Ruby was struggling. She had only the vaguest idea of what 'chiaroscuro' was and she had paid not the slightest attention to Chris's remarks on the subject. "The form. The way the shadow… I mean, when you mentioned, um… you know, the painter who, um…"

"Rembrandt?"

"Yes! Rembrandt! You said, um… well, what you said was most interesting but I don't think I quite grasped it all. I was wondering if you could explain it again. There are one or two details I think I may have missed."

Chris was looking uncomfortable. His male students had already settled themselves at a table at the other end of the pub. Tom Crockley was buying a round of drinks and Chris's pint would now be sitting on the table waiting for him to come and drink it. He did not give the impression that he really wanted to hang around discussing chiaroscuro with Ruby, Rona, Muriel and Maggie. But Ruby had already found a spare chair and was putting it next to their table, clearly with the expectation that Chris would sit upon it.

"Just a minute," he said, "Someone's got me a pint. I'll go and get it. Back in a tick."

"You are very keen on getting Chris to join us tonight," Muriel Greenalge commented.

"Sucking up to the teacher," Maggie Pountice said.

"Trying to seduce the teacher more like," said Rona.

Maggie laughed. "Chance would be a fine thing."

"Now then, Ruby," Chris had returned, a pint of dark ale clutched in his hand. He sat in the vacant chair, "What was it you wanted to know about chiaroscuro?"

Ruby sighed. She did not want to know anything about chiaroscuro but, having gone thus far with the pretence, there was no alternative but to continue with her deception. She and Chris talked in a dull and desultory manner until, having launched upon a long and incomprehensible description of the secret techniques of the Dutch painter Gerard van Honthorst, Chris was interrupted by a growl of impatience from Maggie Pountice: "It's your round, sunshine. Mine's a pint of best. These three ladies will have another bottle of white wine. And you can get us some salt and vinegar crisps while you are about it."

Chris was so startled by Maggie's gruff, sergeant-major-like orders that he complied without a moment's hesitation. While Chris was at the bar, Maggie told Ruby that if Chris went on babbling about art, she would either scream the place down or hit him over the head with her beer glass – and quite possibly both. "If you've got something to ask him about the murder, get on with it, for goodness' sake."

Ruby had to agree. A more direct approach was called for. When Chris returned with the wine, beer and crisps, Ruby came straight to the point. "I gather you were painting a portrait of Sir Clifford."

"Oh. Who mentioned that?"

"It's a well-known fact," Ruby said airily, "Anyway, as you were doing his painting up at Coot Hall, I suppose you must have seen quite a lot of him."

"Yes, I suppose so."

"Why would he go off in the middle of the night, do you suppose? To the cliffs, I mean."

"I don't know. Odd, isn't it."

"Did he commit suicide, do you think?" said Muriel.

"Nah. He was murdered," said Maggie.

"Murdered?" said Chris, "I thought the police had concluded that he died of natural causes."

"There's to be an inquest," said Maggie, portentously.

"Ah. Is that usual in the circumstances?"

"I think he was being blackmailed," Ruby added.

"Really?" Chris looked genuinely shocked, "What about? I mean, I'd never heard of any scandal."

"Well, you wouldn't have *heard* of it, would you?" said Maggie, "That's why he was being blackmailed. To keep it quiet."

"Ah."

"He kept something in his desk, everyone knew that," said Rona.

"His desk? How do you…? Oh, of course," Chris gave the impression that the thought had only just occurred to him, "You work at Coot Hall, don't you, Rona."

"You know damn' well I do," she said sulkily, "I brung you tea and sandwiches often enough, haven't I?"

"Well, yes, but…"

"Apparently, he always kept his desk drawer locked," Ruby said, "Unless you saw him open it? I suppose you may have. As you were painting his portrait in his study."

"Yes, well, I think I may have. Seen him unlock it, I mean. I don't recall anything particularly suspicious."

"What did he keep in there?" said Muriel.

"Oh, you know, the usual things."

"Usual things?" said Ruby.

"Yes. Papers. Cheque book. Receipts and invoices. That sort of thing."

"That's all?" said Ruby.

Chris shrugged. "That's all I ever saw. All rather mundane, I'm afraid. No poisoned daggers or secret documents." He smiled as though he had said something amusing. The three faces that stared back at him were grim and his smile faded rapidly.

"What did you argue about?" said Ruby.

"Argue? Who said we argued?"

"So you didn't?"

"I don't recall. We may have. He could be a cantankerous old git at times. Kept wanting me to make changes to his portrait. He wanted me to make him look younger, I think. People often do."

"You made *her* look younger," Rona said.

"Who?"

"The portrait you did of Lady Coot. You missed out the wrinkles and you took pounds off her weight."

"Ha! Ha!" Chris tried to smile but it looked more like a grimace, "Well, ladies, this has been nice. To have a few drinks, I mean, and talk about… art." The faces were still grim. "We should do it more often." He pushed back his seat and stood. "If you don't mind, though, I'll just go and sit down at the men's end now. It's been, er… lovely to have a chat."

"He knows more than he's letting on to," said Maggie Pountice when Chris had left them.

"You think?"

"You think Chris and Lady Coot were having an affair?" said Rona, "That would explain the flattering portrait he did of her."

"Surely not!" said Ruby, "Think of the age difference."

"Some women likes them young," said Maggie.

"I am led to believe," said Ruby, recalling what Rod the hairdresser had told her, "that Chris and Lady Coot might not be entirely, well, compatible."

"He's bisexual," said Rona.

Ruby nearly spat out a mouthful of wine. "What? Chris? How do you know?"

"I can tell," Rona said, mysteriously.

"I wonder if Sir Clifford left something for Chris in his will?" said Muriel.

"You think Chris might have bumped him off?" Ruby mused, "Wouldn't that be like killing the goose that laid the golden egg? I mean, Sir Clifford was paying Chris to paint his portrait, wasn't he? What will come of that now, I wonder?"

"And then there's the boathouse," said Muriel, "Who's to say what will happen to that now that Sir Clifford's gone?"

"Boathouse?" said Ruby, "What are you talking about?"

"It's where Chris lives," Muriel explained, "In the old boathouse on Southbay Rocks. You must have seen it, with all the walking you do down on the beach. Perched right over the sand at far the southern end of the bay it is."

"Ah? I think I know the place you mean. But what's the boathouse got to do with Sir Clifford?"

"Sir Clifford owns the boathouse," Muriel explained, "Owned, I mean. It was built right on the edge of the land so they could launch a boat when the tide was high enough. It's been many a year since it's been used for boats though. Sir Clifford's father had it converted into a cottage. Chris rents it. I don't think her ladyship has ever really liked Chris, though. So who knows what'll happen to him now? Give her a month or two, I reckon, and she'll boot him out."

"That's just the sort of thing she would do," Maggie agreed, "She was always mean even when she was a little girl."

Ruby wondered if there was any significance in all this or was it an irrelevant detail? She quickly came to the conclusion that she would need to do some more investigation into the matter. In the meantime, she noticed that their wine glasses were empty. "Another bottle, ladies?" she suggested.

CHAPTER 37

"See you next week, ladies!" It was just after half-past ten and Chris was leaving the pub.

No sooner had the front door closed behind him than Ruby got unsteadily to her feet. "Well," she said, "I think I'll be off." She put on her overcoat with some difficulty (How many bottles of wine had they drunk? Three? Four?) and, swaying slightly, staggered towards the door.

"You haven't finished your wine," Muriel said.

"You have it," Ruby slurred.

Muriel was all too happy to oblige and the last thing Ruby remembered seeing before the cool night air struck her in the face, was Muriel carefully pouring the contents of Ruby's wine glass into her own glass.

Ruby shivered. The night was not remarkably cold but the pub had been remarkably warm. Due to the wood fire blazing away in the grate, no doubt. Or, quite possibly, because of the wine that was making Ruby feel decidedly flushed. It took a few moments for her eyes to become accustomed to the darkness. It took a few more moments for her eyes to become accustomed to the two overlapping images of everything around her.

"Ruby," she said to herself, "you are tipsy."

There was no sign of Chris. Which was all to the good. Ruby was working undercover. It was imperative that she should not be observed.

"Which way to go?" she muttered.

"You all right, Ruby?" It was Tom Crockley. Two of him. Ruby stared at the two images, willing them to merge into one. After a few moments, there was indeed just one Tom Crockley standing in front of her, albeit with somewhat blurred edges.

"Just taking the night air," Ruby replied.

"You look a bit peaky, my love. You're feeling all right, are you?"

Ruby assumed a dignified air. It was the air she had assumed when playing Lady Bracknell in The Importance Of Being Earnest in a provincial tour a few years earlier. "The whole theory of modern education is radically unsound," she said, quoting from the play, "Fortunately, in England at any rate, education produces no effect whatsoever."

"Aye," said Tom Crockley, not seeming entirely convinced, "Just as well we're in Wales, then. Well then, I'll be on my way."

He walked along the road to the right which, Ruby worked out after some hard thinking, would lead him towards the northern end of Clogwyn Bach Bay. The boathouse, however, was at the southern end of the bay which meant that she would need to walk down the road to her left. This she now proceeded to do.

She was not familiar with this route. It led through a couple of streets lined with terraced houses and then it turned into a tree-lined road, not unlike Fern Hill but less steep, less narrow and benefitting from the illumination of street lamps. It occurred to Ruby that, since she was working undercover, approaching the boathouse via a well-lit road would not be good policy. Covert operations demanded stealth. She would therefore approach the boathouse along the beach. She turned around and walked back towards the village. Once there she was able to descend some steps from the High Street onto the sand of the beach. Looking to her right she saw, outlined by moonlight, the rocky promontory at the northern end of the bay where she had discovered Sir Clifford's body. To her left, at the southern extremity, the beach ended at another, lower, tree-covered promontory. It was just below the treeline that the boathouse was situated. From where she stood, she could see two pinpoints of light which, as she walked towards that end of the beach, gradually resolved into two lighted windows of the boathouse. Ruby was pleased to discover that there were indeed two windows and not just one which meant that the effects of the wine must have begun to wear off.

The sand was wet and firm for walking but the tideline was strewn with weed and flotsam and, as she drew closer to the boathouse, increasingly more rocks protruded from the sand so that she was obliged to use her torch to avoid them. She hoped that Chris did not chance to look from his window and notice her light as she approached.

As that thought occurred to her, Ruby suddenly stopped in her tracks. Her torch! She would have had enormous difficulty making her way through the darkness without her torch even though the moon that night was almost full. And yet, Sir Clifford had gone wandering up on the clifftops, on a night without a moon. Ruby had not heard of any torch being found among his possessions. Of course, he might have dropped it. It might have been swept away by the sea. Yes, that was in all probability what had happened. Still, she would need to look into that.

She was now standing at the bottom of a stone wall that rose ten feet above her from the level of the beach to the base of the boathouse. The boathouse was a small, two storey dwelling made of whitewashed quarried stone. There were some steps leading up from the beach and some more steps leading from the house up through the trees that covered the steep hill behind it, towards the road that led out of the village. Of a boat there was no sign.

Through one of the windows, Ruby saw a man silhouetted by the light from the room. Chris, obviously. Then there was a second silhouette. Someone was with him. Suddenly Ruby felt a sense of guilt. She was acting like a Peeping Tom! She had come to take a closer look at the boathouse, not to pry into Chris's private life. She was about to begin the walk back to the village when a face appeared at one of the windows above. In a panic, Ruby switched off her torch. When she next looked, the curtains had been drawn across the window. "Did he see me?" Ruby wondered.

As she began the long walk back home, she resolved to make a return visit to the boathouse at first light. She was always awake at the crack of dawn and even if Chris should notice her walking near the boathouse, there would be nothing unusual about that since she made a habit of early-morning walks along the beach.

*

The next morning, Ruby leapt out of bed and looked at the clock. It was half-past eleven. "Good grief!" she said, stifling a yawn, "I overslept!"

Chapter 38

"A torch?"

"That's right. A torch."

Bessie drummed her fingers on the table top. "But I thought it was keys you was looking for."

"Now I'm looking for a torch as well."

Ruby and Bessie were sitting in the kitchen of Rose Cottage. Ruby was holding a mug of tea in one hand and her mobile phone in the other. She brought up a list of phone numbers on the screen of the phone. The more she thought about the torch, the more important it seemed to her. If Sir Clifford had gone walking on the clifftops at night, he would have had to have taken a torch with him. But when the police had returned his effects there had been no torch. If he had not had a torch with him, then what did that mean? That he had not gone walking on the clifftop? Or that he had not been alone? That he had met somebody else who had a torch and the two of them had gone walking together?

"You can't be sure he didn't have a torch. Maybe he took one but lost it," Bessie said.

"Or maybe the police did find a torch on his body," Ruby added, "According to Bronwen, the police returned his wedding ring, his wallet and the mysterious sheet of music. Maybe she forgot to mention the torch?"

Ruby found the phone number she was looking for and pressed an icon to dial it. It rang a few times before Bronwen answered. Ruby asked her if a torch had been returned with Sir Clifford's effects. Bronwen was sure that none had. Then was there a torch missing from Coot Hall? Could he have taken one and lost it? Browen did not know but she was pretty sure that she could find out.

Ruby had planned to go down to the boathouse that morning to have another look by the light of day but it was now almost half-past twelve and she had more important things to do. She was trying to solve the problem of the missing keys. The only place left to search for them was in the funeral parlour in Clogwyn Mawr. Bessie told her that she knew the undertaker there – a man by the name of Dewi Jones who was universally known as 'Dai Jones The Death'. This was in order to distinguish him for all the other Dewi, Dafydd and David Joneses (all of whom would be known as Dai Jones) who lived in the area. Ruby phoned the funeral parlour, asked in her most brisk and business-like tone to speak to Mr Jones and told him to expect a visit within the hour.

The two women got into Bessie's bright yellow Mini Minor and by one o'clock they were on the road. The car huffed, puffed and chugged its way down Fern Hill into Clogwyn Bach, then up over the northern headland towards Clogwyn Mawr.

The road over the headland, Ruby observed, ran parallel to the clifftop path where it was assumed that Sir Clifford had taken his final walk on the night of Wednesday, May the 12th.

"But nobody saw him."

"Saw who?"

"Sir Clifford. Nobody saw him on the night of his death. Doesn't that seem odd?"

"Not really," said Bessie, "Not many people walk along the clifftops even in the daytime. You'd have to be mad to walk there after dark. It doesn't seem likely that anyone else would have been out there that night."

"But people must drive along this road quite a bit."

"True. I suppose there is generally a bit of traffic going between Clogwyn Bach and Clogwyn Mawr."

"Matt told us he'd gone to Clogwyn Mawr that Wednesday night, if you remember. He was very cagey though. But for the fact that I said that Muriel Greenalge had seen him, he wouldn't even have mentioned the fact."

Bessie laughed. "And why should he? He went for a night out. For someone his age, there isn't much to do in Clogwyn Bach of an evening. You're not going to tell me that there's anything suspicious about Matt, are you?"

"Muriel said there was someone with Matt. In his car."

"Maybe so. And maybe that's his own private business."

"And maybe that someone was Sir Clifford Coot?"

Bessie looked at Ruby with an expression that seemed to say, yes, and maybe pigs can fly.

"Matt isn't local, is he?"

"No. He came from the valleys originally. He moved here a couple of years ago."

"So," said Ruby, "you don't really know much about him at all?"

"I know even less about *you*!" said Bessie. Then, realising how aggressive that sounded, she added, "Sorry, I didn't mean to snap. All I'm saying is that if you think Matt could have killed Sir Clifford, you are mistaken. I'd trust that lad with my life."

"Hmmm."

By that time they were heading down into the town of Clogwyn Mawr which sat in supercilious splendour over its bay ("like the Caribbean in South Wales" according to the tourist brochure). The Jones, Jones, Jones and Chittlehampton Funeral Parlour occupied a choice spot directly between the Fun Palace Slot Machine Arcade and the Salty Sailor Burger Bar. It overlooked the long, sandy bay which, on that warm, sunny afternoon was doing its best to live up to the tourist brochure.

Bessie parked her car in the small carpark and she and Ruby made their stately way to the undertaker's establishment.

"Yes, my dears! How can I help you? We do burials, cremations, coffins in mahogany, oak or, for the more cost-conscious buyer, pine with an oak veneer, we cater for all religions or none at all. We accept cash, cheque and all major credit cards, easy terms are available on application."

The man who greeted them upon entry was small, wiry and remarkably jolly. He gave every impression of enjoying his work.

"I phoned earlier," Ruby said.

"Oh, yes. You're the lady whose husband choked on a gherkin, are you?"

"No, we've come to, well, pay our respects to…"

"Oh, Sir Clifford, is it? Family, are you?"

Ruby had not specified her relationship, or lack thereof, to the deceased when she had telephoned that morning. She had not been sure of the correct protocol for viewing a body. From the look the man was giving her, she was starting to form the impression that it might not be quite the done thing for complete strangers to turn up out of the blue with the intention of ogling a corpse.

"Dewi Jones!" Bessie suddenly bellowed, fixing the small man with a gimlet eye, "You are not going to tell me that you've forgotten who I am, I hope!"

The little man suddenly went pale and backed away a step.

"Oh, Miss Morgan!" he said, "I never recognised you for a minute there. You've had your hair done different."

"It must be twenty years or more since you last saw me so I'd say there may be a few other differences as well and it is 'I didn't', not 'I never'. It makes neither grammatical nor logical sense to say that you 'never' recognised someone 'for a minute'."

A broad smile broke out on Dewi Jones's face. "She always was a clever one," he told Ruby, "Strict though. And just listen to the way she talks! Proper, like. Better than them that's on the BBC if you ask me."

"That's as may be," Bessie said, "We have come to pay our respects to the late Sir Clifford Coot and I should be very much obliged if you could assist us in so doing by showing us through to the room in which the corpse is laid out!"

"For you, Miss Morgan, it won't be no problem at all."

"Double negative," Bessie muttered under her breath, "How many times have I warned you about double negatives?"

"She was my teacher, see," Dewi confided to Ruby.

Ruby raised her eyebrows to indicate that she had independently arrived at that deduction.

Dewi led them past a display of coffins – "French oak, this one. Silver satin lined. Combining both elegance and comfort."

"Comfort?" said Bessie, "Do the occupants ever complain?"

Dewi opened a pair of double doors at the back of the showroom and led them into a small dimly lit chamber festooned with red satin drapes.

"Looks like a bordello," said Bessie.

At the centre of the room an ebony-dark coffin lay on a white satin-draped trestle. Ruby instinctively glanced away. She had momentarily caught sight of the body in the coffin and even though she had already seen Sir Clifford lying dead on the edge of a rock pool, it seemed more macabre to see him lying in a box as though sleeping while dressed as though for a wedding. Bessie had no such qualms. She went straight to the coffin and had a good long look.

"You've gone a bit heavy on the makeup," she said.

"It's the lighting that makes it look that way," Dewi replied, "See him by the light of day and he'd look as natural as me and you."

"What's the point of that? Nobody's going to see him by the light of day, are they? Unless he makes an unscheduled escape from his coffin on the day of the funeral."

"The family like to see their loved ones looking healthy," Dewi insisted.

"Healthy? He's dead, for God's sake. Why would anyone want him to look healthy?"

"It's as they remember him, see."

"They must have short memories, then. With that colour of lipstick, he looks like a second-rate drag queen. I remember Sir Clifford very well and I can tell you that he wouldn't be seen dead in bright red lipstick. If he'd had any say in the matter, that is."

"If you'd copped a look at the state of him when he arrived, you'd be glad we done him up so good," Dewi said, defensively.

"Why, how bad was he?"

"Oh, terrible. His skin was all white. And he was as wrinkled as a prune. He'd been in the water for hours, so I heard. And his arms and the back of his head was bashed about a bit too."

"Bashed about?" said Ruby, "You mean as if someone had struck him?"

"I mean," said Dewi, "as though he'd fallen off the cliffs and got sploshed about by the waves on the rocks. Why? You don't think there was foul play, do you?"

Ruby was flustered. "No, no, of course that's not what I mean."

"You solved that other murder, didn't you. So you got to wonder, haven't you."

"Wonder no longer," said Ruby, "My murder solving days are behind me."

"Oh. Shame. Well, then, have a good gawp at the corpse. Or 'the deceased' as we prefer to call 'em in the trade. You got to admit we done him up a treat."

Hesitantly, Ruby drew close to the coffin and peered over the edge. In spite of a somewhat liberal application of foundation powder and rouge, Sir Clifford looked in much better shape than when she had last seen him. Dewi looked at Ruby with a pleading expression like that of a dog waiting to be told he's a good boy.

"He looks…" Ruby struggled to think of an appropriate description – "…lovely."

Bessie put her arm around Ruby's shoulder. "Poor dear, you're overcome, aren't you?"

"What? Oh…" Ruby took a paper handkerchief from a pocket of her coat and dabbed at the corners of her eyes. This had been the plan they had formulated on their drive to Clogwyn Mawr. Ruby would be moved to tears. She would ask to be left alone for a few moments so that she could express her grief in private. Then, when alone, she would search Sir Clifford's clothing to find out if they contained the missing keys. Until Bessie had reminded her, she had completely forgotten about the grief part of the performance. "I wonder," she said, "if I might…"

"Have a cup of tea?" said Dewi, "No problem at all. Come through to the office and I'll…"

"…if I might have a few moments alone."

"Alone?" said Dewi, as though the concept was unfamiliar to him, "With the corpse, you mean?"

Ruby sniffed. "I'd like to say a private farewell."

Bessie took Dewi by the arm, "Come on. I'll help you get the tea on."

"I only have to flick a switch," he protested, "to turn on the kettle."

"We can talk about old times," Bessie said and launched him out of the room.

The double doors swished smoothly together and Ruby was left alone in the oppressive gloom of the chamber with no one but Sir Clifford for company. He was dressed in a smart black suit, crisply ironed white shirt and scarlet silk tie. His mane of white hair was swept back from his head and, combined with his grim expression, it made him look like a classical composer having a bad day. The effect was spoiled by the brilliant red lipstick. Ruby felt sure that this was of a vibrant hue that neither Beethoven nor Wagner would have countenanced.

With horror, Ruby realised that she would now have to force herself to rummage around in the dead man's clothes; she would actually have to put her hands into his pockets. She winced just thinking about it. Then she noticed a problem. The problem was a small green light. The small green light was attached to a plastic spherical object about the size of a golf ball. The spherical object was fixed to the wall, just above the double doors through which she had entered. It was a camera. Anything she did in that room would probably be recorded. Picking the pockets of the deceased was, she strongly suspected, an activity of which an undertaker would strongly disapprove. It was, in fact, in all probability illegal. Just as illegal as picking the pockets of a living person, though she had never heard of anyone being prosecuted for the offence. She did not want to be the person to establish a legal precedent.

She considered the possibilities. There were a couple of wooden chairs in the room. She wondered if she might be able to stand on one of the chairs in order to reach the camera. And then what? Rip the camera from the wall? Put her coat over it? Smash it to pieces with her bare hands? Even if any of those alternatives were possible to accomplish without attracting attention (which she doubted) she would still end up being recorded as she went about her nefarious activities. There was nothing for it. She would have to call the whole thing off. She felt such a failure. At that very moment, the missing keys might be within arm's reach, nestling inside Sir Clifford's jacket or trousers pocket, and she dared do nothing about it. The clue – maybe the *vital* clue – that she was seeking, would elude her. It would be buried along with Sir Clifford; and his murderer would go free.

"Oh, come on, surely there must be some way to do this!"

She was still trying to figure out what to do next when there came a knock upon the door. Ruby jumped. She felt like a cornered criminal. "Come in," she said.

The door opened a crack. It was Bessie. "Tea's ready."

"Bessie, I haven't…"

"Tea," Bessie insisted, "is ready." Silently, she mouthed, "Come on! Come on! I'll explain later."

*

"That's all there was," said Dewi, passing a large manila envelope across to Bessie.

They were sitting in the funeral director's office at the back of the showroom. It was a small, cluttered little room furnished with four upright chairs and a cheap, tatty desk on which sat an equally cheap, tatty computer.

Bessie took the manila envelope and opened the flap. Inside there was a half empty packet of fruit gums and a red ballpoint pen.

"Dewi took those from the suit that Sir Clifford is wearing."

"We always check the pockets before we dress the body, see," Dewi explained, "You'd be amazed at the stuff we find sometimes. Had a bloke in a few days ago, had a half a cheese and pickle sandwich in his pocket. He'd been eating the other half at the time of death."

"Choked on it, I expect?" said Bessie.

"Fell off a ladder," Dewi said.

"Broke his neck," Ruby added.

Both Dewi and Bessie stared at her with owl-like eyes.

"I overheard someone talking about him in the hairdressers."

"How did you know it was the same person?" Bessie asked.

"Well, unless there's been a mass outbreak of people dying while eating cheese and pickle sandwiches, I thought it was a reasonable guess."

"Have another Garibaldi biscuit," said Dewi. They were drinking mugs of thick, tepid tea and nibbling at soggy, tasteless biscuits that appeared to be covered in dead flies which Dewi insisted were in fact currants.

Bessie declined Dewi's offer. "So there were no keys in his pockets, then?"

Dewi shook his head.

"No torch?"

Dewi shook his head again. "Only a half empty packet of fruit gums and a red ballpoint pen."

Ruby sighed and drank her tea.

*

"That was a waste of time," Bessie commented on the drive back to Clogwyn Bach.

"I disagree," Ruby said.

"But there was nothing of significance in his clothing."

"The fact that there was nothing of significance is hugely significant."

"Is it?"

"Oh, yes. The question we now need to ask is, where are his keys?"

CHAPTER 39

"Besides which, Chris is taken."

It was Saturday morning and Ruby had walked down to Karenz Kutz to have a word with Rod who was, she was increasingly coming to realise, the fount of all knowledge where local news and gossip were concerned. If Rona had been right and Chris was bisexual, might Sir Clifford have discovered that Chris had been having an affair with his wife? That would, at least, explain Sir Clifford's argument with Chris.

"Chris is taken?" Ruby said, "By whom?"

"What I mean is, he's got a boyfriend."

"You?"

"Me? And Chris? Ooo, no, love. Not my type at all. No, a bloke called Matt. You probably heard of him. Writes books. Matt Jones."

"I know him!"

"Matt's more my type than Chris, to be honest. Lovely eyebrows."

"I noticed."

"But, like I say, Matt's already spoken for. Chris and Matt have been as close as two ferrets in a bag for the last six months or more."

"Ah. Where did they meet? I shouldn't have thought there were many suitable social venues around here."

"You mean, is there a gay bar in Little Cloggy? No, there damn' well isn't. But there is in Big Cloggy."

"Clogwyn Mawr? Oh, really."

"Well, it's not a hundred per cent. But it's about fifty-fifty most nights. And on Wednesdays and Fridays they have a disco upstairs. So those are the best nights to go."

"I'll bear that in mind," Ruby said, wondering whether or not this might have any relevance to her investigation.

CHAPTER 40

"You won't find a Llanwenog ram better than Casanova this side of Swansea," Tom Crockley said and he practically glowed with pride.

"That's his name, Casanova?" said Ruby.

"Oh, aye, well, you see, that's on account of..."

Ruby interrupted. "I think I can guess. I don't need a technical description."

Early on Sunday morning, Bessie had phoned Tom Crockley and arranged to take Ruby to meet him at his farm. The excuse she had given was that Ruby was keen to see his prize ram. Tom needed no excuse to show off his ram. He could not have been prouder of that ram if it had climbed Everest and won the Nobel Prize for Physics. The ram was, to Tom Crockley, what a 1933 Bentley is to a vintage car fanatic. It was the love of his life, the apple of his eye, a thing of beauty and a joy for ever.

At that moment, the ram was standing in the corner of a field munching a mouthful of grass. Various other sheep were standing around in other corners of the field munching other mouthfuls of grass.

"So, what do you think, then?" said Tom, smiling broadly, clearly waiting for Ruby to give voice to a string of glowing compliments.

"He's very nice," said Ruby.

Tom sniffed. This compliment was not, perhaps, quite as glowing as he had been anticipating.

"Nice face," Ruby added. Tom sniffed again. "Um, good fetlocks." Ruby was not sure if sheep had fetlocks and, judging by Tom's expression, her praise of their quality did not do justice to the ram's excellence.

Ruby ransacked her memory for something more poetic. "Age cannot wither, um, him," she mumbled, "Nor custom stale his infinite variety." The ghost of a smile shimmered over Tom's lips.

"This is the noblest sheep of them all," Ruby continued, "His life is gentle, and the elements so mixed in him that Nature might stand up and say to all the world, 'This is a ram.'"

Tom was rubbing the grey stubble on his voluminous chins and pondering on Ruby's words. "Aye," he said, eventually, "People are always saying that about him."

"Oh, really?"

"He's a good fat fella, that's for sure."

In Tom's opinion, the ram's stoutness was a high compliment. Ruby nodded enthusiastically.

"He's certainly a very fat ram," Bessie said.

Tom broke out in a broad smile. "I'm glad you noticed that. But he'd be fatter still if he was in his proper field. I do my best for him but I'll tell you the honest truth – that ram is a shadow of his former self. And all because of Sir Clifford stealing my rightful field away from me."

"Ah yes." Ruby was much more interested in the field than in the ram. "Which exactly is the field in question?"

Tom Crockley pointed at a scrubby area of grass adjoining the field in which Casanova and his harem were contentedly munching grass. "That's it. The Old Hog's Back field." Beyond the field, through a screen of trees, the turrets and crenellations of Coot Hall could be seen. "Been in the Crockley family as long as anyone can remember, that field has."

"I thought you said that your grandfather bought the field from Sir Clifford's grandfather," said Ruby.

"He did," agreed Tom, "That's as long as anyone can remember, isn't it?"

"Yes, well, I suppose it is."

"A decent old bloke his granddad was. His dad was a decent bloke too. Clifford though..." Tom spat heartily onto a particularly egregious thistle.

"The black sheep of the family?" Ruby suggested.

"More like the sheep scab of the family," Tom said, "Even as a boy he was a bad 'un. Well, you remember what he was like, Bessie. We was all in the same class back then, Cliff, Bessie and me, in the old Primary School."

"I remember he stuck chewing gum in my hair," said Bessie.

"Worse than that. He stole my potato gun!"

Ruby tried to imagine what sort of gun might be used to hunt potatoes. Seeing the confusion on Ruby's face, Bessie explained, "It was a toy gun that fired pellets made of potatoes."

"I was the only one in school who had one," Tom said, "That spud gun was my proudest possession. Cost a fortune, it did."

"And did you ever get it back?" asked Bessie.

Tom smiled again. "Oh aye, I did. I gave Cliff a good hammering and threw him in the pig pond. I reckon he never forgave that. Which is why he stole my rightful field!"

Suddenly there was a loud bag. A gunshot. Ruby gasped. A flock of wood pigeons flew from a nearby tree in a clatter of wings. In the distance, across at the other side of the Hog's Back field, a man with a gun could be seen.

"Is that a rifle he's using?" said Ruby.

Tom chuckled. "A shotgun of some sort. For shooting pigeons."

"Isn't it dangerous?"

"It is if you're a pigeon."

The man was walking across the field towards them. He was dressed like a typical country gent: tweed hacking jacket, tweed cap, corduroy trousers, green Wellington boots.

"He's an amateur," Tom said.

"How do you know that?" said Ruby.

"He 'an't got a dog with him, has he? How's he going to find any pigeons he shoots if he 'an't got a dog?"

"It's Lady Coot's friend, I think," said Bessie.

"Not," added Tom, "that he's got any chance of shooting any pigeons anyway. Not the way he's going about it."

"Hello there!" Yes, Ruby could see now that it was definitely the unctuous Ronald, "Haven't seen any birds fall down over here, have you? I bagged a couple, I think."

Tom laughed so violently that he nearly spat out his bottom set of dentures. He caught them just in time and discreetly slipped them back into his mouth. "His best chance of bagging a bird is to buy one in Tesco's," he muttered.

"Nice weather!" Ruby called out for want of anything more interesting to say.

"I say!" said Ronald, "That's a fine specimen you have there!"

Ruby assumed that Ronald was talking about Casanova the ram. But then she noticed that Ronald was pointing to a part of Tom Crockley's field which, while visible from the Hog's Back field where Ronald was standing, was hidden from Ruby's sight by a beech hedge. She stepped around the hedge to see what Ronald was pointing at. There, in her own fenced-off enclosure, stood the biggest pig Ruby had ever seen.

"That," said Tom Crockley, almost swelling visibly with pride, "is Myfanwy."

"Lovely name," commented Bessie, "Why did you call her that?"

"I named her after an old girlfriend," Tom said, "But don't tell the wife!"

"If you named your pig after a girlfriend, I hardly think she'll be jealous," Ruby said.

"You'll make some fine sausages from that pig," enthused Ronald.

Tom went red in the face and shouted at him, "Don't you dare say such a thing about my lovely Myfanwy."

Ronald smiled sheepishly. "Sorry. Spoke out of turn, don't you know. Wouldn't want to offend the old girl for the world."

This pretty much brought the pleasantries to an end and Ronald went stalking off across the Hog's Back field in the direction of Coot Hall with his gun tucked under his arm.

"I suppose he thinks he'll be inheriting that field now," said Tom, "Supposing he gets married to Patsy Coot."

"You really think that's likely?" said Bessie.

"Bloody near certain, I'd say. They are gold-diggers, the two of them. But he's not getting that field so easy. I'll get my solicitor onto it. I got prior rights to that field. I intend to get that field back if it's over my dead body. Or someone else's dead body, come to that!"

As they were walking back in the direction of Bessie's car, which she had parked in a muddy yard just outside the old, stone-built farmhouse, a plump, cheerful woman came out of the door, wiping her flour-covered hands on her polka-dot-spotted pinafore.

"You're not rushing off are you," she cried out to them, "without having a cup of tea and a Welsh cake? Just baked a fresh batch I have and they are best warm from the bakestone I always think."

"That's very kind of you, Gwladys," Said Bessie, "but we have to be getting along."

"I'll have their Welsh cakes, mam!" Frank Crockley was striding towards the house from the direction of the Land Rover which he had just parked in the yard. He was carrying a big sack of potatoes slung his shoulder as easily as if it had been a bag of popcorn.

Ruby was struck again by how different Frank Crockley was from his father. Frank was tall and muscular whereas Tom was short and fat. Frank had dark curly hair whereas Tom's was straight and sandy. Frank had a distinctive Roman nose whereas Tom's nose was no more than a squat blob at the centre of his face.

"Right you are then," said Gwladys, "How are you these days, Bessie? Rheumatism better, is it?"

"Oh, mustn't grumble," said Bessie, "How's the sciatica?"

"Oh, could be worse," said Gwladys.

That's how people are around here, Ruby thought. They take what life gives them and just get on with it. Except for whoever killed Sir Clifford. That was someone who wasn't content to take what life gave them. It was someone who was prepared to do whatever it took to change their life for the better. If only Ruby could work out who gained the most by killing the elderly composer, she would have found the murderer!

*

"So, what did you make of that, then?" said Bessie.

They were driving down Bayview Hill which took them right past the arched gate leading to Coot Hall. Although the Coots and the Crockleys were neighbours, the difference between Coot Hall and Crockley Farm could hardly have been more striking. The farm was a collection of ramshackle outbuildings and muddy fields which, at night, would be plunged into pitch darkness at the centre of which was a small and cosy farmhouse. The land around Coot Hall, by contrast, comprised an elegant avenue which, at night, was brightly illuminated by lines of Victorian cast-iron streetlamps leading to manicured lawns and orchards at the centre of which stood an architectural monstrosity whose cold, damp interior was bleak and loveless.

"What?" said Ruby, who had not been paying any attention to what Bessie was saying, "The prize ram, you mean? He looked like any other manky old sheep to me."

"You surely can't think that Tom Crockley would have done away with Sir Clifford just because of an argument over a field."

"Who's to say? Tom is still angry about it. It all depends on how angry, I suppose."

"I've known Tom Crockley all my life. He's a cranky old bugger when he sets his mind to it. But he's no killer."

The car had passed Coot Hall by now and was heading down a steep part of the tree-lined hill towards the village.

"You knew Sir Clifford pretty well, didn't you, Bessie?"

"I wouldn't say so. I mean, I knew him as a child. We were about the same age, you see."

Ruby was too discreet to ask what age that might be. She was fairly sure that Bessie was in her seventies but she was as bright and active as many people half her age and she did not like to be reminded that she was no longer in the first flush of youth.

"Tom Crockley, Clifford Coot and I were in the same class at primary school as a matter of fact."

"Really? I'd have thought a family as wealthy as the Coots would have sent their brats to public school."

"Sir Clifford's father wasn't as pompous as his son turned out to be. Clifford had to mix it with the ragtag local kids in those days."

Ruby wondered how long a resentment might fester. Could Tom Crockley have nurtured a toxic grievance for being ill-treated by a childhood friend?

"Did Sir Clifford Coot have a Roman nose by any chance?" Ruby asked.

"Now what made you ask that?" Bessie swerved the car suddenly to avoid a rabbit that was sitting in the middle of the road, "As a matter of fact, he did. Quite a prominent Roman nose. He was also tall and, in his younger days, he had a mop of dark, curly hair."

"Not unlike Frank Crockley in appearance, then?"

"There is some similarity."

"Any explanation for that?"

"None at all," said Bessie.

"What about his mother's family? Any tall, curly-haired men with Roman noses there?"

"Short, red-haired and snub noses mostly. Gwladys had beautiful auburn hair when she was a girl. She's put on a bit of weight now and the hair's gone grey. But she was a mightily good-looking woman in her youth."

"And there she is, living right next door to Coot Hall. Any connection, do you think?"

"Gwladys used to do some work at Coot Hall, as a matter of fact. Cleaning and tidying and that sort of thing. Of course, Clifford didn't live there in those days. He was away teaching in universities and the like. But he came down to the Hall during the holidays. There were a great many holidays, as I remember."

"Frank Crockley is Sir Clifford's illegitimate son, isn't he?"

Bessie swerved the car for no obvious reason. "I wouldn't let Tom hear you say that. He may seem harmless enough. But you wouldn't like to be on the wrong side of his temper."

"I don't think Tom Crockley killed Sir Clifford."

"I'm glad to hear it."

"But I'm not so sure about Frank. He could have killed Sir Clifford, put the body in the back of his Land Rover, driven up to the headland and thrown it over the cliff. He's strong enough to do it. You saw the way he was carrying that huge sack of potatoes."

"But why would Frank do that? It's his father who was annoyed about the business with the field, not Frank."

"His father? Do you mean Tom Crockley or Sir Clifford Coot? I suppose that if Frank could prove that Sir Clifford was in fact his father he might be able to contest the will. In which case, Frank might end up being very rich indeed."

CHAPTER 41

"I looked everywhere. No sign of a torch." It was Monday morning and Bronwen was artistically redistributing the dust in Ruby's kitchen. "His bedroom, his study, the kitchen, the hallway table, the shelf by the back door. All the places he'd be likely to keep a torch. No sign of one. There was one in the potting shed though."

"The potting shed?" said Ruby, "Was Sir Clifford a keen gardener?"

Bronwen laughed. "You have got to be kidding. Wouldn't get his hands dirty, not for anything. The potting is done by Maldwyn Placket."

"The gardener." Ruby remembered the strange, wizened little man who had accosted her first with an aspidistra and subsequently on Fern Hill in the darkness. It was he who had written her the note about the supposed secret in Sir Clifford's desk.

"Then I asked Lady Coot," Bronwen said, "She said they had only one torch and she kept it in her bedside cabinet. It's still there. So Sir Clifford can't have taken it, can he?"

"He might have taken the torch from the potting shed though?"

"That's still there too. I asked Maldwyn and he went and got it for me."

Might there have been some grudge between the gardener and his employer, Ruby wondered? Could Maldwyn have accompanied Sir Clifford on his final walk, using the potting shed torch for light, done away with Sir Clifford and then returned with the torch?

"Isn't it odd," said Ruby, "that there is only one torch in the house? What if there were a power cut? What if they needed to go out after dark?"

"There's a generator they use if the power goes off," Bronwen said, "As for going out at night. Neither of them was big on taking exercise. And even if they fancied a walk, there are lights all along the driveway between the house and the road so they wouldn't need a torch."

"The driveway opens onto the main road into Clogwyn Bach," Ruby said, "There are street lamps all the way along that, aren't there? So he could have walked from the house all the way down to the village without any need of a torch."

"Yeah. No problem. If you fancy a cup of tea, I can put the kettle on."

"What?"

"I was saying if you fancy…"

But Ruby was already on her way to her front door. She had solved the mystery of the torch and she wanted to tell Bessie about it.

CHAPTER 42

"Bessie! Bessie! He didn't fall off the clifftop path. Because he was never on the clifftop path."

"Calm down, calm down, girl. Sit down while I put the kettle on. Now start again. What are you talking about?"

"He didn't take a torch and the beach ball explains the rest."

"Oh, there's lovely. And what beach ball would that be?"

Ruby explained how she had heard about the water currents in the bay and had conducted an experiment to see where a beach ball thrown into the water on the southern end would end up. "I thought it would be swept around to the north end of the bay by the following morning."

"And was it?"

"No. But it was by the morning after that."

"Which means?"

"It doesn't really mean anything."

"Ah."

"But it explains something. Something that was puzzling me. You remember that when I first found Sir Clifford's body, everyone assumed that he must have gone out walking early in the morning and slipped off the cliff edge? It was Matt who told me that wasn't possible because Sir Clifford's clothes were soaking wet but the tide hadn't come in yet that morning and it hadn't rained so he must have been in the sea before the tide went out. That was confirmed later on when the police said he had drowned."

"So he must have fallen off the cliff the night before," said Bessie, "Yes, I know that but I can't see what difference it makes. Not really."

"Oh, it makes a world of difference! Why did he go walking on the clifftops after dark? It makes no sense. And why did go without a torch? That doesn't seem merely foolish; it seems close to impossible. It was a new moon, so the night was impenetrably dark.

How could he even find his way to the cliff edge without a torch? No, he must have drowned somewhere else. Somewhere light. And then, like my beach ball, his body was washed ashore at high tide and stranded beneath the cliffs when the tide went out again."

"That's possible, I suppose. But still I don't see…"

"There are lights along the drive of Coot Hall. There are lights on the road from the Hall into the village. Sir Clifford could have walked from the house to the village without needing a torch. What he could not have done is walked from the village up over the cliff path on the north because there are no lights. So the question we have to ask is where would be light enough to walk by the sea on a moonless night? Not on the shore itself. I tried. Even when the moon was waxing, it was still too dark to see where I was going. On the night of a new moon it would be pitch black. But the road that leads to the boathouse is brightly lit."

"The boathouse? Where Chris lives? That's on the southern end of the bay."

"And the sea currents washed the body up on the northern end. Just as they washed up my beach ball."

"But if someone had killed Sir Clifford down by the boathouse, surely Chris would have heard or seen something? Unless he wasn't at home, of course." Bessie suddenly paused. A terrible thought had occurred to her. "Wait a minute – you're not suggesting that Chris…"

"I can't discount anyone, Bessie. Of course, if Chris was with someone on the night of Wednesday the 12th, that would give him an alibi."

"So you are going to ask Chris, I suppose?"

"No. I think someone else might know. Your writer friend with the eyebrows."

"Matt? Why should he know?"

"Oh, my hairdresser mentioned that… well, I believe Matt and Chris might be on friendly terms, shall we say. At any rate, I think it wouldn't do any harm to have a quiet word with Matt. Meanwhile, the remaining mystery is the sheet of music. That's where we need to concentrate our efforts.

"One of the puzzling things is the name, handwritten in the top corner of the score: 'Eve G'. If only we could find the mysterious

Eve, maybe she would be able to tell us why that page of music is so important?"

"By all accounts Sir Clifford was a bit of a womaniser," said Bessie, "Maybe Eve was one of his old flames?"

"But why would she write her name on a sheet of his music?"

"Maybe it was the other way around. Maybe he wrote her name there? As a dedication?"

"Oh, that's an idea! He wrote his greatest ever piece for the mysterious Eve but kept it secret all these years. Quite romantic, when you think about it."

"And then, someone discovered their secret?"

"Lady Coot? Yes, that's certainly a possibility. And, in a frenzy, she takes her husband down to the cliffs, or to the shore somewhere and… pushes him into the water. So it was a crime of passion!" Ruby tried to make this sound plausible but somehow she could not. Apart from anything else, Lady Coot did not seem to care much at all about her late husband so it seemed unlikely that she would get into a jealous frenzy over one of his affairs.

"Maybe," suggested Bessie, "it was Eve who found out that Sir Clifford was two-timing her."

"You mean he'd promised to marry Eve but then Eve discovered that he was already married?. Then again, maybe she'd been having an affair with him, he'd promised to get a divorce but he never did and finally she decided to take her revenge?"

"For the sake of argument," said Bessie, "let's assume that Sir Clifford composed Ouverture Celtique for Eve. Then maybe the page you stole was the original manuscript. That would explain why there are mistakes in it?"

"It would?"

"It could be his first draft, you see. The absolute original. By the time it was performed he might have made changes."

"So the version the world is now familiar with is a later revision? Bessie, you are brilliant. If that is true, we might be able to find Eve. We would need to find out when Sir Clifford wrote the music, then we can find out where he was living at the time. He used to teach at a university, didn't he?"

"Cambridge. Maybe Eve was one of his students?"

"Not 'maybe', Bessie. Definitely. I'm convinced of it. That has to be the explanation. Do you know which college he taught at?"

Bessie did not know. But Wikipedia did. Wikipedia was also able to confirm the date of the first performance of Ouverture Celtique, thirteen years earlier, which was at the start of what became known as Sir Clifford's Golden Era – a period of extraordinary musical creativity during which he wrote his finest works. Two years after Overture Celtique came Symphonie en Gris. In the next five years there were various orchestral, choral and chamber pieces, almost all of them popular successes.

That gave Ruby all the information she needed to begin her search for 'Eve G'. That afternoon, Ruby phoned the porter's lodge of Sir Clifford's old college and was put through to a department which, she was assured, would be able to help her with enquiries about past students.

The woman who answered the phone was most helpful. Yes, they had lists of past students. In fact, they also had matriculation and graduation photographs. The matriculation photographs showed every student who had begun their course of study in any given year and the graduation photograph showed the same students (assuming none had fallen by the wayside or failed to pass their final examinations), three years later.

Ruby asked if there had been an Eve, who had graduated say twelve to fifteen years ago. The woman asked for Eve's surname. When Ruby waffled, the woman started to sound suspicious. Why did Ruby want to trace Eve anyway? Was Eve a relative? Had they been friends? Had Ruby been a fellow student? Ruby, of course, was unable to answer "Yes" to any of those questions. She improvised: "I'm helping a friend of mine. It's a bit personal, really. We were hoping you might have a photo."

"Just a moment. I can check the matriculation lists. I can sort them by first name. Let's see. Fifteen years ago, Ellen, Evan, no other Es. Fourteen years ago, Eleanor, Emanuel, Evelyn…"

"Evelyn. What would the surname be?"

"Gonfort. Evelyn Gonfort."

"Studying? I mean, which subject?"

"History of Music. Oh, in fact, Evelyn Gonfort was the college organ scholar at the time."

"You said you have a photograph?"

"Matriculation or Graduation?"

"Either. Well, both, if possible."

"Would you like to order a copy? It will take a week or two to get it printed and sent to you but, of course, there is the online archive too."

"The photographs are online?"

"On our web site, yes. Not the final ones. The reference shots."

"What's the difference?"

"Well, before the photographer takes the final picture, all the students have to hold a numbered card in front of themselves. We use the numbers on the reference photo to identify each student. Then the students' names can be printed in the correct orders under the final photograph. Of course, they don't hold numbered cards in the final photo."

"Oh, wonderful! That's exactly what I want. I don't suppose you have contact information for Evelyn? Address? Phone number, that sort of thing."

"I'm afraid we don't keep up-to-date information on old students. I could ask the porter if you like. It's possible he may have been given a forwarding address for mail."

"I'd be grateful if you would. Thank you so much. In the meantime, the photograph might be useful. Where can I see it?"

"I'll email you the link to the online archive."

Half an hour later, Ruby rushed next door clutching three sheets of A4 paper, fresh from her printer. "I've got it, Bessie! I've got it!" she cried.

"Got what?"

Ruby laid two pieces of paper side by side on the table to form the photograph which she had found online. The photograph showed five rows of smiling young people holding numbered cards. "This is the matriculation photograph," Ruby explained, "I had to print it onto two sheets of paper because it wouldn't fit onto one." On a third sheet of paper there was a numbered list of names. "To find out who's who, you just have to match the number in the list to the student holding the same number on a card."

"And Eve is here?"

Ruby handed the list of names to Bessie. "There. Number 11. Evelyn Gonfort."

Bessie reached for her reading glasses, put them on and scanned the photograph. The numbers started with number 1 at the far left of the back row. Bessie stared long and hard at the undergraduate holding the card numbered 11. Then she picked up the list of names and double-checked that she had read it correctly. Then she looked at student number 11 in the photograph. "That can't be right. It must be a mistake."

"It is right. It's we who've been wrong. Evelyn Gonfort is a man. It's not a common man's name. There was Evelyn Waugh, of course…"

"You think Sir Clifford had an affair with…?"

"Oh, but that's not the most peculiar thing I discovered. You see, while I was browsing through the college's archive of photographs on their web site, I decided to take a look at graduation photographs too. All being well, Evelyn Gonfort should have graduated three years after matriculation. But he wasn't on the graduation photograph."

"Maybe he was ill?"

"I thought of that. I phoned the college offices to check. They told me that Evelyn did not finish his degree. He went down – left college – never to return, one year before he was due to graduate."

"This is making my head spin," Bessie complained, "What does it all mean? Maybe there was a scandal? Evelyn and Sir Clifford? Maybe the college hushed it up?"

"Oh, but I haven't told you the most interesting part yet."

"You haven't?"

"As I was browsing the graduation photographs, I happened to glance at the one taken the year before Evelyn was due to graduate. There was a face there that looked familiar. Younger, of course, so I wasn't sure at first. Here, look."

Ruby put another A4 sheet onto the table. This one showed the left-half of a graduation photograph. The students in this photograph were all wearing their black academic gowns and formal white bow-ties with bands, in preparation for their graduation ceremonies.

"Look at number 27" Ruby said.

Number 27 was a young man, three along from the left-hand side of the row immediately beneath the back row. Although the print-out was a bit grainy, he seemed to be a good-looking young man with fair hair and a broad smile.

"Yes, he does look familiar, I think," Bessie conceded, "But I can't quite place him."

Ruby produced one final A4 sheet with a flourish worthy of a magician pulling a rabbit from a top hat. "Here's the list of names. See who's at number 27."

"My God!" said Bessie.

"Yes, quite a coincidence, isn't it. None other than our local art teacher, Chris Chamberlain!"

CHAPTER 43

Ruby had wanted to go straight down to the boathouse and have a heart to heart talk with Chris. Bessie, however, argued that it would be better to act with more caution. "If there was anything going on between Sir Clifford and Evelyn, what's to say that Chris wasn't involved too?"

"So?"

"So it might be something that Chris doesn't want to talk about."

"Why ever not?"

"Because we don't know what sort of scandal might have been involved."

"But if Chris can tell us about Evelyn, that will be the key to unlocking the entire mystery."

Bessie sighed. "According to you, just about everything is the key to unlocking the entire mystery. The page of music, the missing keys, the missing torch, the locked desk drawer, now this Evelyn person."

"But I feel sure I'm on the right track, Bessie. And since Chris knew Evelyn…"

"He was at the same college as Evelyn, you mean. How many hundreds of other students were there? They might not ever have spoken to one another for all we know."

"Oh, Pish!"

"I beg your pardon."

"Pish! It's a thing actors say to express incredulity or dissent."

"Ah."

"Look, it is too much of a coincidence that the name 'Eve G' was written on the page of music, that the organ scholar at Sir Clifford's old college was called Evelyn Gonfort and that our local artist just happened to be at the same college at the same time as both Sir Clifford and Evelyn. It's odd that Chris never mentioned that he knew Sir Clifford in the past, isn't it?"

"None of our business, I suppose."

"It is now," said Ruby, "Chris might not be as innocent as he looks."

"Now wait a minute," said Bessie, "You don't want to go making unfounded accusations about Chris. You said before that you wanted to have a word with Matt. Well, if Matt was with Chris on the Wednesday night, that means Chris can't have had anything to do with Sir Clifford's murder. So before you do anything else, go and have a quiet word with Matt."

*

It was mid-afternoon when the phone rang. It was the woman from Chris and Evelyn's old college. By great good fortune, the porter had kept a forwarding address for Evelyn's mail. Ruby wrote it down. It was a flat in London. Rented from the owner, a Mrs Winstanley. "Of course, this was many years ago," the woman reminded Ruby, "I suspect he may have moved on by now. But good luck anyway."

Ruby searched the web for the address she had been given, which was in Belsize Park, North London. It was listed as a guest house and it was still in business. The web page included the phone number which Ruby immediately dialled.

A nice, friendly-sounding woman's voice answered. She announced herself as Mrs Winstanley. Oh yes, she remembered Evelyn very well. He had been such a nice lad. And so very clever. Wrote music. Very good music. But of course you can't make a living from writing music, can you? So he had to take whatever jobs he could find. Working in pubs, supermarkets, quite menial jobs really. He seemed depressed. He so desperately wanted to have some success with his music. He was obsessed with the idea that someone had stolen his work; Mrs Winstanley could not recall the name of the person. Some quite famous composer. "Sir Clifford Coot?" Ruby suggested. Yes, yes, that was the name. Ridiculous, of course. It was a sort of unhealthy fixation. That was why Evelyn became more and more despondent. Which explains, no doubt, why he did what he did.

"What he did?" said Ruby, "What did Evelyn do, exactly?"

"Oh!" Mrs Winstanley took a deep breath, "You don't know, then?"

"No, I'm, afraid I don't."

"Oh." She paused again, "Were you very close friends?"

"No," said Ruby, "No, we weren't close. Let's just say I know someone who knew Evelyn and I feel close enough to care about him."

"Well, there's really no easy way to say this, I'm afraid. He killed himself."

"He… Are you sure about that?"

"Oh, yes. Quite sure. Eleven years ago. It was a beautiful summer's day. On the underground. He threw himself under a train. Camden Town. On the Northern Line."

CHAPTER 44

"What's this, then? A social call?" Maggie Pountice was standing in the doorway to her house, dressed in a knee-length, flower-patterned pinafore, her hair in curlers with a headscarf tied over the top. In her arms she held a fat tabby cat that purred loudly as she stroked it.

"Actually," Bessie said, "we were hoping to have a few words with your lodger."

"Matt? What's he been up to?"

"Up to?" said Ruby, "He hasn't been up to anything. As far as we know. It's just..."

"The book he's writing," Bessie said, "I've been helping him with the punctuation and grammar. There were one or two things that needed correcting."

Maggie put down the cat which promptly ran back inside the house then she tapped a forefinger on the side of her noise and said in a hoarse whisper that could have been heard a hundred yards away, "You can be straight with me, love. Found some clues, you have, haven't you, to the murder? Well, you'd better come inside then."

Maggie looked to the left and she looked to the right to make sure no neighbours, spies or freelance assassins might be lurking in the doorways of the terraced houses that ran the length of the street and then she hustled Ruby and Bessie into her passageway which smelt strongly of furniture polish and joss sticks.

"He's got crabs," Maggie said.

"I'm very sorry to hear it," said Bessie.

"Keeps them in the shed out the back. Funny little buggers. They live in whelk shells. After the whelk has moved out."

"Hermit crabs?" Bessie suggested.

"Don't ask me, love. You'll have to ask Matt. There isn't nothing that he doesn't know about crabs that isn't worth the knowing of."

Matt was in the shed at the back of the house. He was crouching on one knee, holding a camera, when the three women entered. In front of him was an aquarium on a stand and he was in the process of photographing its inhabitants. These included two hermit crabs, a few shore crabs and several types of fish.

"Blennies," Matt said, pointing to one of the fish.

"And let me guess," said Ruby, pointing to another fish, "Gobies?"

"Exactly right. You know more about marine life than you let onto. You've come to check the semicolons, I suppose." This final remark was addressed to Bessie.

"You can give me a few pages and I'll check them when I get home."

"He writes books, see," Maggie Pountice said, proudly, "My previous lodger was a freelance septic tank emptier. He kept his room tidy though, which is more than I can say about Matt."

"However," Bessie continued, "the semicolons are not the principal reason for our visit."

"We want to know about you and Chris."

Matt blushed. "Me and…How did you know about me and Chris?"

"For goodness' sake, Matt, love," growled Maggie Pountice, "Everyone in Clogwyn Bach knows about you and Chris."

"Really?"

"Really. Now let's go into the front room, shall we, where we can have a sit down and delve into Matt's private life in comfort."

*

"Yeah, well, we decided to go to the Dandy in Clogwyn Mawr. Chris hasn't got a car so I gave him a lift."

"What's the Dandy?" said Ruby.

"It's a pub. The Dandy Highwayman. It's a place where, you know, men go."

"Men?"

"To meet one another."

"How often do you go there?" Ruby asked.

"Not often. We're both too busy mostly. I have to write my books. Chris does his painting. He's doing the illustrations for my next book, you see."

"You didn't see Chris earlier that week, then? Monday, say, or Tuesday?"

"No. I rang him on Tuesday but he was too busy. Besides which Wednesday is the best night. Either Wednesday or Friday."

"What's special about Wednesday and Friday?"

"Those are the nights when they have a disco. In the Dandy. Upstairs."

"So, let me get this straight. The Wednesday before last, the night before I found Sir Clifford's body on the rocks at the north of the bay, you and Chris were in the Dandy Highwayman pub, in a disco. What time did you come back?"

"I don't know. About half-past eleven, I suppose and then…"

"And then?"

Matt stared at Ruby. He seemed to be mulling over the implications of her line of questioning. "You think Chris had something to do with Sir Clifford's death?" he said at last, "That's what this is all about, isn't it?"

"Not necessarily," Ruby said, "I'm just…"

"Well, you can put that right out of your mind. We were in the pub and the disco all night. Then I drove back to the boathouse. We must have got there at just past midnight, I suppose."

"And then you left?"

"Not that it's any of your bloody business, but no, I didn't. I stayed the night. I left just before dawn to go and get my collecting equipment."

"I heard him come in," Maggie confirmed, "The crack of dawn it was. Heard him go out to the shed."

"To get my collecting equipment. And then, half an hour or so later," he fixed Ruby with a gimlet stare, "I was on the rocks down by the headland."

"Which is when I took the photo of you," Ruby said.

"So Chris has a watertight alibi, I'd say. Unless you think we are both in it together."

CHAPTER 45

"I know who did it, Max!"

Max had phoned Ruby to find out how her book narration was progressing. The fact of the matter is that it was not progressing as rapidly as it should have been due to Ruby spending so much time on her investigations.

"You've solved the murder?" said Max, who sounded doubtful, "OK, so who was it?"

"I wouldn't say I have actually identified the murderer yet. I've certainly narrowed down the field to, well, half a dozen or so suspects…"

"Half a dozen?" From the tone of his voice, it sounded as though Max was starting to lose interest.

"But the thing is, Max, I've found the method and the motive."

"You have?"

"Yes. Sir Clifford was pushed into the sea…" (Ruby thought she heard the sound of a suppressed yawn at the other end of the phone line) "…but not necessarily from the clifftop path."

"Ah."

"That's the method. The motive was the music. Possibly accompanied by a spot of blackmail."

Ruby waited for Max to say something. She was greeted by a large expanse of silence.

"Max. Are you still there?"

"What? Oh, yes, I, er… So what do you propose to do next?"

"Well, all I need to do is work out who did it…"

"Ah."

"And then I suppose I had better inform the authorities."

"You'll need a library."

"What?"

"That is how it's always done. You must assemble the suspects in a library and then point the finger of guilt at the culprit. You might want to invite the press along. May as well get some publicity, I suppose."

"Don't be absurd, Max. How would I possibly persuade all those people to come to a library? Oh, wait a minute, though. I know when they will be all together. At the funeral."

"The funeral?"

"Tomorrow. Sir Clifford is being buried. Just about the whole village will be there from what I can gather."

"Now, just a moment, Ruby, I'm really not sure a funeral would be the best occasion to…" Max loved publicity, he adored publicity, he would have been entirely happy for Ruby to have made a complete fool of herself if it had generated publicity. Max had always been of the opinion that there was no such thing as bad publicity. He had just revised that opinion.

"Don't worry, Max. I shall be very discreet. I shall only make a public accusation of murder once I am completely sure I know who did it."

"Oh, that's nice to know. Now if you could just get that book narration finished before the funeral…"

"You're worried I'll end up behind bars for defamation of character or libel or something, aren't you?"

"Well, you never know what might happen…"

"Fear not, Max! I can assure you I won't end up behind bars. But I have a distinct feeling that someone will."

There was a long, miserable-sounding groan on the other end of the line.

CHAPTER 46

It was a lovely day for a funeral. The sun was shining, the birds were singing, there was not a cloud in the sky. The hearse progressed slowly and majestically from Coot Hall, then down through the streets of Clogwyn Bach and up the narrow, twisty, tree-lined hill that led towards St Drogo's Church.

Behind the hearse, a trail of reverential cars bore the mourners, very few of whom (had you been looking closely) had mournful expressions on their faces. In fact, in the first car, Lady Patricia Coot was positively beaming. She had always loved a nice bit of public ostentation and, since she was never called upon to preside over the Changing of the Guard or the State Opening of Parliament, the funeral of her dearly departed husband was as nice a bit of public ostentation as she could reasonably wish for. She waved a regal hand at onlookers as the car passed them by. One or two of the onlookers made slightly less regal hand gestures in return.

St Drogo's Church is one of those typically English churches which finds itself mysteriously built upon Welsh soil. With its lichen-dotted grey stone walls, it is well supplied with arched stained-glass windows and it is dominated by an imposing bell-tower at one end. There is a cemetery surrounding the church and it is blessed with a small but resonant organ which, as the mourners arrived, was rumbling its way through some sonorously melancholy dirges.

All of Clogwyn Bach's high society and a fair smattering of its low society were in attendance. Lady Coot was escorted to the front pew by her friend, Ronald Masters. While they were both dressed in black, their outfits were of such a stylish cut that they looked as though they had been expecting to go to racing at Ascot rather than to a funeral. Ronald Masters wore a bespoke tailored suit set off by a red silk tie and matching breast-pocket handkerchief. Lady Coot was elegantly attired in a calf-length black skirt with a Spanish bolero-style jacket and a broad-brimmed black hat sumptuously decorated with Arum lilies.

"She's having the time of her life," Bessie commented as she and Ruby settled themselves in a pew towards the back of the church. Ruby had deliberately chosen that pew as it gave her a first rate view of the rest of the congregation. Maggie Pountice and Muriel Greenalge were there (Maggie waved to Ruby as she walked past to take a pew towards the middle of the church). Bronwen and Rona were suitably sombre in matching black dresses, though Rona's white foundation powder and black eyeshadow with matching lipstick made her look uncomfortably like Elsa Lanchester in the film, 'The Bride Of Frankenstein'.

Lady Coot's gardener, Maldwyn Placket, seemed horribly uncomfortable in a dark suit which, from its well-pressed shabbiness, gave a strong impression of having been hired for the occasion. Tom Crockley, the sheep farmer who occasionally posed nude at the art class, sat in one of the middle range of pews along with his son, Frank.

Gwendolyn Gormly was wearing a lime green satin dress, split to the thigh. Had this been the finals of Celebrity Come Dancing, she would have looked stunning. At a funeral, Ruby thought lime green satin was perhaps a touch on the bold side.

Rod the hairdresser was sitting just behind Tom and Frank Crockley. Finally, Matt and Chris entered the church together and sat in the second row back from the front. Chris smiled and nodded to Ruby and Bessie but Matt either did not see them or he chose to ignore them. Ruby suspected the latter. Matt, she felt, resented the inquiries that Ruby had been making.

Elfyd Davies the doctor and Ian Tucker the policeman both appeared to be absent – no doubt, Ruby thought, due to the demands of their professions but in that assumption, as she was soon to discover, she was wrong. Ruby was disappointed that Ian was not there as she felt that the presence of an officer of the law might be useful should certain circumstances arise. She was about to ask Bessie if Ian would be along later but Bessie was otherwise occupied. She appeared to have a piece of white Wensleydale cheese in her hand from which she was crumbling fragments onto the floor beneath her pew. In horror, Ruby saw that there sat a fat church mouse which was alternately eating the cheese and wiping the excess crumbs from its whiskers. Ruby was about to suggest that feeding church mice was not in accordance with the dignity of the occasion when she was interrupted by the start of the service.

The vicar droned on in that nasal way that only Anglican vicars have truly mastered. Ruby wondered if this was the same vicar who, according to Bronwen, had become inebriated at last year's Summer Fayre and performed an impromptu striptease. If so, that must, Ruby felt, have been a singularly unedifying spectacle but would, nonetheless, have been a good deal less soporific than his sermon.

Ruby devoted her attentions to the congregation. Tom Crockley, she noticed, was chuckling to himself. His shoulders kept bouncing up and down as he tried to restrain laughter but every so often his best efforts failed and he made a distinct snorting noise. Perhaps he was delighted to see the end of Sir Clifford, the man he believed had stolen two acres which were rightfully his.

Bronwen and Rona were paying no attention to the service at all preferring instead to have a long whispered conversation throughout. Bronwen had brought a packet of sweets which she was sharing with Rona. Ruby wondered if Lady Coot would continue to employ Bronwen as a housekeeper and Rona as a cook? As she could not imagine her ladyship doing any dusting, she thought Bronwen's job was probably secure. But as for Rona's position as the cook, well, that might depend on what sort of food Ronald preferred. Maybe his tastes ran to more exotic dishes than were in Rona's repertoire.

What was Ronald's position in all this anyway? Lady Coot had claimed that he was a family friend who had stepped in (rather briskly, Ruby thought) to help arrange Sir Clifford's affairs and deal with matters pertaining to the funeral. However, he had a tendency to leer at Lady Coot – and indeed, at any other female – in a way that looked a little improper for a mere friend. Ruby recalled Bronwen saying that she had seen Ronald entering place of decidedly ill repute by the name of the Hellfire Club in Clogwyn Mawr. She felt that Ronald had hidden depths.

"…join together our voices in prayer and remembrance with the great hymn, 'Guide Me O Thou Great Redeemer'."

Ruby had been deep in thought. She had not heard a word of what the vicar had been saying. She gathered that a bit of hymn singing was now expected. Everyone was standing. Some were holding bits of paper with words written on them. Ruby wondered where these hymn sheets had come from. Maybe you were supposed to pick one up as you entered the church. No matter. She had gone to church regularly as a child. She knew most of the popular hymns word perfect. The floor vibrated as the organ let loose a might blast of bass notes. Ruby opened her mouth and let loose with gusto: "Guide me O Thou Great Redeemer, Pilgrim through this barren land…"

There was something wrong. A woman in the pew in front of Ruby turned to glower at her. Bessie was digging Ruby in the ribs with her elbow. With horror, Ruby realised that everyone else was singing completely different words. Oh no, they were singing it in Welsh! Ruby smiled with embarrassment at the woman in front of her who, with a parting scowl, turned around again leaving Ruby to move her mouth silently like an asphyxiating goldfish in the hope that anyone who chanced to notice her would think she was at least miming in Welsh.

The service dreared on endlessly. There were several moments when Ruby felt her eyelids grow heavy and her head droop. She only hoped she had not snored. She awakened with a start. The pew was shaking and the ground was vibrating beneath her feet. This was caused by the reverberating bass notes of the church organ. Ruby admired the mighty organ which rose massively behind the pulpit, looking altogether more impressive than its dilapidated cousin in the semi-derelict Methodist chapel in the village. For the first time, Ruby noticed that there was a balcony running around the upper level of the church. The front balcony comprised several levels of raked pews behind which rose the numerous pipes of the organ.

Suddenly the sonorous notes of the organ were joined by a prodigious chorus of voices. A choir of some thirty or forty men stood in the upper balcony in front of the organ. Ruby noticed that Elfyd was among them. So was Ian. The elderly men she had seen at the choir rehearsal in the chapel were there too. As for all the others – she assumed they must be the fabled choir of Clogwyn Mawr.

Ruby did not recognise the piece they were singing. Whatever it was, it was wonderful – majestic, ethereal, rousing, magnificent. She listened enraptured. After the final thundering chorus the silence came as a shock. Then someone shouted "Bravo!" and someone else started to clap. Soon the entire congregation was on its feet stamping and applauding, Ruby among them. She was not at all sure that this was proper etiquette in a church and she was pretty certain that it was not at all the done thing during a funeral. But it was so spontaneous and it felt so *right* that nobody seemed to care.

When, at last, the applause subsided and everyone was sitting again, Lady Coot ascended to the lectern. "That," she said, "was the Dies Irae from my husband's final composition which is called The Welsh Requiem," (there was another smattering of applause). She then put on her spectacles and began reading, from notes, in a curiously dull and unemotional tone of voice, what Ruby supposed was intended to be a eulogy. Two minutes into this and Ruby was dozing off again. The words drifted over her… "He brought music into the lives of so many people… drew inspiration from nature… when he died, a light went out… his music will live for ever…"

Once the service was over, a small group of family and close friends stayed for the interment while everyone else headed towards their cars. Lady Coot had invited the mourners to what she called "a small and solemn buffet" which had been laid on at Coot Hall. As Ruby was about to clamber into Bessie's little car, she noticed a scrawny, shambling character wearing a crumpled trench coat and a grubby trilby hat scurrying up towards her. He looked like Hollywood's idea either of a down-at-heel private detective or else of a shabby newspaper reporter. He proved to be the latter. He had no doubt watched the same old Hollywood films as Ruby.

"Mrs Lake, Mrs Lake!" he called out.

"Miss," Ruby corrected him automatically.

"Tegwyn Pritchard I am, from the Clogwyn Carrion. You will no doubt remember me."

"I do indeed. You wrote a very fanciful, overly dramatic and largely fictitious report which completely distorted the so-called interview that I gave you."

"Oh, thank you very much, Mrs Lake. I do my best, see."

"If you are looking for any more quotable quotes, I'm afraid I am going to disappoint you."

"There's rumours going around, see, that you think Sir Clifford was murdered. That's right, is it?"

"I have nothing to say."

"You don't deny it, then? Oh, that's good, that is. Very good. A scoop, that what that is, I'd say."

"No, it isn't."

"Who's the prime suspect, then? Someone local, is it?"

"Even if I had a prime suspect, I wouldn't tell a reporter, would I? It could be interpreted as a libel."

"You are living in fear of retribution, then? Well, indeed, this is just the sort of stuff the readers of the Clogwyn Clarion will lap up. So what more is it that can you tell me, now then?"

There were a few things that Ruby desperately wanted to tell Tegwyn Pritchard but she clenched her teeth and struggled against the urge to say anything. What she wanted to say was not, in any case, germane to the case and might be construed as a threat against the Clarion's star reporter.

Once they were on their way to Coot Hall, Bessie told Ruby that, in her opinion, it was a great mistake to talk to reporters unless she wanted to feature on page one on a regular basis.

"I'm not worried, "Ruby replied, "The next edition of the Clogwyn Clarion isn't out for another week. The murder of Sir Clifford will be old news by then."

"You think so?"

"Oh, yes."

"How are you so sure?"

"Because I know who killed him, how it was done and what the motive was. And I am about to reveal all!"

CHAPTER 47

There was a penetrating scream. It came from the direction of the Italian Garden. "What the blazes?" said Bessie.

"Don't worry," said Ruby, "It's only the peacock."

Another scream rang out. This one was accompanied by a colourful range of vulgar expressions which do not generally form a part of the peacock's vocabulary.

"Correction," said Ruby, "It's Gwendolyn Gormly. From the fact that two distinct voices are rending the air, I'd say that an altercation is taking place."

"Should we go and see what's going on?" said Bessie.

"I believe we should," said Ruby.

Bessie and Ruby were at that precise moment, standing in the sitting room of Coot Hall, drinking glasses of astringent red wine the disagreeable flavour of which they were attempting to neutralise by eating indefinable nibbly things that tasted of fish but looked like miniature sausage rolls.

All around the room, people were sympathising with one another and muttering meaningless platitudes. Over the swell of muttered conversation Ruby heard the same old, time-worn phrases... "He will be missed... a remarkable man... we shall not see his like again." But nobody was crying or sobbing or even sniffling. In fact, Ruby had the distinct impression that nobody really missed Sir Clifford at all. In fact, she strongly suspected that several people were extremely glad to see the back of him.

It was into this solemn throng that the screaming intruded. When the first scream rang out, all heads turned in the direction of the loggia and the garden that lay beyond. When the second scream rang out, a few of the more concerned mourners wondered aloud whether they should go and see if everything was all right. When a third scream rang out, accompanied by a range of insults whose anatomical specificities might have caused an obstetrician to blush, most of the assembled mourners decided that it was of no immediate concern to them and so they returned to their wine, nibbly bits and meaningless platitudes. All except for Bessie and Ruby. Without a moment's hesitation, Bessie set off in the general direction of the Italian Garden as fast as her stumpy legs could carry her, trailing Ruby in her wake.

"It was you who killed him!" screamed Gwendolyn, her elaborate pendant topaz earrings rattling with the ferocity of pent-up anger that trembled through her entire body.

"Me!" Squeaked Lady Coot, attempting to retain a degree of dignity in a difficult situation, "Don't be preposterous. I was devoted to him."

"Devoted? Ha!" retorted Gwendolyn, "You were two-timing him with that pensioned-off gigolo, Ronald whateverhisnameis…"

"Ronald Masters," Lady Coot said.

"So, you admit it!"

"I do no such thing. I was merely providing you with his name."

"Oh, hello!" The aforementioned Ronald Masters slithered from behind a rhododendron bush at the other side of the garden, "Did somebody want me?"

"No!" screamed Gwendolyn.

"Yes!" shouted Lady Coot, "I should be most grateful if you could escort this hysterical harpy somewhere where she can sit down and calm down."

"Delighted," Ronald chuckled, "Absolutely delighted."

Ruby assumed that Gwendolyn would now turn her anger upon the hapless Ronald. Such was not the case, however. Ronald slipped his right arm beneath Gwendolyn's left elbow, simpered at her from beneath his greasy moustache, crooned, "So, dear lady, how may I be of assistance?" and, the next moment, the two of them were sidling away, all smiles and giggles, in the direction of the nearest wine bottle which, as it happened, was back in the lounge.

"Awful woman," Lady Coot commented when she was left alone with Ruby and Bessie, "She is a nymphomaniac, of course. I do hope the caviar puffs are to your satisfaction."

Ruby realised she was referring to the fishy sausage roll nibbly thing which Ruby was holding in her hand. "Delicious," she replied, unconvincingly.

Pulling herself to her full height, which did not take a great dull of pulling, Lady Coot then strode off, like an empress inspecting her empire, through the french windows and into the house.

Seeing a stroppy looking peacock striding across the lawn towards them, Ruby and Bessie decided to follow. As they entered, they were accosted by Maldwyn Placket the gardener. "It's in the drawer," he said, "The secret's in the drawer."

Ruby smiled. "Yes," she said, "Possibly."

"Not just possible. I'm telling you…"

Tom Crockley arrived then. "If he hadn't stole that field," he said, "My poor old pig Myfanwy would never have got the croup."

Ruby had already heard more than enough about the health problems of Tom Crockley's pigs and rams so she smiled in a way that she hoped looked sympathetic and sidled off into the house. Opposite Sir Clifford's study, the elaborately carved door of another room stood slightly ajar. Ruby could hear voices from inside the room – a man's voice and a woman's voice.

"Oh, of course I shall be able to see you. Frequently." The man's voice was instantly recognisable as Ronald Masters. He spoke with an oozing, oleaginous quality that made it sound as though he had a mouthful of custard.

Ruby pushed the door open and strode boldly in. Bessie chose not to follow. It was a well-upholstered room full of stuffed furniture that would have brought joy to anyone with a passion for red velvet and gold brocade. Two people who had been ensconced in a huge red velvet sofa stood as soon as they heard the door open.

Gwendolyn Gormly smoothed the wrinkles from her lime green satin dress, said "Oh, it's you again!" to Ruby, then said, "See you later, ducks," to Ronald and attempted to sashay out of the room, an attempt that was frustrated by the tightness of her dress.

"An old friend," Ronald said, when Gwendolyn had left the room.

"I believe Gwendolyn has quite a few old gentlemen friends," said Ruby. She immediately regretted saying it as it sounded much ruder than she had intended. But Ronald guffawed.

"You're right!" he said, "She's quite a girl, isn't she!"

Since Gwendolyn was certainly the wrong side of fifty, Ruby did not think that "girl" was an accurate description but she let that pass. "Yes, she is," she said, "Rather wealthier now, of course."

"Really?"

"Due to her inheritance, I mean," said Ruby.

"By Jove! An inheritance, you say? Who from?"

Ruby looked momentarily confused. Ronald was, after all, the executor of Sir Clifford's will. Either he was very forgetful or else he was being exceptionally discreet. "It is my understanding," persisted Ruby, "that Sir Clifford Coot left a sum of money to Gwendolyn in his will."

"Good Heavens, no. Not a penny."

"You are sure?"

"Absolutely. Not a sausage. Why should he? They were not, as far as I am aware, on particularly intimate terms. If you get my drift."

"Whereas you and Gwendolyn…?"

"I say! That's a bit near the knuckle, isn't it. Gwendolyn and I are friends of old. We meet from time to time. Socially."

"In the Hellfire Club?"

Ronald spluttered. It was the first time that Ruby had seen the slightest disturbance in his suave, nonchalant manner. He recovered quickly. "So you know about the club? I don't suppose you've ever…?"

"Been there? No. I know it only by its reputation."

"Clifford mentioned it to you, did he? You must have been a *very* close friend."

Ruby chose not to respond.

"That being so, I expect he told you, then?"

Ruby smiled inscrutably – she had no idea what Ronald was talking about and she thought the best policy was to say nothing and let him keep on talking.

"It was at the club," said Ronald, "that I first met Sir Clifford, as a matter of fact."

So Sir Clifford had been a member of the Hellfire Club!

"You and he were close friends?" asked Ruby.

"Inseparable. Which is why I rushed over here to help Patricia, Lady Coot, in whatever way I could. Really, it's the least I could do."

"You'll think I'm being very nosy," Ruby said, trying to keep the inscrutable smile fixed onto her face, "But one hears so many rumours. About the Hellfire Club."

"About what goes on there, you mean? Well, it's all quite harmless, really. It's just an after-hours drinking club. For mature gentlemen. Though once in a while there are, how shall I put it? Certain entertainments."

Ruby was just about to ask about those entertainments when…

Ting-Ting! Ting-Ting!

A sound like a teaspoon being struck upon the rim of a cut crystal wine glass rang out. Ronald strode to the door of the room and flung it open. Standing in the hallway, just beyond the door, was Lady Coot. She was indeed striking a teaspoon upon the rim of a cut crystal wine glass.

"Ladies and gentlemen," she called, "May I have your attention, please! Could you all please gather in the study. Thank you. You will find the study at the front of Coot Hall to the left of the staircase. I should like to say a few words."

As Ruby went across the hallway she saw that Bessie was deep in conversation with Gwendolyn Gormly. Catching sight of Ruby, Gwendolyn sashayed off, grimacing as though she had been sucking lemons.

"I get the feeling Gwendolyn doesn't much care for me," said Ruby, "You two seemed to getting on like a house on fire, though."

"I know enough about her past for her to worry about getting on the wrong side of me," Bessie explained.

It was just as well that the study was constructed on a monumental scale because by the time all thirty or so people had trouped into it (allowing space for the settee, chaise-longue, numerous chairs, grand piano, the gigantic desk and other assorted furniture) there was very little room to spare.

"I've just learned something about Gwendolyn might be of interest to you," Bessie said.

"Oh yes?"

"The money she has come into. It wasn't left to her by Sir Clifford."

"I had heard that rumour too but I wasn't sure if it was true. So where did the money come from?"

"She won it on the Lottery, so she says."

"And you believe her?"

Before Bessie could answer, the wine glass was *ting-ting*ing again to call the mourners to order. Lady Coot stood between the desk and the covered easel with the light of the large window illuminating her dramatically from behind – a theatrical effect of which Ruby approved and which she was quite certain had not been accidental. This was Lady Coot's big scene and she was going to play it for all she was worth. She heaved back her shoulders, heaved forward her bosom and launched into her prepared oration:

"Ladies and gentlemen, in honour of my late husband, there is something I would like you all to see."

"You dropping dead," Gwendolyn Gormly muttered, none too quietly.

Lady Coot affected not to have heard. "Sir Clifford was of course admired by countless millions of people throughout the world and it is gratifying to see so many familiar faces here to pay homage to his memory."

Oh no, Ruby thought, this is going to be a re-run of her tedious eulogy in the church. She felt her eyelids growing heavy.

"My husband was inspired by the people and the landscape of this lovely part of Wales and, as you know, most of his greatest pieces were composed here in Coot Hall during what has become known as his Golden Era, when, rather late in life, after he returned here to the village of his birth, where he…"

Ruby sat up straight in her seat, her eyes wide open. In an instant she was fully alert. Not that she was interested in listening to any more of Lady Coot's dreary ramblings. It was that phrase which had caught her attention – Sir Clifford's "Golden Era". She had heard that mentioned before. It was in his Wikipedia entry. It said that Ouverture Celtique was Sir Clifford's first great popular success. Written at the age of 61, thirteen years earlier, it had ushered in a period of unsurpassed creativity during which Sir Clifford had written all of his most successful pieces.

That must be rather unusual, mustn't it? For a composer to blossom suddenly in his declining years? After all, Mozart was busy writing masterpieces before he was out of nappies. Mendelssohn was knocking out symphonies before he was a teenager. Ruby was pretty sure that Bach and Beethoven, Verdi and Vivaldi didn't hang around until they were collecting their pensions before churning out the hits either. It wasn't just that Sir Clifford Coot had continued to write successful music in later life; he had only *begun* to do so in his early sixties and thereafter he had carried on doing so until his death.

With a flash of insight, Ruby realised that the dates were important. Sir Clifford had composed Ouverture Celtique during his final year as a don at Cambridge. Apart from that single piece, all of his most popular music had been written since his return to his family home, Coot Hall. Why should that be? He had devoted his life to music. And yet the only music that had brought him fame and (Ruby supposed) a reasonable amount of fortune, had been written in the past thirteen years.

Lady Coot was still droning on. "As The Bible says, 'There is a tide in the affairs of men which, taken at the flood, leads on to fortune'"

Bessie laughed. Lady Coot affected not to notice. "That's Shakespeare," Bessie whispered to Ruby. "Yes, yes, I know!" Ruby whispered back though, in truth, she could not place the source of the quotation.

"'Julius Caesar'," Bessie whispered.

But Ruby was no longer listening. A tide in the affairs of men. Of course. The tide! That explained everything!

With a flourish, Lady Coot whisked away the cloth that had been draped over the portrait of Sir Clifford. When Ruby had peeked at it before, the portrait had been incomplete. In the intervening period, Chris had obviously returned to Coot Hall to add the finishing touches. In the picture, Sir Clifford sat upon his fine mahogany desk, holding in his left hand, a musical score.

The dates, the tides, the desk. Of course, it all made perfect sense. "That's it! That's it!" Ruby exclaimed.

Heads turned to look at her. Ruby realised it was her big moment. She stood, pointed an accusing finger, then turned to look at Police Constable Ian Tucker and declaimed, "Officer, arrest that man. He killed Sir Clifford Coot. I know how he did it and I know why."

A bright flash of light momentarily illuminated the room. Ruby saw the local reporter, Tegwyn Pritchard, smiling toothily over the top of his camera.

An astonished murmur ran around the room. Faces turned to look at Ruby, then they turned to look at Constable Tucker. Then finally they turned to look at the man at whom Ruby was pointing. He stood, his face flushed with anger – "The woman's mad," he said, "She doesn't know what she's talking about."

"Sit down, Chris," Matt said, "This must be a practical joke."

"Oh no," said Ruby, "I assure you, it is no joke." And she proceeded to explain everything.

CHAPTER 48

"It's a most unflattering photograph."

Ruby and Bessie were sitting at a table on the terrace outside Gino's Wine Bar. It was the bar's opening night and it was doing brisk business. Ruby was scrutinising the front page of The Clogwyn Clarion. It was dominated by a photograph of Ruby, her arm extended and her finger pointing accusingly beneath a headline that screamed: "Clogwyn Crime Queen Catches Killer!"

"I look like Lady Macbeth in one of her grumpier moods," Ruby said.

"Can I get you ladies some more wine?"

Ruby glanced up at the man who had silently drifted alongside their table. His name was Gino Ricci and he was the owner of the wine bar. He was, thought Ruby, utterly charming. Square-jawed, tanned, with a mop of curly, dark hair, he looked Mediterranean, though in fact he came from Betws Y Coed.

"Oh, perhaps just a half-bottle," said Ruby.

"Certainly," Gino said, smiling through a set of improbably white teeth.

"On second thoughts, make it a full bottle."

"A very good choice, madam."

The evening was mild and, in the bay below the terrace, the calm aquamarine sea glittered with golden twinkles from the light of the sinking sun. Most of the tables on the terrace were already occupied. At the far end, nearest the shore, Ruby noticed that Elfyd, along with Ian Tucker and the other members of the choir had pushed together a couple of tables and were now earnestly dedicating themselves to testing the limits of their wine consumption. At another table, Gwendolyn Gormly was drinking something fizzy in the company of a stout man in a pinstripe suit. Alone, at a table directly overlooking the beach sat Matt. Bessie had invited him to come and join them but Matt had declined her offer. He made a lonely-looking figure. Matt had envisaged his future life with Chris only for those hopes to be cruelly shattered. At the table next to Matt sat a young, dark-haired girl with sultry good looks and a figure that Ruby envied.

"Who is that?" Ruby asked, nodding in the girl's direction.

Bessie shrugged. "Not a local girl. A holidaymaker maybe. I doubt if she'll be sitting alone much longer, though. I notice that Ian Tucker can't keep his eyes off her." Nor, as far as Ruby could tell, could the other members of the choir. In fact, even Gwendolyn Gormly's gentleman friend appeared to be spending more time looking at the mystery girl than at Gwendolyn.

"You really put Ian Tucker on the spot," Bessie smiled at the memory, "'Officer, arrest that man!' you said. I wasn't sure if he knew how to arrest someone. I don't think he's had much experience."

"Luckily Frank Crockley was there to help him," said Ruby, "Chris took one look at Frank and realised it was in his interests to come quietly."

Ruby had, of course, explained everything to Ian Tucker before he had arrested Chris. Ian had warned Ruby that making a false accusation of murder at the funeral of the deceased is not looked upon kindly by the British legal system. But Ruby had never for a moment doubted that her theory was correct. The clincher was provided when it was found that a key on Chris's keyring opened the locked drawer of Sir Clifford's desk. As it turned out, there was nothing of interest in that drawer. Ruby had not expected that there would be. The secrets which it had once contained had already been taken out and destroyed.

"I still can't figure out how you knew it was Chris," said Bessie.

"I thought that the drawer might be important because of the note that Maldwyn sent me telling me that the secret was in there," Ruby explained, "I supposed that Maldwyn knew because he'd seen Sir Clifford locking the drawer and making sure that nobody saw what was in it. And then there was the business about the letter. Maldwyn told me he'd heard Sir Clifford shouting at someone in his study: 'For God's sake, I've got the letter!'"

"What letter was that?" said Bessie.

"The more important question is, who was he shouting at? Bronwen told me that Sir Clifford often worked in his study and nobody would dare to disturb him. So who else was likely to be in the study with him? His wife, of course. Bronwen or Rona, possibly. And then, when Lady Coot unveiled the portrait, I was reminded that, in order to do his the painting of Sir Clifford sitting upon his desk, Chris and Sir Clifford must have spent some considerable time sequestered together in that study.

"But more significant than that were the dates. They were the final piece of the puzzle. Sir Clifford had been writing music all his life but he only achieved popular success thirteen years ago when Ouverture Celtique was first performed in London. The year after that, Evelyn Gonfort, the organ scholar at the same college, left Cambridge without completing his studies. Chris Chamberlain, who was also at the same college but in a year above Evelyn, graduated that same year. The correspondence of time and place was too convenient to be a mere coincidence.

"When I found out that Evelyn had killed himself, that was another date that seemed more than a coincidence. That happened eleven years ago. It was also eleven years ago that Sir Clifford Coot returned to Clogwyn Bach. Shortly after Sir Clifford came here, Chris arrived. And, all of a sudden, Sir Clifford started writing a string of successful compositions. Coincidence after coincidence!"

Gino returned with a bottle of chilled sauvignon blanc. "There you are, ladies," he said, his perfect teeth gleaming seductively, "Shall I pour or…?"

"Thank you so much," said Ruby (and Bessie could have sworn that Ruby had fluttered her eyelashes at him),"I'll do it."

"As you wish, madam."

"Handsome chap, isn't he?" said Bessie.

"Passably so," Ruby agreed, "And just about my age."

Bessie gave her a knowing look.

"Oh, for goodness' sake!" Ruby spluttered, "I didn't mean…" She topped up their glasses.

"Make that another one!" Muriel Greenalge was standing there, holding out an empty wine glass. Maggie Pountice, who was with her, was holding a pint of lager. "Filthy stuff, that wine," said

Maggie, "Mind you, this foreign beer isn't no better. Give me a pint of foaming ale any day of the week, that's what I say."

"Have you heard the news about Coot Hall?" Muriel asked as she took a vacant seat.

"No," said Ruby, "What?"

Muriel picked up the copy of the Clogwyn Clarion which was lying on the table and flipped to the advertisement section at the back. "Up for sale," she said, "And just look at the price!"

"Three and a half million pounds!" Ruby gasped, "Who would pay that kind of money for that old monstrosity?"

"I hear that her ladyship and her fancy man is planning to buy a house in South Kensington," said Maggie, "Very posh area in London, so they say. People round here is too common for her, I s'ppose."

"South Kensington," said Ruby, "Three and a half million probably wouldn't go all that far in that part of London."

"What I'm worried about is the Summer Fayre," said Muriel, "I mean, if the Hall is up for sale, I don't suppose Lady Coot will be wanting people erecting marquees and throwing their beer cans in the fountain."

Muriel, Maggie and Bessie reckoned that the Fayre might have to be cancelled. Ruby secretly hoped it would be. She had never relished the prospect of trying to put on a play. The idea of auditioning the local talent and then rehearsing them until they were word perfect had filled her with dread.

"So, go on then, girl," Maggie said to Ruby, "Spill the beans. How did you know it was Chris?"

Ruby explained again the importance of the dates.

Maggie took a long slurp of lager. "I has to be honest with you, Rube," she said, "I can't see no connections."

"I phoned Mrs Winstanley, Evelyn's London landlady. She told me that Evelyn thought that Sir Clifford had stolen his work. At the time I assumed that must have been some sort of paranoid fantasy on Evelyn's part. But now I know it wasn't. The sheet of music that I found in Sir Clifford's scanner gave the game away."

"'Eve G' had been scribbled in the corner. The music itself was almost the same as the opening section of Sir Clifford's first big success, Overture Celtique. *Almost* the same but not quite. Why not? Because it was Evelyn, not Sir Clifford, who had written the music. Evelyn had been one of Sir Clifford's most brilliant students. Sir Clifford recognised the genius of the music and decided to adapt it slightly – hence the slight differences – before passing it off as his own.

"Evelyn's music brought international fame and considerable wealth to Sir Clifford. Meanwhile Evelyn's attempts to make a name for himself failed because people said his music was 'derivative'. In other words, it sounded like the kind of music Sir Clifford Coot would write."

"No wonder the poor bugger killed himself," said Maggie.

"But what became of all the music that Evelyn had been writing while he was in London?" Ruby asked, "The music that sounded so much like Sir Clifford Coot's compositions?"

A lightbulb came on in Bessie's head. "Sir Clifford stole his bloody music!"

"Not quite. He didn't steal it. He bought it. When Evelyn died, Chris, who had been Evelyn's closest friend, kept all his unpublished music. He made a deal to supply that music to Sir Clifford, at a price. But not all at once. The value of the music relied upon its scarcity.

"Chris moved to Clogwyn Bach, and Sir Clifford let him live in his boat house. Rent-free, I have no doubt. Whenever Sir Clifford needed some new music, Chris would provide it. But one day, a few months ago, the supply of music came to an end. Chris had nothing more to sell to Sir Clifford. So he changed tactics. He tried blackmail instead. He threatened to reveal Sir Clifford as a fraud unless he continued to finance Chris's comfortable lifestyle."

"That don't explain why Chris bumped off the old geezer," Maggie said.

"Sir Clifford wouldn't go along with Chris's demands any more," Ruby said, "Because he had finally written a piece of music that surpassed anything Evelyn had written."

"The Welsh Requiem?" Bessie asked.

"Exactly. I'm pretty sure that was all Sir Clifford's own work. Which is why Elfyd and the choir were so surprised by it. It was nothing like the music on which Sir Clifford's reputation had been founded.

"Sir Clifford went to see Chris with an ultimatum. If Chris went public with the story of Sir Clifford's musical deceit, then Sir Clifford would go public with Chris's threat of blackmail. Sir Clifford planned to show Chris the copy of the first page of Evelyn's music to remind him that he had the original manuscript and would, if the worst came to the worst, use that as evidence that Ouverture Celtique had indeed been composed by Evelyn. It was also a reminder that Sir Clifford had a stack of other original manuscripts which he kept in the locked drawer in his desk."

"'Ere, wait a minute," Maggie protested, "Why would Chris care if people knew that Evelyn had written that music? Didn't make no difference to Chris, did it?"

"I suspect," said Ruby, "that Sir Clifford also had some incriminating correspondence locked away in his desk drawer. Which brings me back to the letter. Maldwyn Placket told me that he'd seen Sir Clifford hiding a letter in his desk and then, not long before Sir Clifford was killed, Maldwyn heard him taunting someone – 'For God's sake! I've got the letter!'

"Why would a letter be so important? It must have been a letter from Chris. It is my guess that when Chris first contacted Sir Clifford, all those years ago, to tell him that he had a secret hoard of Evelyn's unpublished music and that he was prepared to sell it, he did so in a letter. Sir Clifford kept that letter, possibly realising that it might one day be useful if Chris ever tried to blackmail him. Sir Clifford sent a copy of the page of music to his agent and wrote in an email message that there would be a letter to follow. He wanted his agent to have proof of Evelyn's authorship no matter what happened."

"Good God!" said Maggie with feeling, "Who'd have thought that Chris could be such a conniving bugger?"

"You just can't tell, can you?" Muriel agreed, "To look at him, you'd think he was such a nice young man. Always well turned out and very softly spoken."

Ruby was about to reply when a cloud of pungent smoke wafted across her face causing her to break into a fit of coughing. She glanced around and saw that the source of the smoke was the cigar being smoked by Gwendolyn Gormly's gentleman friend in flagrant contempt of the signs forbidding it.

"So how was he going to keep Chris quiet, d'you think?" asked Maggie.

"Sir Clifford went to the boathouse to issue an ultimatum. Which, by the way, is why he didn't need a torch. The drive at Coot Hall is illuminated at night. So is the road from Coot Hall to the village and from the village to the boathouse. I assume the two men argued. Chris probably knocked Sir Clifford unconscious and dumped him into the sea. It was a high spring tide and the sea would have come right up to the wall beneath the boathouse at the southern end of the bay. The body washed up later at the northern end beneath the cliff path, where I found him on the morning of Thursday the 13th."

Bessie did not seem convinced by this explanation. "Lady Coot said that Sir Clifford was at home all Wednesday night. She was certain she had heard him leave on Thursday morning. Why would she lie about that?"

"Oh, she wasn't lying," said Ruby, "She was just mistaken. You see, once he'd got rid of Sir Clifford's body there was one more thing Chris needed to do. He needed to get rid of the evidence – Evelyn's music and any incriminating correspondence. Fortunately, Sir Clifford kept his keys on a keyring and chain which Chris took before dumping the body into the sea. He used those keys to let himself into Coot Hall and take the evidence from the drawer of the desk. It was Chris that Lady Coot heard, thinking it was Sir Clifford, in the early hours of Thursday morning."

"I knew it was him all along," said Maggie.

"Oh?" said Muriel, "You worked it all out, I suppose?"

"Not at all," said Maggie, "It was in the cards. The cards never lie."

"Funny you never mentioned it then," said Muriel. But she said it quietly and Maggie gave no indication that she had heard.

From the corner of her eye, Ruby watched Gwendolyn stroking her gentleman friend's knee and giggling at his jokes. Ruby did not like Gwendolyn but even so she felt a little guilty that she had suspected her of murder. Then again, Ruby had suspected a significant number of the other inhabitants of the little village too. She looked at Matt sitting sullenly at the edge of the deck, nurturing his lonely glass of red wine. Out of sheer coincidence, Matt had been her first suspect.

"There's one thing that doesn't add up, though," Bessie said, "Chris had a cast-iron alibi. He was with Matt all Wednesday evening and all through the night. According to your theory, that's the night when the murder took place."

"I never said that!"

"Yes you did. You said that Sir Clifford must have gone to the boathouse in the evening and that's when he was killed."

"Ah yes, but not Wednesday evening. Remember my experiment with the beach ball. It turned up on the rocks at the northern end of the bay two days after I had set it afloat at the southern end."

"Rip currents," Muriel said, "I'm always warning tourists about them but they never pay any attention."

"Tourists might not," said Ruby, "But I did. You see, it would have been impossible for Sir Clifford's body to have washed ashore on the northern promontory if he'd been put into the sea at the southern promontory on the Wednesday night. Think about it. I found the body at about half past six in the morning. It was low tide then. It had to have been washed ashore at high tide. But high tide was about six hours earlier – a little after midnight. If he'd been killed on the south of the bay, his body can't have been put into the water at high tide that night. It needed at least one low tide for the currents to sweep the body away from the southern cliffs followed by at least one high tide to wash the body ashore at the northern cliffs and then another low tide to leave it stranded where I found it. All of which means that Sir Clifford was not killed on Wednesday evening but on Tuesday evening. So Chris's alibi for Wednesday is irrelevant. Chris had no alibi for Tuesday. Matt told me that he had phoned Chris on Tuesday but he had been fobbed off as Chris had said he was too busy painting to leave the boathouse."

"But if Sir Clifford died on Tuesday, how come nobody noticed that he wasn't there on Wednesday?" asked Muriel.

"Rona gave me the answer to that. Remember she said that he often spent the days locked in his study. He hated being disturbed so nobody bothered going in there. Moreover, we know that he and

Lady Coot had separate bedrooms so his absence by night and by day simply wasn't noticed."

From the corner of her eye, Ruby noticed that the attractive dark-haired young woman sitting at the table next to Matt's was smiling towards the entrance that led from the street onto the terrace and waving her fingers at someone. Ruby glanced to see if the recipient of her attentions was anyone she knew. There was Frank Crockley looking, Ruby had to concede, rather magnificent with his muscular torso straining against his tight tee-shirt. She whispered to Maggie, Bessie and Muriel, "I think romance is in the air."

Just behind Frank Crockley stood Rod the hairdresser. Matt was standing at his table now; he was smiling and waving his fingertips.

"More romance, do you think?" said Maggie.

"Matt and Rod?," said Bessie, "I'm not sure they have much in common, really. Still, after all Matt has been through, I can only hope it works out for him."

But all was not as it seemed. Frank Crockley strode across the terrace straight to Matt's table. Matt stood and kissed Frank on the cheek. Meanwhile Rod the hairdresser had gone to meet the beautiful dark-haired girl. She flung her arms around him and kissed him full on the lips.

"Ladies!" Bessie, Muriel and Maggie had been so distracted by watching the various goings on that none of them had noticed Gino shimmying across the terrace towards them holding a small tray bearing four glasses, "As it is our opening night, please accept a complimentary cocktail. I call it the Clogwyn Bluebell." The glasses contained a fluorescently blue liquid lavishly decorated with paper umbrellas and chunks of pineapple and cherries on cocktail sticks.

"Oh, I couldn't. Really," protested Bessie, "I'm a Methodist, you see."

"Lapsed," said Ruby, taking the glasses from the tray and placing them onto the table, "Very, very lapsed."

"It's gorgeous," Muriel enthused, "But a bit wicked."

"Chin, chin!" beamed Gino.

"Bottoms up!" said Ruby and took a long, invigorating sip of the drink which, surprisingly, tasted of oranges and lime juice.

"Clogwyn Bluebell be damned!" grumbled Maggie, "It looks like a bloody Christmas tree decoration. I'll stick to my lager."

Bessie gave Ruby a suspicious look. "I hope," she said, once Gino had shimmered away again, "that you are not thinking of getting involved with that man."

"Good Heavens, Bessie! Whatever gave you that idea?" It may have been the ruddy rays of the sinking sun that made Ruby's cheeks seem a little rosier than usual, but Bessie thought she looked as though she was blushing.

Bessie made a rapid change of subject. "How's the insomnia these days?"

"What? Oh, I'd forgotten all about that. I'm sleeping like a log."

"That's good. Solving murders must agree with you."

Ruby laughed. "I hardly think I'm likely to be getting involved with any more murders! Oh, and, incidentally, just in case I didn't make myself clear, I can state with absolute conviction that I am also most certainly not going to get involved with Gino Ricci!"

But Ruby was wrong on both counts. She was about to get very involved indeed with Mr Gino Ricci. And she was also going to be involved in another murder.

Bessie's Welsh Cake Recipe

Ingredients

8oz (225g) self-raising flour
1 ¾oz (50g) butter
1 ¾oz (50g) lard
1 ¾oz (50g) caster sugar
3 ½oz (100g) currants
1 teaspoon cinnamon
1 large egg

METHOD

Rub fats into flour, or use a food-processor, until mixture resembles breadcrumbs. Stir in currants and sugar.

Beat egg and add to mixture. Slice the beaten egg into the mixture using a knife. Once the mixture 'comes together', roll it into a ball with your hands to form a dough.

On a floured work surface, roll out mixture using a rolling pin to about 1 cm thick.

Cut the mixture into 2 ½ inch (6cm) rounds using a fluted biscuit cutter. Each Welsh cake should be about ¼ inch (0.6cm) thick.

Very lightly butter then heat the bakestone. When hot (a drop of water flicked onto it should sizzle at once), place Welsh cakes onto stone and allow to brown on one side. Then, using a fish-slice or spatula, flip them to brown on other side (you may need to do this a few times until they are cooked). Typically, each Welsh cake will take between 4 and 5 minutes to cook.

When each Welsh cake is done place it onto a grid to cool. Then dust with caster sugar.

NOTES:

Cast iron bakestones or griddles are available for use with gas and electric hobs.

Instead of self-raising flour, you can use plain flour to which 2 teaspoons of baking powder is added.

You may use all butter instead of half lard but the Welsh cakes may not then be quite so light and crumbly.

You may try nutmeg or mixed spice instead of cinnamon. You can also add a teaspoon of good lemon essence along with the egg.

Instead of all currants, try a mixture of chopped mixed peel and currants.

If the dough is very dry you can add a couple of teaspoons of milk. However, this is rarely necessary. This dough needs to be quite dry so don't be tempted to over-moisten it!

NOW READ ON…

In the next novel, *'Who Killed Inspector Stoat?'*, Ruby Lake unexpectedly meets an old actor friend, Gerald Haven, who has come to Clogwyn Bach for a short holiday after finishing the latest series of the TV show, 'The Inspector Stoat Mysteries' in which he stars. Gerald Haven throws a party for the cast of the show at The Old Watch House overlooking the bay. Everything seems to be going well. Until a dead body is found…

In the following pages, you can read the first chapter of *'Who Killed Inspector Stoat?'*

Who Killed Inspector Stoat?

Ruby was sitting on the terrace of Gino's Wine Bar overlooking the bay, sharing a bottle of chilled sauvignon blanc with her neighbour, Bessie Morgan, when a man's voice suddenly bellowed out, "Ruby Lake! What the dickens are you doing here?"

At other tables, heads turned. The voice was unmistakable. Its rich and fruity timbre had been responsible for causing hearts to flutter and pulses to skip a beat in everything from tender love scenes to shoot-outs with ruthless villains. The voice belonged to Gerald Haven, the actor. You have no doubt seen him in films and on television. He tends to play slightly run-to-seed toffs in Edwardian period dramas, dashing officers in wartime thrillers and, of course, the ever popular Detective Inspector Stoat in the long-running television series.

Bessie looked flustered. "Is that who I think it is?"

"I've no idea who you think it is," Ruby replied coldly, "but I can tell you who it *actually* is. It's bloody Gerald Haven. What is he doing in Clogwyn Bach?"

Gerald was swooping across the terrace like an albatross coming in to land, his arms extended wing-like, his lips puckering up for a kiss. Having been in the acting business for most of her adult life, Ruby responded as unthinkingly as a dog that drools when it smells food: she stood, she extended her arms and she puckered her lips. She and Gerald manoeuvred themselves into an awkward embrace and blew kisses into the air over one another's shoulders.

"And who, may I ask, is your charming friend?" Gerald oozed.

Bessie simpered and blushed like a teenager. Gerald took one of Bessie's hands and kissed it. Bessie simpered some more and told him her name.

"Bessie," he enthused. "What a lovely name!"

"Oh, give over!" said Ruby. "You're not playing Algernon Moncrieff now!"

Gerald smiled. "Ah, so you remember!"

"Gerald and I acted in a play together," Ruby explained for Bessie's benefit.

"One wonderful summer in Norwich," said Gerald.

"Uttoxeter," Ruby corrected. "And it was the middle of winter."

"I played Algernon," Gerald said, "and Ruby played Gwendolen."

"Cecily."

"What?"

"I played Cecily. Buffy Fairfax played Gwendolen."

"Oh yes, of course," Gerald raised a humorous eyebrow. "You were marvellous."

"And then, for the Christmas season we put on that dreadful production of Peter Pan."

"Oh yes! You were Mrs Darling."

"And you were Mr Darling. And Captain Hook. There was that snotty-nosed pop singer chap playing Peter. And that very pretty little girl playing Wendy. Now what was her name?"

"Oh, that pop singer!" Gerald snorted with laughter. "I'd forgotten all about him. We had to let him sing those ghastly pop songs that had nothing at all to do with the plot."

"Rosalynd. That was her name. Our Wendy, I mean. I wonder what became of her? I thought she would go far but I can't say I've heard of her since."

Bessie, who was entranced by all this theatrical repartee, took advantage of a brief pause to inform Gerald Haven that she had seen him in a Jane Austen dramatization on the television and thought he was marvellous and, what's more, she was a big fan of Detective Inspector Stoat. Gerald wafted a deprecating hand in Bessie's direction, seeming to indicate an innate humility which cared naught for the effusive adulation with which he was universally greeted.

"Why don't you two ladies join me?" said Gerald. "We are sitting over by the wall." He pointed towards a corner of the terrace where a gaggle of loud people were in the process of arranging chairs around two tables while Gino Ricci, the proprietor of the wine bar, poured Champagne into crystal flute glasses.

"That's very kind of you," said Bessie, standing. "We'd love to join you…"

"But," added Ruby somewhat abruptly, "sadly we are unable to do so. We are meeting some friends."

"Bring them over too!"

"We have some private matters we need to talk about. You know how it is." Ruby pushed Bessie back into her chair.

"Quite. Quite," said Gerald. "But you really must come tomorrow."

"What's happening tomorrow?" Bessie asked with (Ruby thought) unbecoming eagerness.

"We are having a little party. We've just finished the new series, you see."

"Series?" Ruby said.

"Inspector Stoat."

"Ah."

"A cracking last episode if I do say so myself. It's called 'Who Killed Inspector Stoat?' I get bumped off. Well, I mean, the dear Inspector does. Right in the last minute. Just as the credits come up. A bit of a cliff-hanger, what!"

"Presumably you will be resurrected in time for the next season?" Bessie asked.

"Can't tell you, old girl. I'm sworn to secrecy, you see. But let's just say that since the next series is already in the planning stage and it would seem a bit odd to have an Inspector Stoat mystery with no Inspector Stoat…"

"So," interrupted Ruby, who was supremely uninterested in Inspector Stoat, "what brings you to Clogwyn Bach?"

"We had to do some filming in the Brecon Beacons, do you see. I thought a little holiday by the seaside would round it off splendidly. I brought a few of my actors along by way of a small thank-you. We've rented the Old Watch House. For the week. We'll be leaving next Saturday. I really shall expect you, Ruby."

"Sadly I don't drive and the Watch House is rather a long way…"

"I drive!" Bessie said.

"There you are then. That's sorted. I shall expect the both of you. Eight o'clock or so would be a good time," and off he sauntered back in the direction of the noisy group of people drinking Champagne.

Ruby glowered at Bessie. "Really, Bessie! I was hoping to wriggle out of that. I don't want to go to a party with Gerald Haven and a bunch of actors."

"Why not? You'll be in your natural habitat with that lot, I should think!"

"I came to Clogwyn Bach to get away from that lot! Actors are the most tedious people in the world. They all think the earth revolves around them. If you have to be stuck in a party for a few hours, the last people you'd want to be stuck with are actors. Oh, Hell's Bells! That's Sofie Silk! Don't look!"

But Bessie did look. She not only looked, she also waved.

"Bessie! What are you doing?"

"I'm waving, what does it look like I'm doing? There's a woman over there waving at us so I'm waving back."

Ruby turned to look. Sure enough, there was Sofie Silk waggling her fingers in their general direction. Ruby fixed an insincere smile upon her face and waggled her fingers back.

"'Ey! You'll never guess who I just seen," said a gruff voice from behind Ruby. The voice belonged to Maggie Pountice, a fierce-looking little woman who had become one of Ruby's closest friends during the few months since she had moved to the village.

"Sofie Silk?" Ruby suggested.

"What? No, I just seen that wossisname who's on the telly in that whatchamacallit, you know the thing, with police and murders and whatnot."

"That narrows the field down," Ruby said.

"You must know who I mean," persisted Maggie. "He wears a trilby hat. On the telly, that is. He's not wearing one now."

"She means Gerald Haven." That was Muriel Greenalge, another of Ruby's circle of friends, who had arrived on the terrace with Maggie. "Plays Detective Inspector Stoat."

"I appear to be the only person who has never seen this famous Inspector Stoat," said Ruby. "To be honest, until tonight I'd never even heard of him."

"I'll lend you the box set," Bessie said. "I've got all seven series."

"He was in that wartime series too," Muriel said. "You know the one. About a man who goes away with the Army and when he comes back his wife has fallen in love with someone else."

"Very tragic, I'm sure," said Ruby. "Now get yourselves sat down and decide what you want to drink. There's this bottle of New Zealand sauvignon blanc. I should think that would suit you, Muriel."

"A bottle of Guinness will do me," said Maggie and she snapped her fingers imperiously at Gino as he walked past.

By the light of the setting sun they sat in the warm evening air with the sound of the nearby sea tumbling over sand and pebbles while Ruby told them all about Gerald Haven. She had worked with him almost twenty years earlier in a touring production of The Importance Of Being Earnest. They had played to paltry and indifferent audiences in Rotherham, Uttoxeter and Scunthorpe. Gerald Haven had been a little known, third-rate actor at that time. In the years since, he had become a world famous third-rate actor while Ruby's career had dwindled to the point of insignificance. In Ruby's opinion, Gerald Haven was a self-centred, pompous fool whose entire career was based on the simple fact that he oozed a certain sort of superficial sex appeal which was strangely attractive to women of a certain age. "But don't be fooled by the charm," Ruby warned. "He's a nasty piece of work who'd stab you in the back if he thought it would help his career."

Having finished her character assassination, Ruby paused to allow her friends to comment. But comments came there none. The three of them were staring, as though in a trance, at the rowdy theatrical folk sitting in the corner of the terrace.

"He's better looking in real life than on the telly," said Maggie.

"He smiled at me," sighed Bessie.

"Hasn't he got lovely eyes," cooed Muriel.

"Oh, for God's sake!" Ruby slammed her fist on the table. "You three are like overgrown children!"

A Short Message...

I hope you enjoyed this first visit to the Welsh seaside village of Clogwyn Bach. I am already writing more books in this series and I hope you may be tempted to let me take you there once again to get to know the characters better – and find out if Ruby manages to solve some even more baffling murders!

If you have enjoyed this book, I would be enormously grateful if you could take a few moments to leave a short review on Amazon. You can do that by clicking one of the two links on the next page or (on other Amazon sites) by clicking the 'Write a Customer Review' button on the book page.

Thanks again for reading my book!

K T Mill

LEAVE A REVIEW

Amazon (USA)

https://tinyurl.com/44kh3s4c
or
https://www.amazon.com/review/create-review?asin=191313217X

Amazon (UK)

https://tinyurl.com/m7hps6wk
or
https://www.amazon.co.uk/review/create-review?asin=191313217X